Dragon Mage

Red Dragon Chronicles

Arisha Grabtchak

Dragon Mage: Red Dragon Chronicles

ISBN 13: 9781733444880

Library of Congress Control Number: 2020933422

Cover Image: Arisha Grabtchak

Cover design © by All Things That Matter Press

Published in 2020 by All Things That Matter Press

This book is dedicated to Arisha, the author. While this is not common, neither is the circumstance of the publication of this book. Arisha passed away in 2016 at the age of 23. She was a very bright, remarkable artist with so many interests in her life. Arisha loved nature and animals, she volunteered at dog shelters and enjoyed horseback riding, she collected seashells from every place she visited and could identify every one of them. Since she was little, Arisha was fascinated by dragons—mysterious powerful creatures from a different world. Not surprisingly, dragons became major characters in her fantasy stories. Being a perfectionist, she was constantly scrutinizing and polishing her manuscripts, hoping to publish the whole series. Unexpected death disrupted Arisha's plans but her family keeps working on realizing her dreams. We could only wish that some things would have happened sooner in her life ...

Prologue

Arrows laced with fire streaked through the moonlit night, hitting houses, making flames whoosh through the wooden buildings, forcing the hapless occupants outside. One by one they were felled by arrow or sword as raiders cloaked in black stormed through the village.

"This way," roared their leader. "It's over there." He pointed his men toward a group of houses in the western end of the town, and they kicked their horses into a charge.

A man glanced out the window, clutching something around his neck. "They've come for it. Run!" He grabbed his wife and infant daughter and pulled them out the back door just as their building exploded, crumbing into ashes.

The horsemen turned toward the, even though the fleeing figures were not visible through the thick black smoke. The sound of hooves rang out as their lathered mounts took a sharp turn to cut off the family.

The victims ducked into a smouldering shack and barred the door.

"Here," said the man. His hands shook as he took a chain off his neck and held it out to his wife.

"No, at this range it will do no good," she whispered. The raiders had jumped from their mounts and were hammering at the door with their axes. Flaming arrows were already lodged in the roof; they had t seconds at most. "You know they will still find it." She looked sadly at her daughter. "But not on her."

"No, it's too soon. I can't let her be stuck with the cursed thing her whole life—"

"We have no choice." With trembling fingers, she took the necklace from her husband's hands.

He sighed. "Go. I will hold them off." He turned to face the door just as it exploded into splinters. A ball of light formed at the end of his staff and shot toward one of the invaders, exploding on impact.

The woman clutched her baby to her chest with one arm, using the other to climb out the window in the back. She ran and did not pause even when she heard a familiar scream from the shack she'd left behind.

A raider flipped the dead husband's body over with his foot. "What? He doesn't have it. Find the woman!"

Breathless, she stopped next to an overturned caravan.

"I'd hoped to avoid this for a few years," she whispered as she slipped the necklace around her daughter's neck. The child was too frightened to cry; she simply shook with terror at all the noise and violence around her. "I'm sorry. You'll understand some day." She kissed the infant's forehead and thrust her underneath a flap of loose canvas.

She never even saw the arrow as it embedded itself between her shoulder blades.

Blood gurgled from her mouth. "Take her... please, take her," she croaked to the older woman she knew was hiding in a hole beneath the caravan.

The next arrow pinned her forehead to the wooden pole.

The raiders drew up next to the body. They looked confused.

"I don't get it. It's gone. I don't feel the pull at all anymore. Do you?" he asked his companions. But they shook their heads. "Impossible. It can't have just disappeared. Fan out. Grab all the villagers you can. Slaughter and search them."

Amidst explosions of fire, columns of smoke, and running, screaming people, no one noticed a woman take off from behind the caravan and run down a back path. She splashed across the river and kept running, holding a small bundle close to her chest.

Chapter 1 ~ Orphan

Eiryenne woke with a start. She'd had the nightmare again. The one with the fire and shadows that chased her in endless circles before she herself started to burn.

She gripped the straw that served as her mattress, finding comfort in its familiar texture. Slowly, her breathing eased. Early morning sunlight streamed through holes in the roof while the pigs behind a wooden divider twitched and huffed in their sleep. All was well.

The girl got up and went to the door. Her naturally slender build compounded with a poor diet made her especially thin for a thirteen-year-old. Her brown hair fell to her shoulders in tangled mats, and her bright hazel eyes were bloodshot from a restless night. She wore an old tunic, a worn-out jacket, and breeches that had more patches on them than she could count. Her clothes were stained and tattered, but they were all she had.

Clutching her threadbare jacket tight against her shoulders, she stepped out into the cold wind. It was the middle of autumn and though most of the snow had yet to come, frost already glittered on the fallen leaves, accenting the reds and oranges with streaks of silver. It settled on the roofs and doors of the village that lay spread out on her right. A lone oak leaf, picked up by the breeze, fluttered down and landed in her hair. She brushed it away, the worn leather bracelet on her wrist shifting with the motion. On it was a single opaque bead. A neat oval spun of colourless matte glass, the bead's smooth surface was covered with smudges of dirt and grime. An ornate pattern of scratches garnished one side that cut through the frosted outer layer to reveal a glimpse of clearer, translucent glass.

A stone suddenly struck her between the shoulder blades, making her jump. A peal of laughter sounded out from between the houses. "C'mon, *Airhead,* pick up the pace," yelled a boy. It was the butcher's son and a group of his friends. They continued to throw rocks. "Did they run that slow where you're from? No wonder your parents never got out of the fire."

Eiryenne's face flushed, but she said nothing. She just tucked her fists against her sides and ran faster.

"My cousin probably changed his mind by now. He doesn't need some dirty *orphan* helping him with the flock," added another boy. "Go back to wallow with the pigs where you belong."

She was out of breath by the time she arrived at the shepherd's hut. She fervently hoped that the boy was lying. Unlike them, she had no one to turn to for food or shelter. She had to work for it herself. Being older than most of the village boys, Eiryenne had done the odd jobs around the place for some years. One of the best was helping the butcher. Though the blood made her turn up her nose, her reward was getting first pick of the leftovers and even occasional extra cuts of meat. Those days, she could be certain she wouldn't starve. Then the butcher's son got old enough to do the job himself, and she went to the next person who could use a hand. She learned how to build huts and chop wood, to herd sheep, and to fish. But the lads were getting older and stronger, and hardly anyone would pick her over them for chores now.

"You're late," said the man who leaned out of the window. He was dressed in a faded blue cotton tunic and a wide straw hat. His name was Kal, and he was notorious for his short temper. Eiryenne feared that he'd beat her again for arriving just after sunrise. "But today that won't matter," he continued. "Michael's taking over the flock. He's a far better herder than you anyway."

Eiryenne looked at the ground. It was as she'd feared. Now she'd go hungry for another day. Her stomach growled. She hadn't eaten since last morning.

"What are you standing around here for?" demanded Kal. "Get out! You've lost me enough sheep, you worthless wretch. I did a head count last night, and there were two missing. Two! Can't you do anything right? Do you know how much that will cost me?" He continued to shout. Eiryenne flinched and shrank away. Everyone shouted at her, but she never got used to it.

Sighing, she turned and ran back the way she came, trying to ignore the rocks that pelted her back. She'd lost count of how many bruises there were. Kal had worse aim than the boys, but he hit harder.

She trotted back down the path. The sun had started to rise in earnest, bathing everything in a yellowish glow. For a moment, the flimsy wooden huts appeared gilded, if only by the light that shone on them. There weren't many of them in this small, poor farming community. Eiryenne ran to the one on the eastern edge, an old building slightly taller than the rest but with one broken wall. Of all the people in the village, the only two who'd treated her with some decency lived here.

Though working for the butcher had kept food in her belly, her favourite chore by far was helping out at Hayden's stables. Despite being old, partially blind, and with a crippled leg, he still insisted on keeping his horses and often put their welfare above his own.

He opened the door as she thumped up the stairs leading to it. Though his eyesight was going, his hearing was as good as ever, and he knew her step when he heard it. He'd also learned that she didn't like knocking on doors.

"Hello, hello," he said with a smile. "No luck at Kal's, there, eh? Too bad. But you know, I wouldn't want to work for him anyway," he added. "He don't treat his animals right. Nasty temper. I'm surprised you even got through a few weeks with him. I don't envy that new boy he's got at all. He goes through his workers as quickly as his sheep, that guy. I don't blame those cows for wantin' to stray." One thing Eiryenne liked about Hayden was that he talked enough for the both of them. He never had a problem with her quiet ways. She also didn't have to worry about meeting his eyes.

"Now, seeing as you're here, I'll ask you to take my lads out," continued Hayden. "Neil's gettin' stir crazy, and Horace will sleep until his muscles break down if you let him." He nodded to himself. "There's oats in the usual place, and the hay hasn't moved either, so have fun."

Eiryenne left the run-down house and went up to the barn where the horses stayed. Hayden owned two at the moment; the rest of his small herd had starved in last winter's famine, along with his wife. Horace was Hayden's oldest horse, a big, dark-grey gelding that was so lazy and calm, even his elderly owner could ride him. He barely even blinked as Eiryenne entered his stall and slipped a halter on him, tempting him with oats to get him to move. Once she'd gotten him out to the pasture, she tied him to the fence and went to get the other one. Neil was a young stallion, seal-bay with a white sock on both hind feet. He'd been born on Hayden's property a couple of years before, and his dam had been Eiryenne's favourite horse. She hadn't made it through the famine, but Neil had, and since he'd gotten too much for Hayden to handle, most of his care fell on Eiryenne. But she didn't mind.

Neil needed no coaxing. He pulled on his lead, almost dragging Eiryenne to the field. She tied him next to Horace and set to grooming them both. Once she'd scrubbed off as much mud as she could, she slipped off their leads. Neil immediately took off, cantering around the pasture. Horace continued to crop the grass where she left him.

She mucked the stalls and put in fresh hay before going back to the house. Hayden usually had little to spare for her, but she attended to his horses regardless. It was the one thing she was relatively good at, and she enjoyed spending time with the horses and learning how to ride. Hayden always gave her something each time she came—an apple, some bran, or, if his own stomach was as empty as hers, a story. He'd travelled a lot in his younger days and always had a tale or two about some far-off land. He told her about fantastical creatures such as griffins, unicorns, and dragons. Though she suspected those were more myth than truth, she listened anyway, enthralled by the possibilities that far out there in the world there could be something so much more magical than her mundane life.

Today he gave her an apple and told her about mages, people that could channel the powers of the earth and use magic to do both wonderful and terrible things. A number of creatures had magic, he'd said. Humans were among them. But mages among humans were rare; they hadn't been seen for the last few hundred years.

"Come by later today if you'd like to take one of them for a ride," he said once he finished his story. "I may get on Horace, too, if my bones don't ache so much by midday. Right now they're so stiff I think they're forgetting that they're not in a grave yet." He threw his head back and laughed harshly.

Eiryenne left as silently as she'd arrived. Talking to people, even Hayden, made her nervous. If she really got into the story he was telling, she might ask a quick question or two, but that was about it. At least he didn't mind or try to make awkward small talk like some of the other folk.

Her belly continued to grumble as she walked through the village. A single apple wasn't much, but it would get her through the next few hours. She decided that she'd borrow Hayden's gear and try to go hunting again. She rarely had a successful hunt, but what little luck she had saved her during the famine, and she was hoping things would turn her way again. She would try her luck at the butcher's first, though. She could sometimes get a meaty bone or two from him, or at least steal some food from his neighbour's dogs. They were supposed to guard the houses, but there was one in particular that had warmed up to her and was not as possessive of its scraps as the rest.

But the village boys soon ruined her plans. She heard their muffled footfalls on the grassy hill and picked up her pace. She expected the rock and didn't think this encounter would go any differently. What she didn't expect was the fire. They weren't throwing rocks, they were using metal tongs to chuck red-hot coals, having stolen both from the smith's hut. They'd done it once before, and their parents had scolded them harshly for it. They'd nearly set fire to a hut the first time. But evidently her reaction had been satisfying enough for them to try again.

The coal hurtled through the air, landing at her feet in a patch of dry grass and lighting the tips of nearby leaves. It was a small blaze, but terror had taken hold of her at the sight of the flames. Her vision blurred and throat closed; it suddenly became hard to breathe. Her earliest memory had been of flames and of people screaming and dying in the blaze. Embedded within her was a fear of fire and the death and destruction it represented to her. She screamed.

Her screams turned into shrieks as more coals fell at her feet. She turned and bolted through the village and the woods, running until her legs could carry her no more. She fell to her knees at the base of a tree, breathing heavily, her heart still racing. But her anxiety only amplified her other fears. Something rustled in the bushes, and in her mind, it immediately turned into one of the bloodthirsty wolves from Hayden's stories. The new fear had given her another burst of energy. She screamed again and ran in the other direction, every tree trunk and shadow seeming to reach out to strangle her.

Eiryenne jumped the fence without even noticing that she had skinned her knees. Still in a blind panic, she raced through the pasture until she found the horses. She collapsed against Horace, wrapping her arms tightly around his thick, shaggy neck and burying her forehead in his mane. Neil had spooked at her sudden arrival and was now pacing around the pasture, but the old gelding didn't bat an eyelid.

There were shouts from the village at first, no doubt the elders yelling at the boys for almost starting another fire. Pranks were one thing but putting the entire village in danger of a fire was not taken lightly. They'd all be whipped thoroughly for it. But the thought did not make Eiryenne feel any better.

Eventually, the noises died away, until all she could hear was Horace's steady breathing and the sound of Neil, now calm and chomping some grass nearby. The big horse's sides rose and fell evenly beneath her hands. She forced herself to think of him and not the fire. Horace had been in the village for as long as she could remember. He was a calm, constant presence in what could otherwise be a chaotic environment. The world could be ending, and Horace would still be here, steady as always. It was that steadiness that Eiryenne tried to focus on until it found its way into her, too.

Time passed. Horace continued to stand there patiently. The girl calmed down little by little, until at last she stood back and gave the horse a pat on the nose for his patience.

It had been a while since she'd had a panic attack like this. She'd had a few during the eight years that she'd lived with Aunt Gretchen, but the main ones started when their house burned down after being struck by lightning, taking her aunt with it.

Looking around to make sure there was no one in the field beside her and the horses, Eiryenne slipped a hand beneath the collar of her shirt and closed it around the jewelled necklace. It hung there on a chain, tucked away and hidden, the lower half bunched up inside a small herb bag for concealment.

Carefully opening the bag, she slid out the rest of the necklace and laid it across her palm, gazing at the stones. There were five of them: four small teardrops surrounding the centre piece, a large, gleaming gem with sharp edges and engraved faces. All of them were a deep, dark blue, so dark they seemed to be black when in shadow. But as the sun hit them, it brought out the veins of shifting colour, looking like little blue lightning bolts trapped within the stone. The gems were attached to silver hoops that kept them on the silver chain.

She didn't dare to take it out too often. If anyone so much as glimpsed it, it would be stolen in an instant, so she kept it hidden under her shirt, the stones wrapped up in an herb pouch so that even if the necklace slipped out from the folds of her clothes, it would just look as if she was wearing a spice pouch on a chain.

No one in the village had anything that came even close to it. These were a rich man's jewels, and she knew it. What she didn't know was how she came to have them. Aunt Gretchen seemed to know, but she said little on the matter. She only told the girl that she must not let anyone see the necklace, or they would steal it. And she must never, ever let someone else take it. It always had to be kept under guard; she couldn't take it off. It was important, Gretchen had said. A very valuable family heirloom. The only thing left to her by her parents. She'd tell her more when Eiryenne was older. Someday, when she was ready, she'd find out why it was special.

She never got the chance. Aunt Gretchen died when she was eight. She'd been living in squalor ever since, alternating between Hayden's barn loft and the pig shed. She preferred sleeping near the horses, but the barn was open and cold, so in the chillier months she had to use the pig shed to stay warm enough to sleep.

There were a lot of unanswered questions, perhaps some she could have gotten the answer to if she'd have asked. But Eiryenne was a quiet child even before Gretchen's death, so she rarely ventured to ask something outright. What she did know was that Gretchen wasn't really her aunt, and the circumstances of her parents' deaths were not revealed in full to the other villagers. A raid, a fire. That was all Gretchen said. And she took all those unspoken secrets to the grave with her.

Eiryenne ran her fingers over the stones, marvelling at how someone who had so little could possess something so fine. She'd usually been glad to hide her secret treasure, tucking it deep under the folds of her shirt and rubbing as much dirt into the silver chain as she could, trying to make it as inconspicuous as possible. But sometimes it frustrated her. She wondered, what good was something like this when it was so little? During the famine, she had been very tempted to try to sell it. But that would have been risky since few merchants ever came to her tiny village, and most would steal as soon as they would sell. Something else held her back, too. She couldn't bear the thought of parting with her parents' last gift.

Gazing into those dark navy swirls could be mesmerizing. It could lure her into a sort of trance, where her thoughts slowed and the only thing in her mind would be the image of the dark, iridescent crystalline depths. It was what she wanted now; it took away the last traces of her panic.

The sound of footsteps on the grass made her jump. She stuffed the necklace back down her shirt and turned so abruptly that Neil spooked. Old Horace just yawned and continued to graze.

She needn't have worried. It was only Hayden coming toward them. He had a difficult time seeing through his good eye, and she'd been on his blind side. If he'd noticed the necklace, he paid it no attention.

"Silly hooligans, nothing better to do than play dangerous tricks that could cost us all," he grumbled. "I lost a barn in a fire once, it's not a pretty sight at all … they should know better by now than to play with fire."

Eiryenne looked at the ground. She wished those boys would find something else to do with their time besides terrorizing her. She wished she wasn't so afraid of everything. She could go on and on about the things she wished for, like a solid meal, warm clothes, a house, friends, parents … but from prior experience, she knew that such thinking would get her nowhere. It was always best to keep moving and do what you could with what you had. At the moment, what she had were two fine horses. It was time to go for a ride.

"Don't let it bother you, girl," the old man continued. He paused, rubbing a hand over his balding head. "Look, I know you feel out of place here. But someday you'll find something you're good at, and you'll know that you got a path set for you. Maybe you just haven't found it yet because it's different than them other kids. But when you finally walk down that path, you'll know. Trust me. You'll just know."

"You really think I have a future, Hayden?" Eiryenne said softly. "I have nothing."

"You're here for something special, kiddo." His face crinkled in a smile. "And don't let anyone tell you any different. Maybe it's horses that are in your future. I dunno. What I do know is that you probably want to go for a ride right now, so I ought to unlock the tack room." And with that he was off to the barn.

He was a strange man, thought Eiryenne. But a good one.

As she walked over to the tack room, Hayden was reaching for Horace's saddle.

"Um, I'll, I'll take Neil today," she said. Though the younger horse was wilder and harder to control, something inside her wanted to be on a horse that could actually run as opposed to just lumber along. She wanted to lose herself in the exhilaration of Neil's gallop.

"All right, if you think you can handle him, go for it."

Hayden stood by the fence, watching with his good eye as she caught the spirited stallion and put on his saddle and bridle.

"I'd also like to borrow your gear," she said, still not looking at him. "Try to hunt."

"Go right ahead. God knows I have no use for those things anymore," he chuckled.

Eiryenne knew where he kept his old hunting stuff. She went into the back room and retrieved a bow, an old hunting knife, a coil of rope, and a small pack. She put the gear into the pack while she planned out her route. She'd let Neil run for a while until they reached the lake. Then she'd tie him up by the big oak and go try to catch something. She wasn't that bad of a shot with the bow; she just usually didn't go deep enough into the woods to find much game. Even the thought of venturing out around the lake by herself frightened her. But her hunger was making her desperate.

She put the pack on her back and swung up into the saddle. Neil pranced on the spot, eager to get going.

"He looks lively today." Hayden said with a chuckle. "You might want to use that rope to tie yourself to the saddle. You know he always bucks when he's that excited."

He had a point. Neil continued to fidget, his hindquarters quivering. He pulled at the rope that still tied him to the fence. Eiryenne knew that if she could ride out the first storm of bucks, it would be mostly smooth sailing from there. So, she did as Hayden suggested and wound a piece of rope around her waist, tying it to the saddle with a quick-release knot that she could undo once Neil calmed down.

Hayden was still talking about the kinds of training Neil could benefit from when the rumble reached their ears. He froze in mid-sentence, listening. Eiryenne listened, too. It sounded like thunder at first, but then she realized it was something different—the sound of hooves. Lots of them.

"Horses," said Hayden. "That's odd."

Eiryenne craned her neck to try to see the riders, her thoughts racing. There had never been large groups of horsemen passing through here. Maybe these were just lost merchants. No reason to worry, none at all.

Then she heard the screams and knew that her worst fears were confirmed; these were raiders.

She could see the outlines of the horsemen. They rode with swords and axes and cut down anyone in their path.

For once, Hayden was lost for words. Instead, he set to untying the rope that bound Neil to the fence. His hands were shaking.

The stables were at the far side of the village; the raiders hadn't reached them yet. But they were coming closer. Eiryenne tried to shut out the sounds of people dying, and homes being destroyed. She tried to keep her gaze on Neil's mane. She could feel a panic attack coming, but her common sense told her that she needed to keep her head if she wanted to survive this.

Then an inhuman screech pierced the air, followed by dull thudding. Wingbeats, Eiryenne realized. She looked up and gasped.

Huge, dark-grey beasts were circling the village. They had wings like a plucked chicken's, lizard-like tails, and squished-up muzzles filled with serrated teeth. Their eyes burned a demonic red, and they took turns swooping down onto the village, demolishing entire buildings with each thrash of their tails. Red beams of light streamed from their mouths, turning the countryside into a single solid blaze of fire.

Eiryenne bit her tongue hard to keep from screaming.

Hayden, too, was looking at the sky. "My god," he whispered. He continued to fumble with the rope. Neil had a knack for untying knots, so Eiryenne had made a particularly tough one to keep him in one place. Now she was wishing fervently that she'd done a simple knot.

One of the demons in the sky turned in the direction of the stable. It extended its wings and dove.

Hayden finally yanked the rope free of the fence, slapping Neil on the rump with it. "Hya! Get going!"

The demon landed next to them.

Neil shot out of the gate like he was on fire. He flew across the field, Eiryenne bent low over his mane. There was a strangled yell from behind them, followed by a sickly crunch. Eiryenne looked over her shoulder to see Hayden disappearing down the monster's gullet. A couple of the raiders had noticed her, too. Now that they were closer, she could see that they were not dressed in the tattered rags of bandits. They all wore dark leather uniforms with silver insignia on the front.

They weren't bandits. They were soldiers.

Her horse jumped the back fence like it wasn't even there. He was as terrified by the invaders as she was, desperate to get away from that scary place. He bolted through the woods, dodging tree trunks, branches were whipping at Eiryenne's face. They were already past the lake when she heard sounds of pursuit. Looking back, she saw that two mounted soldiers were following her. One of the demons flew above them, Hayden's blood still staining its jaws. Its murderous eyes were fixed on her.

Eiryenne grabbed for the reins and heaved on them, managing to turn the panicked horse away from the clearing ahead back toward a thicker part of the forest. He crashed through the undergrowth and squeezed between trees. If it wasn't for the rope, the heavier branches would have knocked her right off the horse.

The sounds of the other horses were getting fainter. Neil's smaller size let him move through the thicket more easily than the big warhorses. Though they could rip through the bushes that tangled Neil, they couldn't follow him through the narrower cracks between trees.

Eiryenne knew none of this. The lack of food and exhaustion had finally caught up to her, overpowering the adrenaline. Her head drooped as sudden fatigue took over her limbs.

Then she heard the screech of the demon overhead and fainted.

Chapter 2 ~ Lost and Found

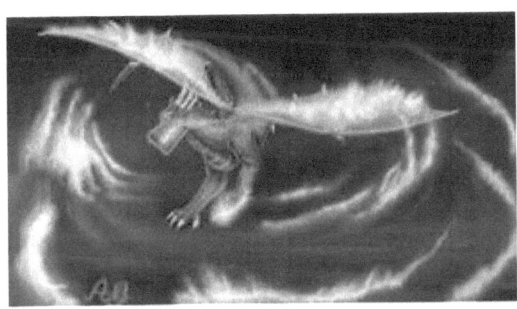

Eiryenne woke to the sounds of chattering birds and swishing leaves. As she opened her eyes an unfamiliar forest greeted her, filled with elm and spruce and none of the oaks she was used to seeing at home.

Then she realized she was lying on something that moved and snorted—Neil. Her body was stretched out in an awkward position. Her feet were jammed into stirrups, a rope held her waist to the saddle, and tangles of mane were still clutched in her hands.

At first, she was confused. Where was her pig shed and bed of straw? Why was she tied to Neil's back? Slowly, the attack on her village came back to her. She shivered and hugged her horse around the neck.

"Clever boy," she whispered. He'd somehow managed to escape them all, even with an unconscious girl as a dead weight on his back.

Her horse nickered weakly. He was hobbling along slowly, limping heavily on his left front leg. The chase had cost him.

Eiryenne sat up and groaned. Every one of her muscles ached, stiff and sore from spending so much time in an uncomfortable pose. Her face and limbs were covered with bleeding cuts and scratches where the branches had torn her skin. The insides of her calves had chaffed against the stirrup leathers until they were raw. But she was alive. And that was something to be thankful for, considering the odds.

She looked around uncertain as to how long she was out.

Most of the day, by the looks of it, she thought. The sun had begun to dip toward the southern horizon, casting a gradient of gold out across the clouds and over the forest. A light breeze blew from the east, scattering leaves in its wake.

Neil stopped to rest his sore leg, taking the weight off his hoof. The girl pulled at the knot securing her to his saddle, thanking the stars that it had held. It took her a few tries, but the stiffened quick-release knot soon fell away. She stumbled from the saddle. Her legs did not support her, and she landed in a heap next to the horse. She expected him to take off, as he usually did when he dumped his rider, but instead he continued to stand there, head hung low. She could already see the swelling setting in around his left fetlock. There were numerous scratches and bumps on him as well from where he'd crashed through the undergrowth. Streaks of dried sweat and blood marred his usually sleek coat, and his eyes were listless.

Eiryenne forced herself to her feet, grabbing on to Neil's mane for balance. Then she took him by the bridle and began to walk. Sitting still would only stiffen their muscles, she told herself; they needed to keep moving.

They were halfway across the clearing when she heard the noise again. Hooves, and lots of them. Terror paralysed her already stiff muscles. She tried raise her foot back into the stirrup, but her other knee folded underneath her. She fell back into a tangled heap.

Suddenly there were hoofbeats right next to her.

"Hey, are you all right?" said a woman's voice.

Eiryenne looked up. A stranger was looking down at her from the back of a tall dun horse. She had kind grey eyes and light brown hair tied back in a ponytail. Her wide-brimmed hat, light green jacket, and leather boots were worn but sturdy, with only a few patches. Two other horses, with saddles but no riders, were tied on a string behind her own mount.

The woman slid off her horse and looked Eiryenne over. "You and your horse are quite a mess," she said. "What happened? Aren't you too young to be travelling by yourself?"

Eiryenne struggled to her feet, ignoring the outstretched hand. She met the stranger's eyes briefly before looking away.

Noting their battered state, the woman spoke again. "Was it raiders?"

Eiryenne still didn't meet her eyes, but she gave the tiniest of nods.

"Hmm. Might be the same ones that almost got me," said the woman. "I hadn't heard of bandits in this area before. Always moved my sheep through without a problem. Anyway, I'm Tina. What's your name?"

"This is Neil," she replied hesitantly, patting her horse's neck. "And I'm Eiryenne." She paused. "You're a shepherd?"

"Yes. The… the raiders took my whole flock, as well as my friends." Tina gestured to the riderless horses. Then she took something out of her saddle bag. "Here," she said, holding out a small white container. "This will help with the cuts. You should put some on your horse, too."

The girl was speechless for a moment. After all the cruelty she'd seen that day, this small act of kindness surprised her. She took the can with unsteady hands. "Thank you." She opened it and rubbed some of the white salve onto her worst cuts. Then she turned to Neil, putting some on his injuries as well. He was so tired that he didn't even mind her poking his wounds.

Eiryenne wondered whether the raiders were still after her. Should she warn the shepherd? If they came for her and killed Tina, it would be her fault. "You should go, they might still come for me."

Tina looked thoughtful. "How did they look like, these raiders?"

"Soldiers. They were soldiers," Eiryenne said quietly. "Black uniforms with silver signs on the front. Dangerous."

Tina laughed. "Well, in that case you're quite welcome to camp with us. The Empire is no friend of mine, trust me."

"The Empire?"

"Those were Imperial soldiers you saw. Probably the same ones that attacked my group. I'd heard that there was a regiment moving through the area, but they were supposed to pass well north of here. I wonder why they pulled off course like that."

It occurred to Eiryenne that she knew this word from somewhere. She'd heard it in Hayden's stories. An Empire. That sounded big. It seemed strange that there could be something that big in the world that had previously only contained her small village and the surrounding countryside. Why on earth would an entire Empire be after *her*? She thought.

"Is this part of the Empire?" she asked after a pause.

"No. It's quite a ways away. But the Emperor is a greedy man. He always had troops out and about, looking for new lands to conquer. He's never shown much interest in Turmain, though. There's just not much here besides a few small towns and farming villages. My guess is that they were heading to neighbouring Lorahira before whatever it was that made them turn caught their attention."

Neither Neil nor Eiryenne were in any shape to go much farther that evening, so Tina decided to stop for the night. They made camp in a small clearing surrounded by alders. Tina untacked her horses then helped the girl slide the saddle off Neil. She found an extra halter and rope to picket him, not that the horse would go far even if he was loose.

"Here," said the shepherd. She pulled two packets of bread and dried meat out of her pack and handed one to Eiryenne. "You must be hungry."

The girl was ravenous. She tore into her food, wolfing down large chunks with gusto. She didn't remember the last time she had such a big meal.

"You're inhaling that stuff like you haven't eaten for days," joked Tina.

"I haven't. Apart from an apple and a scrap of meat."

"Oh." Tina's face grew serious, and she eyed Eiryenne's thin frame with what seemed to be concern. "Slow down, then. If your body isn't used to so much food, then eating too much can overwhelm your system. I knew a woman who, stranded in the desert, nearly starved to death. She just managed to make it to the edge and the town that lay there, only to die when she ate a full meal all at once."

The bread dropped from Eiryenne's mouth. "Okay … I think that will be it for now, then."

Tina gave her some bandages to put on her more serious cuts then went into the woods. Eiryenne was confused when she saw her coming back with an armful of dry timber. The woman piled the wood in the middle of the clearing in a shallow rock-lined pit she'd dug earlier.

A sinking feeling crept into the pit of Eiryenne's stomach, and it was nothing to do with the food. She had remembered similar pits that the villagers dug for their bonfires, so she opened her mouth to say something, but no words came out.

It was only when Tina struck her flint and lit the tinder that Eiryenne yelped. Tina looked up at her, puzzled.

"Is something wrong?"

But Eiryenne's throat had closed again. She'd pushed herself as far away from the fire pit as possible and curled up into a tight, shaking ball against the tree trunks.

The blaze continued to grow, wrapping its tendrils around the smaller twigs. Tina blew on it before coming over to her new friend.

"What is it?" She took the panicked girl by the shoulders. "Eiryenne, talk to me."

"F-f-fire."

"Yes, I started a campfire. It will keep us warm. Good heavens, girl, what is the matter with you?"

The fire began to crackle as it met the bits of sap still stuck between slivers of wood. It expanded until it began to consume one of the logs. Tongues of flame danced up from its burning bark. They seemed to form grasping hands, reaching to pull Eiryenne into the blaze.

"Stop it," she screamed, wrenching herself out of Tina's grip. "It burns. Stop!"

Tina got up, looking from the terrified teen to the campfire. Then she walked back and kicked dirt over the flames. They quickly sizzled out of existence.

Tina looked back, but Eiryenne was already out cold.

***

That night, after her usual nightmares about fire, Eiryenne's dreams turned to her memories. She dreamed about a day several weeks ago when she was at Hayden's house and he was telling her about the wolves.

"Huge," he exclaimed. "As big as a deer, Bigger. They'll eat anything, too." He waved his arms. "Dyre wolves, they're called. Bloodthirsty critters, them."

"You always tell me about the scary ones, Hayden," said Eiryenne. "Why don't you have more stories about unicorns? Or centaurs and pegasi?" Of course, that's all they were, stories, right?

"That's because the mean creatures were usually the ones I heard about," replied the old man. He opened his storybook, gliding through the pages more by feel than by sight. Despite his bad eye, he seemed to know what was on every page as though he was looking right at it. The book was old with crinkled, yellowing paper and faded colours. On every page was a new story, a new mythical creature he could tell his young friend about. She couldn't read the words, but there were far more pictures than letters. And though the coloured inks had grown faint with age, his own words made it easy for Eiryenne to bring the creature to life in her head.

He stopped at one of the pages near the back. "Ah. This one," he mumbled, feeling across the page with a thumb. "Dragons." He gave Eiryenne the book while he continued. "Those are huge, lizard-like beasts with wings that blot out the sky and a glare that turns you to stone."

Eiryenne peered across the page. There were no words at all on this one, just an illustration. It showed a reptilian creature with a wedge-shaped head, a neck twice the length of its snakelike body, and a long, curling tail. It had wings instead of front paws, that took up most of the page. Small scales dotted its body, and its ugly muzzle was wrinkled in a snarl.

She stared at the image and frowned. "It's ugly," she said. "I don't like it."

"No one in their right mind would," said Hayden. "Them dragons, they wolf down people like ants, they do."

But Eiryenne had meant something more by that statement. As she continued to look at the image, she was struck by the inherent *wrongness* of the creature. Its neck was too long. Its jaws were too flimsy. It looked deformed. With every other beast that Hayden had shown her, she'd somehow been able to understand the creature and picture it romping about some distant corner of the world. Not so with the dragon.

"Hayden, is this *really* what they looked like?" she asked, flipping through the book. Pictures of Dyre wolves, griffins, unicorns, and pegasi flashed before her eyes. Now, suddenly, she started to doubt them.

"It's as good a guess as any, comin' from those that lived to tell the tale," he said, chuckling. "After all, dragons breathe fire, did ya know?"

The conversation ended. Eiryenne had put down the book, thanked Hayden for his stories, and gone out to take Horace for a ride. But in her dream, she continued to flip through the pages. Faster and faster, they whipped through her fingers until the creatures on them began to move. They leapt from the paper, growing large and landing around her. But as they turned to look in her direction, they suddenly morphed into the grey demons that had attacked her village.

Eiryenne gasped. She backed away, her frozen legs refusing to run. She dropped the book.

Something sprang out from the last few pages. A serpentine silhouette formed at the edges of her vision. There was fire coming out from between its jaws.

***

When Eiryenne woke, she was covered in cold sweat. She was still sore, but she shivered with a combination of cold and fear. The nights were getting chillier, and the mornings as well. Her breath formed into steam on the crisp morning breeze.

It was well past dawn. The sun was almost a third of the way to the middle of the azure sky. There were few clouds to block its rays today, but the promise of winter was stealing away its warmth.

Tina sat across from Eiryenne on the opposite side of the clearing. She was munching on some bread. As Eiryenne sat up, she put the bread down, looking at the girl in silence. There was something new in her gaze. She was looking at her strangely, almost warily.

She'd seen that look before. Eiryenne realized Tina thought she was crazy.

The villagers gave her that look sometimes when they saw her living in the pig shed or listening to Hayden's stories. It was often the other girls that did it, glancing at her down their noses as they busied themselves in their weaving or embroidery while she toiled away with the sheep or horses. She'd learned to stop caring about what they thought a long time ago.

But for some reason, Eiryenne didn't want Tina to think she was crazy. Her opinion meant something. Eiryenne wasn't sure what that was, but she felt that she owed the shepherd an explanation since the woman was obviously having second thoughts about rescuing someone who did not appear to be sane. After all, normal people didn't shriek and panic at the sight of a small campfire.

"Um …," she began nervously, "about last night." She expected Tina to say something, but the shepherd remained silent, her expression unchanged. Eiryenne took a breath. "About the-the fire." She looked at the ground, uncertain how to explain this. Then she glanced up to where Neil was picketed with the other horses. *Pretend you're explaining it to Neil,* she told herself. "I'm sorry," she continued. She looked Neil in the eye and pretended Tina wasn't there. Now the words poured out, unhindered. "My parents died in a fire a long time ago. It's the first thing I remember. Then my aunt's house burned down a few years ago, killing her and nearly getting me, too. So, fire scares me. And sometimes talking to people does, too. So please don't think that I'm crazy by talking to my horse right now." She let out a breath and made herself look back at Tina.

The shepherd's expression had changed to pity. "It's all right. I understand." She paused. "You know, I used to be afraid of horses, believe it or not. One of them kicked me when I was a little girl and broke my arm. I refused to go near them for years."

"Really? So how did you—?"

"Master the fear?" Tina looked thoughtful. "It took some practice. At first, I just tried standing a way away from the corral. Then I began to move closer. I was scared stiff that first time when I was at the fence." She chuckled. "That was it for a while. I couldn't go past the fence. Then one day my sister came home crying that our brother was mauled by a bear while playing the woods. He was bleeding badly, she said. She didn't know how much longer he'd make it. I ran until I found him, curled up in the grass and covered in blood. His horse saved him, he told me. It drove off the bear before it could finish him. Anyway, the only way to get my brother back was on his horse. And that's what I did. The poor beast was bleeding badly itself. I guess that made me a bit less scared of him. So, I slung my brother across the horse's back and got them back to the village."

"Did he live?"

"My brother did. The physician told me I got him there just in time. But the horse didn't. He collapsed after he brought us back. He knew he'd done his job." Tina looked pensively at the horizon.

"And after that you weren't afraid," guessed Eiryenne.

"No. I'd been forced to confront my fear. And I'd learned about a different side to horses than I'd seen before. I saw the undying loyalty that horse showed to my brother, and that made me change my mind." She paused then looked back at her guest. "So, think about fire. It keeps us warm. It cooks our food. It protects us from regular wildlife. It can be useful."

Eiryenne wasn't sure what she'd meant by *regular*, but she knew that most animals instinctually avoided fire. Still, it was hard to think of fire in this new light that Tina offered.

"It will take time," said Tina. "But you *can* fight fear. Trust me."

"Hmm." She decided to take the topic away from fire for now. "Where are your siblings now? Are they shepherds, too?"

"Tayer and Christine, shepherds?" Tina chuckled at the thought. "No. They each had their own trade. As for their fate," Her face grew sombre. "Christine died in a raid by Imperial soldiers when she was about your age. Tayer was killed later, in a war."

"Is that why you hate the Empire?" Eiryenne asked quietly. Now the reasons for Tina's enthusiasm in helping her yesterday became clearer. She, too, was a victim of the Empire.

"When Tayer died, I decided I needed to make a change," Tina said. "So, I left … I left what I was doing. And I went and became a shepherd. This quiet life suits me." Something in her tone told Eiryenne not to ask more. "At least it *was* quiet until I ran into those soldiers two days ago."

She told Eiryenne to get her breakfast from the pack before finishing her own bread in silence.

The swelling on Neil's fetlock had gone down enough for him to travel, but Tina said it would be best if Eiryenne rode one of the others instead. Still munching her food, she looked over at the two horses that were picketed between Neil and Tina's own horse, Lahu.

The first was a dark-bay gelding. A narrow star of white marked his forehead, and his body was a deep, dark brown that faded smoothly into the black on his lightly feathered lower legs. He was tall, taller than both Lahu and Neil, almost reaching the height of draft horses like Horace. His powerful hindquarters rippled with muscle, and the breeze tossed strands of his jet-black mane into the air.

The horse next to him was almost pony sized. Its chocolate brown coat was broken up by white splotches around its withers and legs. Its long, uncombed forelock almost covered its eyes, and each stubby leg ended with a white sock. The animal nickered to his companion, but it was Neil who answered it first.

Looking at the size of the smaller horse, Eiryenne wondered whether one of Tina's companions had been a child.

"Chief is probably too big for you," said the shepherd. "I'd recommend Reygo."

"Okay."

"And let Chief carry Neil's saddle. It's best to avoid putting any weight on him now."

Once she'd changed Neil's bandages, Eiryenne tied Neil's saddle on top of the bigger horse's and slipped her pack into his saddle bags. Her stiff shoulders would thank her for that as the day wore on. Then she tied a rope to Neil's halter before saddling Reygo and mounting.

"By the way," the shepherd said. "I'm curious; how did you get by without fire? The winters down in the valleys aren't that bad, but I still can't imagine going without a campfire at night."

"When I lived with my aunt, she had a small stove," Eiryenne answered. "I couldn't see the fire inside there, so I was okay with it. After the house burned down, the stove was one of the few items that made it through. I kept it in the pig shed where I spent my winters, only lighting it on the coldest nights where nobody would be out and about.

If the pigs' owner saw smoke coming from his shed, he'd take it away. Too much dry straw." Hayden knew about the stove; he wouldn't let her bring it into the stable. It was part of the reason she spent the winter months in the pig shed. "After the house burned down, I started sleeping in the pig shed. It was built up against the back wall of a larger house, which had its own stove and gave off enough warmth to keep me and the pigs from freezing to death."

"I see."

Tina led the way on Lahu. Behind them was their unofficial pack horse, tied on a string. Eiryenne, holding Reygo's reins in one hand and Neil's rope in the other, brought up the rear.

They'd head to the town of Rosfiord, Tina told her. It lay on the Rosen River and was one of the northernmost cities in Turmain. To the south was the capital and to the northwest was the border with Gosrun. It was not where Tina had been heading before the attack, but now that she'd lost the sheep, she saw no reason to continue on her original route. She had some friends in Rosfiord. It was where she spent most of her time when she wasn't out with the sheep.

"It's a quiet, quaint town," she continued. "I think you'll like it. We'll find a place for you and your horse."

"And what about you? Will you continue to be a shepherd?" Eiryenne asked.

"I'm not sure. I'll have to find out more about these raids first. If Turmain is being attacked, things must be very bad on the other end."

"The other end?"

Tina didn't answer.

They rode on, making their way through a winding path between the trees. Eiryenne noticed that the landscape was beginning to change. Instead of the flat fields and low hills she was used to, sharp ridges began to crest the earth, the trees and rocks on their tops thrown into sharp relief against the sky, like the teeth in the jaws of some fearsome beast.

Fallen leaves carpeted the forest floor and spilled onto the trail, muffling the sound of their horses' hooves. It was like someone had spilled a bucket of fiery paint, lighting the moist leaves with the bright autumn shades of red, orange, and yellow.

The colours of fire.

They rode throughout the day, meeting no one besides a squirrel and some whitetail deer that spooked Neil. He almost ripped the rope out of Eiryenne's grip, made slick by the drizzle. Reygo barely blinked. He seemed to be an experienced trail horse, even if he did balk at walking through puddles, no matter how shallow they were.

When they made camp that night, Tina didn't try to start a fire again. Instead, she made one farther out in the forest, out of Eiryenne's sight. But she could smell the smoke. The scent made her uneasy. It got even worse when Tina said that she wanted her to get comfortable with ash for a start. Eiryenne refused at first then thought of how the shepherd overcame her fear of horses. Small steps. She had gone up to the fence of the corral before she'd actually gotten on the horse. So Eiryenne told herself that she could do the same. It was just ash. There was no fire left.

Still, she couldn't stop her hand from shaking as Tina poured in the flaky grey powder. Even though she knew that the embers were long gone, every stir of the wind seemed to threaten to send up a new blaze.

But she felt no heat. Indeed, they'd gotten quite cool. She concentrated on that. It was no different than holding a handful of snow. Not so bad even, because the cold was not enough to burn her skin.

Actual coals took her longer to get used to, mostly because those were what the village boys would throw at her. More than a week went by before she was ready to hold an unlit coal. Tina then wanted to gauge the minimum distance that Eiryenne had to be from a fire to avoid panicking. At first it seemed that any fire, as long as it was within view, would trigger her fears. But Tina was patient; she kept on moving the fire back, and back, until she was on the top of the ridge and the fire was nothing more than a point of light at the edge of Eiryenne's vision. For once, the girl didn't run.

"We're making some progress," said Tina, coming back to the camp. "Next time I'll move it just a little closer. And eventually you'll be sitting right next to it without a problem."

"You really think it'll work?"

"Rosfiord is still a few weeks' travel away. We'll have plenty of time," replied the shepherd. She settled down on her blanket, which was still next to the fire pit, even though there was no fire. Then she reached behind her, fumbling in the back pocket for something.

Eiryenne began to groom Neil. His injuries were healing well, though she still wasn't riding him. In a day or two he should be ready to carry her weight again. Not that she minded Reygo that much; he wasn't too difficult to ride. But he plodded on with his head down as if he thought this trail was the most boring thing in the world. Neil, on the other hand, trotted along like it was an adventure, ears pricked, and nostrils flared at each new sight. Excitement glowed in his eyes, and his enthusiasm was contagious.

She ran a brush along his withers, careful to avoid the cuts on his shoulders. Most of them had already scabbed over, and she didn't want to risk reopening them. She carefully brushed dirt away from the wounds with her fingers and then replaced the few bandages that he was still wearing.

When she finished with him and turned back to the camp, she saw Tina doing something strange. The woman was holding a long, dark stick and using it to make markings in the dirt. At first Eiryenne thought they were drawings, but the lines took no definite shape. And something about the definite way that Tina drew them made her think that they weren't just random squiggles.

The girl walked over and crouched beside her. Something about the symbols looked familiar, but she wasn't sure where she'd seen them.

"What are those?" she asked.

"These?" Tina looked surprised. "Why they're letters, of course. I'm writing."

"Writing?" The word only drew a blank in Eiryenne's head. She'd never heard it before.

Tina slapped herself in the face. "Oh, of course. Most people in those small farming villages never learned to write or read. You probably have no idea what I'm talking about."

"No," admitted Eiryenne.

"Well, I'll show you." Tina scratched out a series of individual, spaced-out symbols and went on to explain how each letter corresponded to a sound, and by putting down the correct order of markings, you went on to make a word.

Now their evenings consisted of a writing lesson as well as fire phobia sessions.

Between learning letters and facing sparks, Eiryenne had little time to think about the possibility that she might still be followed. They'd gone too far, she reasoned. Even the demons couldn't be on them now.

Chapter 3 ~ Chance Meeting

Eiryenne dreamed about Hayden's storybook again. This time it turned to ashes in her hands as she was flipping to the last page. The corner of the page she was holding remained in her grasp. Tina's lessons came into play, and she read it aloud.

Today is the day, she read. *That everything changes. Today I dance with destiny. For as a—* She squinted. The next word, *harbinger,* was not yet part of her vocabulary. She didn't know what it meant.

The ashes at her feet swirled until they formed a long, serpentine shape. It was like the monster she'd seen in the book, but dark brown. It curled its tail around her feet and let out an ear-splitting yowl that made her cringe. There were other shapes moving around in the smoke, but she couldn't see them clearly.

Then there was a deep rumble from above them. The monster, as well as its surroundings, exploded in a burst of ash.

***

She woke quickly and sat bolt upright. The noise was continuing. The sky was covered with thick, dark-grey clouds. There was another rumble, followed by a flash of light.

Eiryenne sighed. It was only a thunderstorm.

Tina, as usual, was already up and eating breakfast. Her usual stores would have run out by now, but the packs on Chief's saddle had yielded a surprising amount of extra food. Eiryenne guessed that whoever his rider had been, he was a hearty eater. In any case, it was enough to get them to Rosfiord, and she was thankful for that.

As she ate, she wondered what she'd do once they got there. She wasn't sure, but she knew that after this trip, she'd have to do *something* to earn her food. And Neil's. He could live off grass on the road, but she knew that Hayden always supplemented his horses' diets with hay and grain, especially in the winter. It was already autumn, and there wasn't much grass left for him to crop. It also occurred to her that she would no longer have a free place to keep him. Most of the peasant kids she'd known did not have their own horses. Judging by the amount of food and care that Hayden put into his stables, she guessed it was simply not something that many kids could do, unless they knew somebody with an extra stall or space in their pasture.

Maybe Tina would help her with that. After all, she had to have a place for Lahu. And Eiryenne wasn't going to give up Neil after all they'd been through.

She was still deep in thought as she saddled Reygo. Whatever happened next, she told herself, she was going to keep Neil.

Her thoughts shifted to the strange dream she'd had that night. "Tina," she called. "What's a harbinger?"

"It's something or somebody that foreshadows the approach of something else," replied the woman. "A sign that tells you of an oncoming event before it happens. Like … geese could be the harbingers of autumn. We know that when they fly south, colder weather is coming." She paused. "Interesting word. Where did you hear it?"

"In a story."

The clouds continued to rumble as they moved out, but rain didn't fall. Instead, there was a strange kind of electrified tension in the air, as if the entire world was holding its breath, waiting for something to happen.

She'd felt this before, right before lighting struck a tree in front of her and set it ablaze. So Eiryenne kept on glancing up at the clouds as they rode, fearful that a bolt of fire would come zigzagging down from those ominous clouds.

But they held.

Apart from the occasional rumble of thunder, all was silent. Their horses' hooves made no noise as they trod along the sodden leaves, and the very sound of their breathing was sucked away by the heavy, humid air.

Up ahead of her, Tina abruptly cut away from their forest path, choosing to follow a narrow trail that led to the top of the ridge. It was a tall, rocky ridge, with a sheer cliff along most of its northern side. There were few points at which it could be breached but crossing it would shorten their journey. At least that was the explanation she gave.

Eiryenne leaned forward in the saddle as her horse fought his way up the incline. Rocks slid out from beneath his hooves as he tried to get his footing. Behind her she could hear Neil scrambling along as well. She thought it was unwise to lead a recently injured horse up this punishing trail, but she trusted that Tina knew what she was doing.

Once they'd gotten to the top, Tina looked around warily before moving out from the shelter of the trees onto the flat, sparse grassy area on the crest. Eiryenne followed her just as carefully. She was beginning to realize that this detour was not the shortcut that the shepherd was making it out to be.

Tina had spotted something. And whatever it was, she wanted to be well out of its way.

They had followed the top of the ridge in silence for a few minutes when the thunder struck up a new rhythm with a vengeance. It pulsed and roared, the pitch so deep that Eiryenne could feel it resonating within her bones. Flashes of light flared up from deep within the clouds. The patterns of orange and green were almost mesmerizing. Eiryenne was so caught up in watching them that she didn't notice that Tina had stopped until Reygo bumped into her horse.

"Why are we—" she began. But the rest of the girl's sentence was muffled by the deafening boom that rang out across the sky. She looked up again.

At the source of the storm, the clouds had thinned. Dark shapes were swirling through the air. They danced about one another and clashed with violent bursts of light.

It wasn't a thunderstorm at all. It was a battle.

Two of the shadows, slightly smaller than the third, made rapid circles around their foe. Green jets of light streaked through the sky but were dissolved in a flash of orange.

The hair on the back of Eiryenne's neck prickled. She tore her eyes away from the spectacle and looked around. The faint sound of closing wingbeats came to her ears. Then she spotted it: a demon, ash grey, flying toward them on bat-like wings. Malice glimmered in its eyes, fixed on her with insane intensity.

"Tina. Behind us," she shouted, kicking Reygo into a gallop. The shepherd whirled about then followed suit after seeing their pursuer.

Running away from him meant running down the ridge, straight under the fighting beasts in the clouds. But Eiryenne hoped they were too distracted with their own plight to notice a couple of riders passing by.

She pressed Reygo to go as fast as she dared on the rocky, uneven ground. Neil cantered along beside them, the whites of his eyes showing as he spooked at every noise and flash.

As they passed beneath the battle in the air, Eiryenne could no longer hear her horse's hooves above the cacophony. In front of them, the ridge widened out into a small plateau before narrowing sharply. Too sharply. It funnelled down into a narrow walkway that reached a dead end some ten feet out.

Realizing this, Eiryenne yanked on Reygo's reins. They had nowhere to go. She spun him around as Lahu and Chief clattered to a halt beside them.

The demon saw that its prey was trapped. It dipped its wings and began to dive.

Out of the corner of her eye, Eiryenne saw Tina pull a short sword out of her bag.

There was another flash of light, and a bolt of yellowish orange light spilled down from the clouds. The demon pulled out of its dive sharply to avoid it, letting out an angry squawk. Angling its wings, it ascended into the clouds. Joining the two smaller figures, it rushed the source of the orange.

There was a booming roar, and a blinding flash of light broke out from the centre figure as the winged beasts collided. Then all four of them came hurtling down toward the ground. They fell so fast that they were just dark, indistinguishable blurs as they sped towards the earth and hit the far edge of the plateau in an explosion of dust and smoke.

Reygo reared, almost throwing off his rider. Eiryenne struggled to keep him under control and hold on to her other panicked horse. She tied the rope around her saddle horn before Neil could yank it from her hands.

But as the dust slowly began to settle, there was only silence.

The unknown combatants had landed on a small ridge that sprouted from the edge of the plateau. It was at an angle to Eiryenne and Tina, so they couldn't see what lay in the craters made by the fallen creatures.

Then movement reached their ears. Something stirred in the centre crater, still obscured by the dust and angle.

There was a brief scrape of steel against leather, and a huge, shining sword appeared out of the dust. It was driven point down in the edge of the crater, and its wielder used it to haul himself out of the hole.

The man stood there, breathing hard. Now that he was on the lip of the crater, Eiryenne could make out his features, illuminated by a ray of light that had come through the parted clouds. Beside her, she heard Tina stifle a gasp.

The stranger's short blonde hair streamed back over his ears. It seemed to catch the sun and make his skin glow. This gave his fierce, angular face a certain ageless, almost ethereal quality. He had thick, sharply angled eyebrows and a short beard covering the lower half of his face, ending in a sharp point at his chin.

His medium-length jacket was dark brown, with a hint of red, reaching halfway to his knees. A thick leather belt was clasped around his waist and on it hung an empty sheath to match his blade. A long, brownish-black cloak was draped across his shoulders. The leather-like fabric shifted slightly in the breeze.

He was bleeding from a large, deep wound on his shoulder, and his left arm hung limply at his side. There were numerous gashes on his torso and legs. Blood dripped down the side of his face as well. But despite all this, his expression betrayed no hint of pain.

"*You,*" Tina said softly. "I remember you. It's been many years, but the images of those days never left me."

"Well, if it isn't the soldier who became a shepherd. Strange place to meet old allies, Tina." The man's voice was deep but melodious, with a faint touch of some strange accent. He limped down the ridge toward them, leaning on his sword.

"Your memory is better than mine, D—" She paused, the word escaping her.

The stranger glanced at Eiryenne as he continued. "My name is Danzi." He narrowed his eyes. "Who's your friend?"

The girl flinched. Her breath caught in her chest as Danzi's piercing gaze looked right through her. Now that he was closer, Eiryenne could see that his eyes were bright amber, with strange, slitted pupils like a cat's, only wider. He scrutinized her for a second or two before turning back to the shepherd. Relieved, she let out the breath she'd been holding.

"Her name's Eiryenne," said Tina. "Her village was attacked by Imperial soldiers. I ran into her shortly after losing my own flock to them." She paused again, looking Danzi up and down. "Now, you look like you could use some bandages."

Danzi shrugged. "Wouldn't hurt, if you have any to spare." He slid his sword back into its sheath, shifting his weight to his good leg.

Tina dismounted and opened one of her saddle bags as Danzi limped up to them. Now that he was level with them, Eiryenne could see just how tall he was. He towered over both women.

The shepherd handed him a fresh roll of bandages and some ointment. "Tell me, Danzi," she said. "What brings you out here?"

"Business, as always."

"Do you know why there are Imperial forces so far east? Turmain's been so quiet all these years. It just doesn't make any sense."

Danzi carefully wrapped up the large cut on his left shoulder. "They're looking," he said. He dipped his fingers in the ointment and spread some onto his other injuries.

"Looking? For what? New territories?"

"In part. Their other objective is the camp."

"Oh." Tina looked away. "I guess it was moved again."

"It is always moved. With an enemy like the Empire, no single place can be safe." The man finished tending to his injuries and looked up at Tina. "Where are you bound?"

"Rosfiord. You are welcome to accompany us, if you are able to ride. I know you're not one to enjoy sitting still."

"Indeed." He nodded.

Tina took a few packs, as well as the extra saddle, off Chief, redistributing the load amongst the other horses. She then handed the gelding's reins to the newcomer. Danzi's movements were stiff as he mounted the horse, but he gave no other indication that his injuries were bothering him.

"There's a trail back there that we missed when we were galloping away from the demon," Tina said to Eiryenne. "We'll take it to get off the ridge. But I don't think we'll go far today. Neil's leg is starting to swell up again." She was right. The uneven path and sudden burst of galloping had taken a toll on the young stallion.

Eiryenne let Tina lead the way, followed by the strange man. The girl was deep in thought. Who was this mysterious man? A soldier of some kind? How did he even get here?

She decided that he must have been riding one of those winged creatures in the battle. That explained his injuries and sudden appearance. Was his partner dead, then? she wondered. He'd walked away from the site of impact without a second thought.

Overcome by a sudden wave of curiosity, Eiryenne pulled Reygo to a stop. She hesitated, then looped Neil's rope around a nearby rock and turned toward the small ridge where the craters lay. There was another patch of raised ground next to it. If she went up there, she'd be able to peek into the craters without getting too close. So, they trotted up the incline, and Eiryenne craned her neck to see what had become of the beasts from the sky.

The first three craters contained badly singed bodies, more ash than flesh. There lay the demon that had pursued her, and next to it what looked like a giant eagle with the hindquarters of a lion: a griffin. There wasn't enough left of the third creature to make out what it was.

The fourth crater was empty.

Eiryenne was not sure what to make of this. She decided that Danzi's partner must have flown away while the dust was obscuring their view. It was alive, then. But why hadn't Danzi gone with it?

She turned her horse and caught up with the other two riders. She supposed the creature was injured by the fall, and maybe, like Neil, couldn't support a rider until it had healed.

The group didn't get far from the ridge before making camp. Neil was limping again; Eiryenne thought that Danzi looked like he'd topple off his horse at any moment. Most of his wounds had bled right through the bandages. After rewrapping them, the man sat down heavily against a tree and closed his eyes. He didn't say it, but he was tired.

Tina unpacked their things while Eiryenne gave their horses a rub-down and tended to Neil's leg. He'd been jittery all day, which hadn't helped his swollen fetlock at all. Even now, as Eiryenne tried to wrap up his leg, the stallion spooked and shied away. He looked around wildly with his nostrils flared. Something had him on edge.

Once she'd finished with him and eaten her evening ration, Tina called the girl over for their usual spelling lesson. Now that Eiryenne was starting to get the hang of her letters, Tina had started to have her spell out entire words in the dirt.

Today, the first task was writing her name.

The girl took her stick and hesitated, then wrote out 'AIR-YEN' in the dirt.

"Close, but you left off two letters," said Tina. She took another stick and added *NE* to the end of Eiryenne's name, as well as changing the *A* to an *E* at the start.

"Two N's? And an E? But why?"

"Well, some words and names are written differently than how they are spoken. Think of those extra letters as silent letters." Tina paused. "My name is pretty straightforward; it's written like it sounds." She glanced over at the man dozing on the edge of their camp. "But try writing Danzi's."

Eiryenne thought for a second then scribbled out 'DUN-ZEE' in the dirt. "Hmm, I got it wrong, didn't I? It doesn't quite sound like a U ... it sounds like something between an A and a U. So how do you write it?" She tried again, writing DAHN-ZEE.

"It's pronounced that way, but it's another one of those names that's said one way and written a little differently." Tina wrote DAN-ZI'with her stick. "Remember that if you ever have to write it. He gets annoyed if you misspell his name."

The girl studied the letters. They were much more legible than her own. "You've had some practice with this. I mean no offence, but where does a shepherd learn to write?"

"Ah, I wasn't always a shepherd," said Tina. "My father was a merchant. He had just enough wealth to send me to school. Later, I put my skills to use as an army scribe, keeping records of supplies and messages."

"You were in an army?" Eiryenne found it hard to picture Tina in the military. Then her brow furrowed as she remembered the raiders that destroyed her village. "The kind that burns down towns and pillages everything?"

"No, the kind that tries to stop people from doing that," said Tina. "It's also where I first came across Danzi." She paused. "But that's another story. Come on, back to our writing lesson. Don't forget those two extra letters on your name this time."

"Okay, but how do you even know that that's the correct spelling?"

"It says it right here, on your bracelet. Look." Tina reached out and took Eiryenne's wrist, gesturing to the worn piece of leather around it. On it was a single bead.

It was the only thing, aside from her necklace, that Eiryenne had from her parents. The bead was covered in dust but was glass underneath all the muck. She had to replace the leather several times as she was growing up, but the bead held together well. She'd thought that the markings in its surface were simply a pattern of scratches, but now that she knew the alphabet, looking closer she realized that they were letters. Letters that spelled out *Eiryenne.*

The neatly carved letters put her own awkward writing to shame. She took off the bracelet and put it on the ground next to a blank patch of dirt, deciding that now that she knew how to spell her name, she'd try writing it properly. Eiryenne leaned forward, trying to concentrate, and slowly started to etch an E into the ground, trying to imitate the straight lines and clean curves that were in the writing on the bead. But her end result was little better than the previous attempt, the lines still squiggly and rough.

"It will take some time," Tina said. "But you can learn to write that well if you practice. Not that you'll be writing on glass anytime soon," she added, glancing at the bead. "That was done by a specialized carver."

Eiryenne tried again, looking often at the bead for reference and trying to keep her hand steady. It was tough; she'd never needed to keep her hands steady for any of the ordinary village tasks she used to do. Slowly, her name began to take shape again, slightly neater than before. She concentrated, bending low over the ground until her nose almost touched the dirt. She didn't even notice when her necklace slipped out from under her shirt and hung in front of her chest.

"There." Satisfied with her work, she put her stick down and sat up, slipping the bracelet back on. The result was still nowhere near as neat as the carved writing on the bead but noticeably better than the first letters she'd scrawled.

"Nicely done." Tina applauded. "We'll make a scholar out of you yet." Then her gaze moved toward Eiryenne's neck. "Oh, that's a pretty necklace. Where did you get it?" She moved to reach out, but the girl instinctively drew back. An impoverished orphan didn't manage to keep a bejewelled necklace safe for thirteen years by letting strangers handle it.

"Family heirloom," she muttered. Then she felt the hair on the back of her neck prickle. There was movement at the edge of her vision. She turned.

Danzi, who'd been napping throughout her writing lesson, had woken up. He was looking right at her. Eiryenne realized that she'd never felt the full power of his gaze until then. He might have given her a glance, but now his complete attention was fixed on her. His amber eyes burned with an intensity that she'd hadn't seen before, resembling flames dancing across those slitted pupils that seemed to look right into her soul. Danzi held her gaze for a few seconds that felt like an eternity as everything around her seemed to blur and glow and her thoughts slowed into a dizzy trance. She could not tear her eyes away. Finally, his gaze travelled down toward the necklace. It seemed like he was examining every detail and crevice on the blue stones, even though he was sitting twenty yards away.

"Too dark to be sapphires, maybe an unusual kind of opal?" Tina continued to talk, unaware that Danzi had directed his attention to them.

Eiryenne mumbled something unintelligible and looked at the ground. She had a sudden urge to tuck the necklace back into the folds of her shirt. But at the same time, wouldn't that be disrespectful to Tina, treating her with the same suspicion as a petty jewellery thief? The shepherd has shown Eiryenne nothing but kindness, and she didn't want to offend her host. Surely, she was just curious about the stones. After all, who wouldn't be? They shone with an iridescent spectrum of blues and blacks, sparkling brightly in the late afternoon sun. It might be a rarity even to someone who hadn't spent their entire life in a small rural village.

"Absolutely beautiful. Definitely haven't seen anything like it before." The older woman was continuing to gaze at the stones, longing starting to creep into her voice. The longer she looked at them, the more she wanted to hold them. "Here, let me take a quick look—" Her hand came up quicker this time. Eiryenne couldn't have been able to grab it if she wanted to.

"*Stop.*" The voice was so deep, it was almost a growl. Tina's hand froze. Then she jerked it back, rubbing her fingers as if she'd been burned. Both she and Eiryenne turned around.

Danzi was staring at them. His face was grim. "Don't touch it." It wasn't a suggestion; it was an order.

Tina backed away from the girl. She shook her head but said nothing.

Eiryenne quickly stuffed the necklace back under her shirt.

***

The rest of the evening went quietly. Tina didn't mention the necklace again. In fact, she barely spoke to Eiryenne and tried to keep away from her. The girl was confused. What was it with this necklace?

The question spun about her head as night crept in, and she tucked herself under her blanket. She'd wondered about it before, but always in the context of how a poor village girl had what looked like a nobleman's gem. Now she was starting to get the feeling that it was more than just lost jewellery. Danzi obviously knew something about it that she didn't. But even the mere thought of asking him made her shiver. Even in his wounded state, the man intimidated her.

She must have been more tired than she realized, because despite all her musings, she was asleep within minutes.

***

Eiryenne woke to the sound of hushed voices. It was still mostly dark, though a faint hint of moonlight crept through the grey clouds that were scattered upon the sky. She didn't move, pretending to still be asleep. The sounds were faint, but if she held her breath, she just managed to make out bits and pieces of speech.

"… necklace. Tairung, very dangerous."

"Had no idea. How did it get here? What should we—"

"Let it be Balon's problem. Take to the castle."

"The properties can constrain them? Someone else should—"

"No, only mage. Reach is proportionate to power…"

"She is? Then by gods, Danzi, teach her! … needs to be prepared."

"Good point … should then … tell her in the morning—"

"No! She's too young, have some pity."

"… honestly think … am capable of pity?"

"… have something that awful hanging over her. Just give her some time. Ignorance is bliss."

"… may be right. She might just panic and throw it away. But will tell her before we reach—"

Eiryenne took a few deep breaths to calm herself before holding her breath again and listening. They were still talking, but she couldn't make out the rest of their conversation. She thought about what she'd heard. What was Tairung? Who was Balon? Where was the mage? What did she need to learn?

Just more questions. Never any answers.

Then she shivered. Most of what she'd heard made no sense to her, but one thing was clear, there was something very bad about the stones that hung around her neck.

Chapter 4 ~ The Necklace of Tairung

The next morning dawned misty and cold. Snaking strips of moisture clung to the ground like small clouds, finding crevices in rocks and within tree trunks and depositing tiny crystals of water that sparkled and flared in the morning sun.

Tina, as always, was already awake when Eiryenne woke up. She figured the shepherd must always get up at the crack of dawn, because Eiryenne was used to waking right after sunup.

Danzi woke up soon after she did. Droplets of water clung to his cloak and hair scattering into what looked like a million diamond shards when he moved. He looked slightly better today, more energized and alert. Condensation had also settled onto his sword, the wet metal and leather gleaming. A large, polished ruby set in its pommel stole Eiryenne's attention. It caught the sunlight and shone with an iridescent crimson light as if holding a small red fire of its own. The hilt itself was inlaid with gold.

So, he was no stranger to jewels. Eiryenne wondered whether that could be why he seemed to know something about her necklace. It also made her wonder about his status. His clothes, though not flimsy, were worn and had no other fancy adornments. But that jewelled sword had obviously belonged to a rich nobleman. Like her, he seemed to possess a gem beyond his rank.

Or did he?

Eiryenne watched him as he got up and limped to the centre of the camp. His leather scabbard and sturdy boots were worn with use. More than anything else, he had the air of a man who'd *done things*. And Eiryenne, with her quiet village upbringing, couldn't even begin to fathom what kind of life someone like that had led.

He bent down by the packs, took out a handful of dried meat, and wolfed it down. Then he looked over at the pile of sticks sitting in the middle of their clearing. Tina had brought them there, planning to have another fire therapy session with Eiryenne. She wasn't done gathering firewood, so she'd brought what she found into their camp.

Danzi didn't know this. He kneeled by the mound, evidently thinking that Tina was planning to light a campfire. He must have had a flint in his hands, because the pile burst into flames.

Eiryenne *was* getting better at handling fire but being within ten feet of one was still too much for her. She just managed to keep the scream from exiting her throat.

A clatter of falling wood sounded from the edge of their camp. Tina had dropped the sticks she was carrying. She ran into the camp, kicking dirt onto the fire until it went out. Danzi looked up at her with a mildly puzzled expression.

"Oh, have some pity on her," she said with a hint of exasperation. "The poor girl's afraid of fire. I was going to make one further out, where it wouldn't scare her as much."

Danzi raised an eyebrow but said nothing. He glanced at where Eiryenne was crouched, shivering badly but forcing herself to stay silent. Then he shrugged.

"Eiryenne." Tina went over to the girl and gripped her shoulders. "Go groom the horses. Come on, up you get."

It took over half an hour before the fear began to ebb out of her system. She groomed Neil, then Reygo, then Lahu, and had started on Chief before her fingers stopped shaking. Still, she was making progress, she told herself. At least she'd avoided a full-blown panic attack.

Once she was calm, Tina called her over. Eiryenne hesitated a little. She was thinking of how the woman tried to take her necklace the day before. But Danzi was standing next to Tina, and something told Eiryenne that she would not try to take it again in front of him. Then there was their conversation from last night to consider; maybe Tina now knew *why* she shouldn't take it.

She walked over to them, stopping just out of arm's reach.

"Well, Eiryenne," Tina began hesitantly. She seemed to be searching for the right words. Danzi stood beside her with his arms crossed and his face impassive. "This necklace that you have," the shepherd continued, "it's … special. Other people might try to take it from you. So Danzi and I have decided that you need to learn some skills, if you ever need to defend yourself."

"Skills?" she asked. "Like using a sword? You're going to teach me?"

"Not quite." Tina laughed nervously. "And it's not something that I can teach. Danzi has agreed to do it."

Eiryenne's confusion was mounting. "What?"

"It's something special that not everyone can do," Tina continued vaguely. "It's … well—"

"Cut to the chase," Danzi told her sharply. He turned to Eiryenne. "You are a mage. And I will teach you to use your magic."

Eiryenne was flabbergasted. Of all the things she expected to hear, this was the last. "Umm … me? A mage? What are you talking about?" she said to Tina because she was uncomfortable with looking at Danzi directly. "Really, I think I'd know if I had magical powers. Besides, aren't mages and magic just legend?" Like almost everything else in Hayden's book, of course.

Then again, she *had* seen a burnt-up griffin the day before, along with the demon and those other two flying creatures that she hadn't been able to make out. Perhaps mages weren't too much of a stretch. But the concept that mages existed was one thing; the idea that she was one of them was something else entirely.

Tina shrugged. "I know it's hard to grasp, but if Danzi says you've got it, that means you do."

Eiryenne backed away from them. "No, that's silly. I'm just a farm girl. An orphan—"

"Who happens to have a powerful magical talisman that would have long since killed you if you weren't a mage," said Danzi. This made the girl pause. He took a step toward her and grabbed her left hand with his right, roughly turning it palm up.

Eiryenne struggled, but his grip was like iron and his hand didn't budge. Then there was a strange, warm tingling on the back of her hand where Danzi gripped her. The warmth spread into her arm along with a faint tugging sensation, and the skin on her hand began to prickle. It all only lasted for a second or two before light blossomed up from her palm. She gasped as two entwined strands of colour swirled in front of her face, one orange yellow, the other bluish purple. They rose higher until they streamed well above her head. Then Danzi let go of her hand, and the light faded.

"You are a mage," he repeated. "Because of the burden you carry, you will be responsible for learning to use your powers. And for better or for worse, the task of teaching you has fallen to me."

Eiryenne flinched, but she held Danzi's gaze for as long as she dared. Tina must have seen her knees start to buckle because she came over and put a hand on her arm, pulling her away.

"Come," she said. "Have some breakfast. Magic will take a lot out of you. It's never good to start training on an empty stomach."

Eiryenne ate her food without really tasting it, her head still spinning. She was a mage. She hadn't really believed it until she saw that light come from her hands. Danzi had called it up somehow. Even now, she had trouble believing what she'd seen. It was a fact that both terrified and thrilled her.

When she was done eating, Danzi called her over to where he sat, leaning casually against an elm tree. "Sit," he told her. "If you faint, it's less distance to fall."

Eiryenne gulped. She nervously sat down facing him, wondering what on earth she was getting herself into.

"The first thing you will work on is calling on your magic. That's what I did this morning, except now you'll need to know how to do it yourself," he said. "For some people it comes naturally, but apparently it doesn't for you since you've lived your entire life with no idea that you're a mage." He looked thoughtful. "Now, you know how blood vessels run throughout your body?"

The girl nodded. She'd worked for the butcher before.

"I want you to visualize that. Except instead of blood, picture that purple light you saw. See it running through your veins in a shimmering network beneath your skin," Danzi continued. "It does actually look like that to the trained eye. Once you are further along, you'll be able to see it."

Eiryenne closed her eyes. She imagined that she had veins filled with purplish blue light. As she concentrated on the image, she thought she felt her arm tingle where she pictured a band of light to pass through.

"Concentrate on it. Tune in to that light you see. Reach for it with your mind."

She focused on her left arm and imagined that she reached over with her right hand and dipped her fingers beneath the rippling, water-like surface that had become her skin. And through it, she pulled the ribbon of light.

"Open your eyes."

When she did, Eiryenne looked down at her left hand. There was a faint glow on her skin. It disappeared as soon as she looked at it, a far cry from the shining ribbon of light that Danzi had summoned from her.

Evidently, he was thinking the same thing. "Bring it back. And make it brighter," he said.

She tried again, concentrating until a small spark of light flitted up from her hand and dissolved. Her next attempts grew steadily weaker, until the magic didn't come up at all.

"Hmm." Danzi sounded disappointed. "I'd hoped that the necklace would go to someone more capable. Quite frankly, that is pathetic."

His words stung. Eiryenne gritted her teeth. What did he expect, that she'd be a master of magic within five minutes?

She tried to focus her mind again, but the light wasn't returning. And moreover, she was tired. Her muscles hurt as if she'd run all morning, and her eyelids were beginning to droop.

"No, she won't do," Danzi said to Tina. "She'll be killed quicker than you can blink." Then he raised his hand and pointed it right at her. Orange fire flickered around his fingers. It was the fire.

Eiryenne's breath caught in her chest, and she became paralyzed. She was going to die—by fire. Just when it looked like she might live through this, Danzi was going to kill her just because she was not competent at magic. By the thing she's been most afraid of.

It was the combination of fear and indignation that did the trick. A small but bright burst of light flared up from her hands, lighting up her face with purple. It flashed for a second before going out and threatened to take Eiryenne's consciousness with it. Blackness filled her sight, and she was dimly aware that she was falling backward.

The last thing she heard before passing out was Danzi's voice, echoing in her ears.

"Magic is controlled by both your mind and your emotions. Remember that."

***

She woke up to find Tina hovering over her.

"Are you okay?" asked the shepherd, sounding concerned.

"Yes, I think so," said Eiryenne. "How long have I been out?"

"Almost all day," replied Tina. She sat back on her heels. "Well, that was an action-packed first lesson, wouldn't you say?"

Eiryenne sat up slowly. Danzi sat at the edge of their camp, dozing. Her lip trembled. "He ... he tried to kill me."

"No, he tried to scare you," said Tina. She frowned disapprovingly. "Which, given all the fears you've got already, I think was rather unnecessary."

The girl couldn't stop her hands from shaking. But now that she thought about it, he hadn't *actually* thrown the fire at her.

"So, how's it feel to be a mage?" asked Tina.

Eiryenne shrugged. "I'm not sure. Strange, I guess." She paused. "How'd he know I had magic, anyway?"

Apparently, Danzi had heard her. "Most mages can sense one another's magic," he said, looking up. "And when you know what to look for, you can see the magic in front of you, both in spells, and in other people. I knew you were a mage the moment I first set eyes on you."

Eiryenne thought back, remembering the look of what had seemed like surprise on his face when they first met. So that was why.

"And I think you might have picked up on mine," he added.

"Well," she said, thinking of the strange effect his gaze had. "There was something about your eyes."

"My ancestors could use their stares to petrify their opponents," said Danzi. "I suppose I may still have a trace of that. Not many people pick up on it, however. Interesting." He turned to Tina. "Now, we better get moving. There's still a way to go to the capital, and we've stayed here for long enough."

"The capital?" asked Eiryenne, jerked out of her thoughts about ancient mages who could petrify you with a single glance. "But I thought we were going to Rosfiord?"

"We *were*," said Tina. "But considering recent events, we've decided to go to Luchork instead. It's a much better route, really. And I just remembered that I have a brother-in-law there who I haven't visited in a while, and I want to show you his stables—"

"It's the necklace, isn't it?" There was a hint of desperation in Eiryenne's voice. She was getting a little tired of Tina smoothing over the truth.

"Yes," said Danzi. "We're taking it to the king. Which means you're coming with us."

Blunt he might be, but Eiryenne found that she almost preferred his brutal honesty to Tina's well-meant lies.

They readied their horses. Tina said that Neil might be fit to ride that day, so Eiryenne put his saddle on as well. She'd start out on Reygo first and wait to see if the younger stallion was well enough to get on.

They'd run out of fresh bandages, so Danzi just tightened his bloody ones and mounted his horse without complaint. Eiryenne decided that they were lucky even to have enough to last this long; apparently, one of Tina's late companions had been moving supplies for a physician's assistant.

The wind picked up as they headed out. It was already midafternoon, but Danzi obviously wanted to make some time that day. They rode down the moose trail at a brisk trot. The sounds of moving branches and shifting leaves filled their ears, making it hard to make out anything else.

A few hours into their journey, Danzi called for a halt. Eiryenne was about to ask whether his wounds had caught up with him before she noticed him point discreetly to the left.

"They're here," he said.

Eiryenne squinted, peering at the clump of trees he was pointing at. But with the light starting to fade and the wind moving the trees, she couldn't see what he'd seen.

Tina shortened her reins. "Are there many squads in the area?"

"Three," said Danzi. "One of them had the griffin that I was fighting. The second, I'm guessing, is the one that found Eiryenne's village. This must be the third."

"Maybe they'll just pass by," said Eiryenne hopefully.

The man shook his head. "No. If they're this close, then they will not pass by."

"Why not? I don't think they can see us."

"Because *that* calls to them," he replied, jerking a thumb towards her neck. With a jolt, Eiryenne realized he was talking about her necklace.

"I don't know," muttered Tina. "She's not very powerful yet. We might be just out of range. I think they would have made their move by now, if they'd sensed it."

That was when two horses and three giant wolves burst out from the bush in front of them.

"Ambush. Run," yelled Tina. The three of them whirled their mounts around and put their heels to their horses' sides. They swerved into a meadow to avoid being herded into the hidden attackers that Danzi had spotted.

But there were soldiers here, too. A dozen horsemen, wolves, and demons waded out from the trees to surround them.

Tina took her reins in one hand and drew her short, curved sword with the other. She used it to block an axe and continued to duel with two other swordsmen who'd surrounded her. Eiryenne kept Reygo and Neil behind her horse, but it was clear that they were being overwhelmed.

She heard a sword being drawn followed by screams, howls, and the scent of burning flesh. Danzi was fighting behind her, but she kept her eyes on Tina, horrified at the sight of the woman being assaulted by three horsemen at once.

A whinny of protest rang out, followed by Danzi muttering, "Stupid farm horse!" and more rings of steel on steel. Then one of the giant wolves sneaked in around the fighting horses' legs and leaped around Lahu, right at Reygo. Neil's lead slipped out of Eiryenne's fingers as her mount shied away from the beast.

"Tina," she yelled. The shepherd was disappearing beneath a swarm of black cloaks and swords.

"Go," her friend hollered. "Get out of here. Run!"

Reygo was still dancing about, trying to avoid the wolf. He needed no extra urging when Eiryenne turned him around and put her heels to his sides. He took off at a wild gallop. With a howl, the wolf pursued. It was joined by two more, as well as a few horsemen who'd broken off from their engagement with Tina.

They galloped through the meadow, Eiryenne barely noticing the corpses that were strewn about — Danzi's work, undoubtedly. Then Reygo stumbled as an arrow buried itself in his hindquarters. The wolves caught up and one of them seized his leg in its jaws while the other leaped at Eiryenne.

Something grabbed a hold of her collar and lifted her off the falling horse, away from the wolf's snapping jaws. Eiryenne turned her head to see Danzi, covered in blood but still riding strong, holding her aloft with his good arm as though she were no heavier than a feather. In a few seconds they'd caught up with Neil, and he tossed her onto the young stallion's back.

Eiryenne grabbed at Neil's reins. "We have to go back. Tina needs help! And Reygo."

"Ride," he ordered.

Neil was so terrified that Eiryenne doubted that she could turn him around if she wanted to. With tears streaming down her face, she let the reins go slack.

There were sounds of pursuit from behind. At least two horsemen were still after them, and perhaps the wolves as well. But Danzi led them on a harrowing gallop through the trees, leaping over logs and tearing past brambles until they finally shook them off. Soon the only sounds were that of their own horses' hooves and breathing.

Eiryenne was about to try slowing Neil down, but Danzi shook his head. He looked behind them. "We're not done yet."

A familiar shriek confirmed her fears. There was a demon in pursuit. She heard its wingbeats getting louder.

Danzi then yanked on the reins so hard that Chief neighed and snorted, wheeling about at an impossible speed. He gave the horse a kick, and they charged right at the diving demon. In a flash, Danzi dropped the reins and drew his broadsword. He whipped the silver blade through the air, slicing clean through the front of the demon's chest. It gave an awful wail before cartwheeling to the ground.

The mage sheathed his sword before picking up the reins again with his good arm and steered the horse back to where Eiryenne and Neil waited. Both he and Chief were lathered with sweat and blood.

The girl gulped. "Are they gone now?"

"That's the last of them, I think." Danzi stopped his horse. Chief stretched his neck down, panting. The man's own shoulders rose and fell quickly as he tried to catch his breath, breathing hard through his nose.

Eiryenne was unhurt, but her heart ached. "Is Tina …?"

"Probably." Danzi shrugged. He didn't seem to care either way.

The girl squeezed her eyes shut tightly, willing herself not to cry in front of him.

"It's not the first life to be lost fighting the Empire," the man said. His voice was harsh. "And certainly not the last. This is a war you've stumbled into, girl. And wars have casualties." He gave his horse a light squeeze, getting him to start walking again. "Now keep moving. We need to put some distance between us and our pursuers. If we stop now, it's likely that they'll get in range of your necklace again."

"In range?"

"I will answer your questions tomorrow," he said, looking weary for the first time. "Right now, we ride."

They continued, weaving in and out of the trees, hiding behind ridges as they went. Danzi didn't stop even when night fell. He ended up having to tie a rope from Neil's bridle to the back of Chief's saddle to prevent the young stallion from wandering off their path. Eiryenne didn't know how he could see the ground at all when she couldn't even see her hand in front of her face, much less follow his horse.

They pushed on through the night and kept going as dawn broke. Eiryenne figured she must have dozed off at some point, because she woke to find a spare lead rope tying her to the saddle. Satisfied that she was not going to slip off the horse, she closed her eyes again, drifting in and out of fitful sleep until Danzi finally called a stop at a rocky overhang beneath a hill. They stripped the saddles off their tired horses, and Eiryenne groomed both of them. She was glad that they were taking a break. Neil had a renewed limp, and she was concerned that his leg wasn't going to be able to heal completely at this pace. He refused to put any weight on it, cropping the grass with his bad hoof aloft. Chief had some fresh cuts, but there was no more ointment to put on them.

Danzi slept like a rock through most of the morning, but Eiryenne tossed and turned on her blanket when it was his turn to go on watch, unable to calm her restless mind. Her stomach growled, reminding her that she hadn't eaten since the previous morning and that their food rations were running low. She'd have to start putting that bow to use soon. Hunting was never easy for her, but now she had the added risk of running into soldiers while foraging. For the moment she settled for the last of Tina's bread and a bit of dried meat.

When the sun rose fully, Danzi opened their packs and finished the rest of the meat in a few bites before emptying his water skin. He looked up at the girl, pointing to a bundle of half-dried herbs peeking out from beneath the yellowing grass.

"You can apply those to the horses' injuries," he said. "It will make them heal faster."

As she tore off the leaves and went over to the horses, she saw Danzi take a handful and put them on his own wounds.

"You know a lot about herbs?" she asked. It seemed like an unusual knowledge for a warrior to possess.

The man shrugged. "I used to know an herbalist. I picked up a few things from her."

When Eiryenne finished with the horses, Danzi called her over.

"Tina didn't want you knowing the truth about what you carry," he said. "I thought the knowledge was necessary, but now that I see your fearful nature, I think it is optional. So, you decide, do you want to know about your necklace or not?"

It occurred to Eiryenne that this was the first time he was giving her a choice about something. She hesitated. It would be so easy to say no and just to go on blindly doing whatever he told her the rest of the way to the castle.

Ignorance is bliss, Tina had said. Part of her agreed.

But another part argued that she deserved to know the truth, the reason behind all this death and violence. Putting it out in the open would at least take the threat of the unknown out of it.

"I want to know," she said, sounding braver than she felt.

"Very well," he said. "It is called the Necklace of Tairung, named after the unicorn who created it."

Unicorn? That didn't sound too bad, she told herself.

"Tairung, is also known as the Shadow Unicorn. He was one of the few unicorns in history to become corrupted. Unicorns are powerful magical creatures, but usually oriented toward light. When one goes bad, well, he goes very bad. Tairung gathered an evil army with which to sweep the lands. He himself was host to several powerful demons. He led his army across what later became the Empire, conquering and destroying entire nations. And to prevent his downfall, he put a curse on his army and himself at the cost of his own soul. No soldier would truly die as long as he lived; their aura would merge with his, and he would absorb all of their power.

"Anyway, when he finally did fall, his last deed was forging that necklace. He bound the stones with the souls of all those he led and conquered, an army waiting to rise again. And when he died, he had the last bit of his horn put into the central stone." Danzi paused, looking pensive.

"So that one day he might rise again. But the necklace, along with most of the other terrible treasures he'd gathered over the years, was locked away in the Shadow Unicorn's Vault for the next seven hundred years." He shifted slightly where he sat, making himself more comfortable before he continued. "But once the Emperor rose to power, he heard of this ancient vault, hidden away from the world and containing magical artifacts beyond his wildest dreams. So, he had the necklace stolen. He wanted to have Tairung's army and use his power to finally quench the resistance that had risen up against his reign. He almost succeeded. But the necklace was in turn stolen from him. That much we knew, and we assumed that it had been returned to the vault. But judging by its present location, I see that was not the case. Instead, I think a secret clan of human mages, of whose existence no one knew, took the necklace for safekeeping. They brought it as far from the Empire as they could, to Turmain. They must have thought it would be safe here; Turmain is an empty land. It was one of Tairung's first hunting grounds back in the day, and there are few remaining inhabitants, none of them magical. It's worthless enough and so far away from the Emperor's lands that his soldiers would have little cause to be here."

Eiryenne kneaded her forehead with her knuckles, trying to process all that she was hearing. *Keep breathing*, she told herself. *Just keep breathing*. With another deep breath, she asked, "So what happened, then? Why was it discovered?"

"You see, Tairung wanted the necklace to be found by someone powerful and just as corrupt as he was. If it is worn by an ordinary person or discarded completely, Tairung's horn would send a beacon directly to the greatest source of evil it can find and that would be the Emperor. He would recognize its aura instantly. The power of the necklace can only be held in check by a mage—but with a twist. It would still be able to call out to nearby evil, just not as far. It would be restricted to a certain radius. The more powerful the mage, the farther its reach would expand. That is why you alone must ferry it—if anyone else except an even weaker mage so much as touches it, the Emperor will zone in on it and send his army in. Once he locks on to it directly, there will be no escaping him."

"That makes sense, I guess," Eiryenne said. "And my parents ... they died protecting it. They passed it to me so that nobody could tell that it was there."

Danzi nodded. "I assume it was passed from generation to generation of these mages, probably disguised as farmers in some remote Turmain village. Their plan worked, too, because no one heard of the necklace again until about thirteen years ago, when a regiment of soldiers chasing the Empire's enemies accidentally wandered into its range."

"Right. That would be when my parents died. No, they were murdered. Murdered by a power-hungry Emperor. One other thing ... do you know if the holder of this necklace will suffer any side effects?" She looked down at the stones beneath her shirt with a newfound respect, suddenly very conscious of all the evil that hung around her neck. It was a terrifying prospect, really. A deranged unicorn and his undead army were in there.

"I know that it has a reputation for corrupting minds with the mere lure of its power," Danzi said. "But I doubt you are interested in world domination, so don't concern yourself with that. No, it shouldn't be a problem. Apart from calling over all the evil creatures in the area, the only inscription written on the box it was in said, *Whoever bears this necklace shall hold the power of Tairung and be a harbinger of doom.*"

An unhappy realization came over Eiryenne. "So that means Tina, my parents, and everyone in my village died because of me. I drew those soldiers to us."

"Yes," he replied, his face still impassive.

"I'm a harbinger of doom."

"Indeed."

It was all her fault. This time she didn't try to hold back her tears.

Danzi continued to stare out over the horizon, keeping watch for more soldiers. After a little while he spoke again. "Stop crying already, girl, and put your grief toward something useful."

Chapter 5 ~ Warrior Mage

Danzi insisted on continuing Eiryenne's magic lessons. But now that the enormity of the situation was known to her, it hung over the girl like a terrible omen, threatening to suck her mind into the madness that lay within the stones around her neck. Her thoughts were scattered and uncooperative, and her anxiety built up until it burst into another panic attack. Her control over her magic was nonexistent; she could manage a small spark, but that was it.

Her mentor seemed annoyed at this. He told her to snap out of it. She needed to learn how to defend herself if she was to successfully carry the necklace.

"I don't *want* to carry the necklace," she suddenly snapped, her frayed patience finally gone. "You take it!" She moved her hand to grab at the chain, but Danzi caught her wrist before she could even blink.

"*You have no choice,*" he growled, making her flinch. "You know what will happen if you take it off. The Emperor will send his forces after it and eventually gain control of Tairung's army. Then the Empire will truly be victorious. Is that what you want?"

"I," she began, not really knowing how to respond, why can't you find another weak mage?"

"I already told you, there are no other mages in Turmain." Danzi's eyes flashed as she tried to grab for the necklace with her other hand, thinking that he was still unable to use his left arm. She was correct; he just squeezed painfully tight with his good hand, making her cry out and abandon the effort. "If you take it off, the Empire's forces will kill you when they come for it," he said. Then he saw her eyes flit to the horses. "Let me correct that; take it off, and *I* shall kill you!" He let go of her arm and stalked away.

Eiryenne shivered involuntarily. She'd already had demons, soldiers, and wolves after her. But for some reason the thought of Danzi turning against her scared her even more.

She made a fist, torn between terror and frustration. The man was right; she didn't have a choice. She had to bring the necklace to the castle or risk losing both her own life and endangering whatever lands remained free of the Emperor.

Getting up, she slowly walked over to Neil and hugged him. He nickered softly, still refusing to put any weight on his injured foot.

"Why me?" she whispered, pressing her face against her horse's soft, warm neck. Neil's winter coat was starting to come in, and clumps of his old summer fur spilled out onto the girl's hair. She spent the next few hours rubbing him and Chief down. Going through the familiar grooming motions calmed her.

Once she dared to face her teacher, she walked back to the overhang. He was sitting cross-legged beside a boulder, his hands on his knees and his expression serene. Apparently, he had calmed down, too, because when he opened his eyes there was no sign of the hostility that had gleamed in them earlier.

"Sit down," he said. "I think it will be useful for you to learn how to meditate. In fact, I should have started it sooner. If your mind is in turmoil, your magic will be, too."

She sat down, copying his position.

"Close your eyes," he said. "Steady your breathing. Concentrate on it. Empty your mind."

That was easier said than done. Eiryenne told herself to think of nothing, but some stray thought or another would always interrupt her. She would wonder how long it would take them to reach the capital or what the king would do with her once they got there.

"Distance yourself from your thoughts," he continued. "Picture yourself looking at them from afar. Like looking at pictures and words on a page."

She imagined a storybook, like Hayden's, only bigger. She stowed her worries into one chapter, imagining the ink drying and carrying her emotions away with it. On the next page she put the image that was most intrusive: a picture of herself running away from the soldiers. As she looked at it, pretending that she was looking at it from a distance, the person in the picture began to change, until she was looking at a different girl. Not her. She was just an observer—neutral, impassive, calm.

Her head felt clear. Clearer than it had been in weeks.

"That's right," he said, his voice slow and calm. "Now *breathe*."

They exhaled in unison. Eiryenne focused on the air emptying out from her lungs. She then inhaled deeply, matching Danzi's rhythm. Within a few minutes, the unfamiliar deep breathing made her light-headed, but she was still calm.

"Now find that light inside yourself. Reach for it."

It came more easily than it did the first time. Eiryenne looked, and she found that her brain already knew where to look—the place that had been hidden by the clutter of her thoughts and emotions. She concentrated, and soon a small sphere of bluish-purple light floated in her hands.

"Better," Danzi said. "Now, have it move up. Keep your focus taut but concentrate your will on moving it."

Eiryenne focused on the mesmerizing light in her hands. She willed it to move, but it wouldn't budge.

"Try harder. But don't get frustrated. Don't lose your focus."

She tried again, wanting it to move, picturing it moving. And inch by inch, it drifted skyward.

Danzi had her repeat that exercise several times before switching to manipulating the light in other ways—changing its shape, varying its intensity. She lost control of it a few times and had to start over, but overall it was the most successful lesson she'd had.

"You need to familiarize yourself with these mental motions and how they affect your magic," Danzi said when they'd finished. "Once you do that, you can start getting it to do specific things that you want it to, rather than just sit in your hands like a decorative candle."

Eiryenne raised an eyebrow. Had he just made a joke?

"We're done for now. Let's head out."

"Okay," she said, getting up. "This meditation thing. Do you do it often?"

"When I can," he replied, rubbing his forehead. "Sometimes it's the only way to keep myself sane."

"And when you can't?"

Danzi didn't answer.

He unfolded his legs gingerly, the motion making his thigh start to bleed again. He had to grab on to the boulder for balance, but even his fresher wounds wouldn't make him cringe with pain. Looking at the nasty cuts on his shoulders, Eiryenne decided that he must have had a spell to numb his nerves.

When they got out to where the horses were picketed, Eiryenne saw that Neil was down. He obviously didn't want to put any more strain on his leg.

She ran to his head, pulling at his halter. "Come on, boy, get up. It's time to go." But Neil tugged his head away and sunk deeper into the leaves. Eiryenne was concerned; it was never a good sign when horses were lying down.

"His fetlock's gotten pretty bad," she said to Danzi as he limped over. "I don't know if I can get him to use his leg, let alone ride him."

The man walked up to Neil and got down on one knee, feeling the horse's swollen leg. "Stand back," he said to Eiryenne. "He won't like this."

The girl backed away, unsure of what he was about to do. Surely Danzi wasn't about to kill her horse?

He put his hand over the horse's fetlock then took a couple of deep breaths. His eyes narrowed. Then fire blossomed around his fingers, engulfing the stallion's leg in bright orange flames.

Eiryenne and Neil cried out at the same time. The horse stumbled to his feet and kicked out, but Danzi narrowly avoided his flailing hooves by rolling out of the way. Then the stallion bolted away on all four legs, fleeing to the end of his rope, almost breaking it.

"You healed him?" she asked, gazing at the horse in wonder. His leg steamed, but the cuts were gone, and the swelling had disappeared.

Danzi nodded and got to his feet. "It's not one of my greater talents, but I can manage when the situation demands it." He went over to his own mount. Neil shied away from him. "You can saddle him now. He might still be sore, but functionally his leg is fine now."

Indeed, the horse was soon cantering along like nothing had ever happened to him. They rode for most of that day, only making camp when the sun began to dip toward the horizon. Danzi had her practice magic again the next morning, and the one after that, until she started to grow proficient at manipulating her magic and calming her mind. It was slow progress, but it was still something.

The forests were beginning to dwindle, and the ground became rockier and the ridges steeper. The night, too, grew colder. Danzi had taken to starting a campfire after Eiryenne was already asleep or when he knew she'd be too tired to be afraid. Their food supplies had run out, so the fire now served the double purpose of both warmth and cooking the birds that Eiryenne managed to snare with her bow. She kept her distance, but it was obvious that she was beginning to overcome her fear.

As the days went by and Danzi's wounds began to heal, he started joining in the hunt as well. He would sometimes bring a larger animal to the camp—a deer, a hog. Eiryenne supposed that he caught them with his magic, since he had no bow, which explained their singed fur. In any case, his kills let her bring her butchering skills to bear, skinning and quartering the animal as best as she could before setting out strips of meat to dry or cook. Danzi took no such finesses with his own meals; he tore off random chunks off his portion with unusually sharp teeth and gobbled the meat down, sometimes without cooking. Eiryenne had heard of hunters who could eat their meat raw like that, but she still found it disturbing.

A little over a week after the loss of Tina, Danzi and Eiryenne came to the banks of a narrow, winding creek. Though they had not had any water that day, Danzi stopped Eiryenne before she could drink. He sniffed at it suspiciously then bent down and slid something out of his pocket, waving his hand over the water. Eiryenne couldn't see exactly what he did, but she heard a quiet hiss.

"It was poisoned," he said, getting up. Whatever had been in his hands went just as quickly back into a pocket on the inside of his jacket. "Someone's expecting us." He glanced back at the girl. "I cleared it. You can drink now."

"You used a spell to do away with the poison?" she asked, bringing a handful of water to her mouth as he did the same.

He wiped the water off his beard with his sleeve. "I've made it safe for us to drink."

They pressed on. There was no sign of any hostile forces as the day wore on, so by late afternoon they made a stop to try to catch some supper. There was little game in the area, and neither of them had had much luck hunting over the past few days. They tied the horses by the trees before Eiryenne strung her bow and headed away from the clearing. Danzi followed at enough of a distance that he wouldn't spook any animals, but close enough to spot anyone hunting *her*.

He spotted a small, fat fowl that had escaped the girl's attention. It hid beneath a low-growing bush, half-covered in fallen leaves. Danzi turned toward it, deeming the detour too short to be of much danger. He moved quietly for his size, slinking through the leaves toward the bird.

Eiryenne kept walking, peering into the shadows of the trees, hoping to find something. Her stomach growled and she felt light-headed; it had been too long since her last meal. Now that she was hunting in this land to survive, she saw why Danzi had called it barren.

Then she heard the rustle of leaves and a frightened squawk. Her companion had caught something. There was more rustling and muffled footsteps coming closer. Danzi was probably coming to tell her that he had their supper. She turned, about to ask him if she could cook it properly this time. Instead she found herself staring into the face of a short, stocky man with a muddy face and an axe in his hands.

Eiryenne froze. Then the man took another step toward her, and she'd released an arrow before she realized what she was doing. It hit his thigh, and he staggered, grunting with pain. The girl raced past him, sprinting as fast as she could as more figures emerged from the trees.

She tripped over a log and just managed to stop herself from falling head over heels. Righting herself, she continued to run, looking frantically around for Danzi. Where was a mage when you needed one?

After a few tense moments, she finally spotted him, coming toward her with long, quick strides. Once she'd reached him, Eiryenne realized she could go no further. She let her weakened legs collapse, falling to her knees and breathing hard.

Danzi stepped toward the men coming out of the trees, his sword drawn. There were about a dozen of them, but now that they were closer, Eiryenne saw that these were not the same uniformed soldiers that had chased her. Their clothes were worn and ragged, and their rusty weapons didn't gleam with the professionally polished steel of an army.

"Since when are there bandits in Turmain?" she muttered to herself.

The apparent leader of the group, a man with a thick red moustache and bones hanging on a rope around his neck, approached Danzi. "Give it up, you're outnumbered," he drawled. "Give us the girl and we'll let you keep yer own sorry hide. Those Imperial soldiers put a handsome price on her head, and we mean to collect it. Ain't that right, boys?" The other men let out a jeer, shaking their weapons.

"And no bounty on me? I'm insulted." Danzi looked almost amused. He shifted the blade in his hand. The long, deadly stretch of steel glinted as sunlight ran along its edges and pooled in the blood groove running down its lower length. It had to be over three feet long, and the girl wondered how the man could hold it in just one hand with such ease. Then Eiryenne saw a glimmer of something else, a streak of orange light, coming up from the hilt. It ran the length of the sword, merging with the sunlight and giving it a foreboding gleam. The weapon hungered for blood as much as its master did.

The leader of the bandits barely had time to lift his axe before Danzi moved in, swinging his sword in a wide arc that beheaded him, continuing to block the sword of one of his companions. The blonde man sidestepped the next blow and dug his own blade into the bandit's gut, wrenching it free with a shower of blood. He jumped at the next bandit, ducking beneath his sword and gutting him.

Eiryenne stared, her eyes wide. She'd never seen much fighting before, save for the attacking soldiers and the jerky swings that Tina made with her sword. But now she realized she was watching a master at work. Danzi turned with inhuman speed, his flashing blade taking down two more men before either had a chance to hit him. An archer, keeping out of the reach of his sword, fired an arrow. Danzi turned his head at the last instant, and the projectile whizzed by his cheek.

None of the bandits could so much as touch him as he whirled and danced around their weapons, dealing out death with every strike. His sword moved in a blur, flowing like a river of molten silver around his hands.

Four bandits rushed him at the same time. He leaned out of the way of the first one's club, thrusting his sword through the second's torso in the same motion. Avoiding the remaining two swords, he swung. His sword sliced clean through the chest of the first man before moving just as easily through the second. Both dropped like rocks, the death rattle sounding in their throats as blood filled their failing lungs.

The archer paled. He strung another arrow and shot it at Eiryenne. Danzi jumped forward, arm outstretched. A small thud rang out as the arrow hit the flat of his blade and bounced off, catching the wing of a finch as it flew by. He cut the next arrow in half before turning his gaze to the archer and the remaining bandits crouched around him. Most of them were picking up crossbows.

Danzi turned as the first bolt sailed toward him; this arrow he couldn't avoid. It hit the thick leather of his jacket hard, but the material held. As he held his dripping sword aloft, the fire that danced beneath the surface of the metal burst into view. Orange flames lined with yellow and red ran down the length of the blade, burning the blood off in a matter of seconds. He made a swinging motion, and a ray of fire broke off from the sword, flying toward the bandits. It almost instantly burned them and the trees they crouched behind to ashes.

The fire on his blade went out as quickly as it had appeared, and Danzi slid his sword back into its sheath.

Eiryenne was aghast. She sat where she'd fallen, her muscles tight with fear and shock. She could barely wrap her head around how so much destruction and death could come from just one man. Seeing

Danzi kill so easily and ruthlessly scared her; the fire that was his magic unnerved her even more.

She couldn't help but flinch as the mage turned back toward her. Then he walked back and picked up the fowl he'd dropped when he saw the bandits coming.

"Supper?" He looked up nonchalantly. The man hadn't even broken a sweat.

"Umm …" She tried not to look at the corpses, feeling her stomach turn. How could anybody have food on their mind after they'd just taken half a dozen lives? "Maybe, but not now."

He shrugged. "Suit yourself, but the last thing we need is you passing out on the trail." Then he began to walk back toward their camp.

She got up and followed him, running out of that bloodstained clearing as quickly as her cramped legs would carry her.

Eiryenne didn't say a word for the next hour. After Danzi had eaten most of the bird, he told her that they would have another magic lesson now.

"We will reach the castle tonight," he said. "And I want you to know at least one or two proper spells when I leave you there."

She nodded, meeting his gaze. Now that she was used to it, she found that she did *not* fall into a dizzy trance every time she met his eyes. Or perhaps that was just because he was getting used to her. It was still there, but she could control it better now.

"You've gotten better at calling on your magic and moulding it into different shapes. It's now time to ask something of it. Start by calling up a handful of magic."

Eiryenne tried to concentrate, but every time she closed her eyes, she saw flashes of blood and fire and mutilated corpses. She shook her head, trying to get the fight out of her mind. Actually, it hadn't been much of a fight. More of a massacre.

"Concentrate. Put any stray thoughts into the book," Danzi said. As he watched her unsuccessful tries to calm her mind and summon her magic, he frowned. "I knew you were progressing slowly, but don't tell me we have to start over from scratch."

Eiryenne gulped. She wondered if he'd punish her when he realized that they weren't getting anywhere. Now that she'd seen what he could do, she did not want to displease him.

She focused that fear, using it to drive her thoughts away. It still took several tries, but she was finally able to once again generate a blob of bluish-purple light floating in her palm.

"Form it into a ball." Danzi reached for a twig and stuck it in the earth a few feet away from Eiryenne. "And throw it at this. Think about blowing the stick to pieces. It takes a certain kind of thought to give your magic a destructive edge."

She condensed the light into as tightly packed a circle as she could then made a throwing motion. The light stuck to her fingers like glue. Embarrassed, she tried again, trying to move the light toward the twig with her mind. This time it fell off her hand and slumped to the ground, dissipating before it made contact with the earth.

"Try again. You have to learn how to form your magic into an offensive spell," he said.

She sighed. It wasn't working. After seeing so much violence that day, she wanted to cause no more, even if it was just to a lifeless piece of wood. Her next attempts were no better.

"I told you that emotion affects magic," her mentor said. "If you are unable to do this with your will alone, add some anger. In general, it is unwise to rely on your emotions to direct your spells, since they are hard to control and more unsteady than magic cast by a clear-headed mage. But if needed, they can give you a boost."

Anger. What made her angry? She mostly felt fearful about this situation. But wasn't there frustration as well? Those soldiers had robbed her of her parents. She'd never have a normal life because of some distant, greedy Emperor that forced this accursed necklace to destroy her family and be passed on to her. Why did she never have a choice in these things?

Seizing that speck of anger and concentrating on it, Eiryenne tried again. This time the magic came to her more readily, though it was harder to form it into a ball. She threw it, her mind set on destroying that twig. It fell through the air in a sloping diagonal arc then settled onto the twig and broke off its top.

"Hmm." By his tone, Danzi had expected better results. "Better than nothing, I suppose." He had her practice it several more times, but her results got little better. Then he switched to the next spell: a barrier. He told her to stretch out her magic into a thin, wide net, a net that would catch and stop anything that fell into it.

She concentrated again, thinking of immovable walls and impenetrable rocks and trying to make the essence of those fortresses seep into her magic. Then a new thought occurred: how was Danzi going to test this? She suddenly realized that she wouldn't put it past him to throw a handful of flames at her, then and there. The jolt of terror made her flimsy barrier pulse and contort. Her sweaty hands began to shake when she saw Danzi reaching for something; the flashing light of her barrier made it hard to make out what he was doing.

Something struck her barrier, and it disappeared with a flash of light. Small pieces scattered onto her lap. Opening her eyes, she realized that they were little chunks of wood. Danzi had tossed a small stick at her.

Eiryenne sighed, rubbing a piece of wood out of her hair. She realized that she was being stupid. Killer mage or not, Danzi had made it very clear that his mission was to protect her and the necklace she carried; he would not risk losing it by something as simple as a dangerous training exercise.

Then she glanced up at the sword at the mage's belt, and suddenly she was not so sure.

"Not bad. Seems that you're a bit better at barriers than offensive spells. That's to be expected; different mages have their strengths in different places. Still, you should work to be proficient in both. You'll have to keep practicing on your own time," he said. "As I said, we will be at our destination soon, but you still need to know how to defend yourself. Reaching the king will still not guarantee that no one else will come after the Tairung Necklace."

"Are you expecting any more trouble?" she asked.

He shrugged. "I'm not sure. The soldiers knew very well that the bandits would be no match for me, especially now that I've rested a little. I think they simply put them to the hunt so that they'd be able to track us, either by picking up our trail at the corpses or seeing my flashes of magic. That's why I kept it to a minimum. But they still could have spotted it."

Eiryenne was silent for a few minutes, thinking of all the dangers that faced them. She suddenly wished that she was home. She wished she *had* a home. Whether it be with Tina in Rosfiord or with her aunt in her own village, she wanted, more than anything, to have a normal life again. To be rid of this stupid necklace that everyone was after.

Danzi had her practice the barrier spell again, but her thoughts were jumbled, and her spells collapsed even before he had a chance to throw something.

"You are distracted," he said tartly. "Concentrate!"

But this time it did no good. She tried to cast a spell until tears ran down her cheeks, but soon she was back to barely being able to summon a spark.

"Enough for now," he said with a frown and turned away.

Disappointed with herself, she tried to think of something else. Eventually, her mind settled down and drifted back the spells he'd just tried to teach her. Her little, twig-crushing sphere of light was still a far cry from Danzi's flames of death. And truth be told, he had not touched upon the type of magic that she was most curious to learn.

"Danzi, can you teach me to heal?" she asked quietly.

"Healing is a more advanced application of magic. I doubt you would have any success if you struggle with even the basic concepts." He paused, looking thoughtful. "Still, I suppose it wouldn't hurt to try."

"There was a finch," she said, "when the arrow bounced off your sword, it hit a little finch. He's probably still there. I could practice on him, if he's still alive." She bit her tongue, hoping that Danzi wouldn't ask her to get the bird. The thought of going near all those corpses made her cringe.

Thankfully, he decided to go get the bird himself, in case the soldiers had caught up and found the bodies. When he returned, Eiryenne first thought he'd come empty-handed. Then he opened his hand and cradled within his large palm was a tiny brown finch with black splotches. A trickle of blood ran down its wing. He put it in front of the girl and sat down.

"All right," he said briskly. "Healing is much like fixing something. The better you know what you're trying to fix, the better it will work, especially with more complex injuries. I assume that with your hunting and butchering experience, you are familiar with a bird's physical structure."

She nodded.

"Then begin the spell. Let your magic flow into the bird. First, figure out what exactly is wrong."

She put a hand over the bird, letting the light pour onto it. Concentrating, she found that she could spread her awareness beyond her own hand. She became aware of the bird, its tiny heart beating fast with fear and its wing hanging limp. Dipping her consciousness toward the wing, she focused in on it, looking closer and feeling deeper. There, among the down of its chest, she felt a flash of wrongness, like a gap in its life energy. There was a tear in the muscles that ran from its wing to its chest.

She relayed this to Danzi.

"Now that you know what is wrong, concentrate on how you know it should be instead. Calm your mind and fill it with the thought of fixing this finch."

She examined the torn muscle with her magic, becoming aware of the ripped fibres. Thinking back to a fowl she'd butchered; she knew exactly how those fibres should look. Now she willed them to stitch themselves back together.

The finch peeped weakly. The pitiful sound sent a stab of pity through her heart. Remembering what Danzi had said about emotions, she let the feeling fill her. She felt sorry for the bird, a victim of something he had no part in and no control over, just like her. The desire to take his pain away was strong; she would heal him, and then she'd go on and heal others, other victims of this otherwise cruel, unforgiving world.

There was a tingling on her skin, and she felt the finch's feathers quiver beneath her fingertips as warmth flooded her palms and flowed into the bird. The next thing she knew, the bird struggled out of her grip and flew away.

The spell took more of her energy than ever before, and she collapsed onto her side.

"Hrmm, looks like we finally found something you have a knack for," she heard Danzi mutter. Then she fainted.

Chapter 6 ~ The Lord of Fire

She was seated in Hayden's stables, the storybook in her hands. Horace and Neil were in their stalls, along with all the horses that had died in the famine.

Wait, what famine?

She blinked. Hayden's wife was there, too, giving her mare Yandy a handful of oats.

"There's a good girl," she murmured. "Tina, pass me the water, please."

"Coming." The shepherd filled up a pail of water and gave it to her. Then she glanced at the girl. "Are you going to sit there all day, Eiryenne? You know your mother told you to get home early. She and your dad wanted to take you to the bonfire, remember?"

"My parents?" she said, utterly confused. Her thoughts were muddled. Why did something that simple seem so strange?

She looked down at the book. It showed a picture of three people: a tall, brown-haired man with a thin moustache and green eyes next to a fair-skinned woman with dark hair and hazel eyes. Between them was a girl, about thirteen years old. She had her dad's hair and her mom's eyes. She was smiling.

Me. She realized. *That's me.*

"Eiryenne!" A voice sounded from the doorway. "Time to go, sweetheart. You don't want to miss the bonfire. I know how much you enjoy them."

She turned. Two people stood in the doorway; their faces obscured by the sun. But they sounded distant, vague. Suddenly, all the sights and sounds around her blurred until they were slightly out of focus, a watery image that floated in and out of her sight.

"Get your head out of that nonsense." Unlike the others, this voice was clear and deep, ringing through her dazed thoughts. It sounded like the speaker was standing right next to her. Turning, Eiryenne saw Danzi. His features were crisp and clear, his figure solid and real. His amber eyes blazed as he knocked the book out of her hands. It burst into flames. "They're gone," he continued. Now their surroundings began to burn as well. "Forget them. Stop living in the past. If you do not focus, you will join them in their graves."

***

"Get up!"

The girl woke with a start.

Danzi was saddling Chief. His face was grim. "I saw movement in the hills behind us," he said. "It's time to go."

Eiryenne made herself get up and haul Neil's saddle onto his back. She couldn't have been out for more than an hour or two, judging by the sun. Her head still spun with a mixture of fatigue, grief, and fear. She thought, Was that really how my parents looked like? She bit her lip. Thanks to this necklace, I will never know. And thanks to me, Tina and Hayden will never see this day.

Guilt wrapped its tendrils around her mind, settling almost like a physical weight around her shoulders. It slowed her fingers, making her fumble with the leather.

"I'm waiting." Danzi's sharp voice cut through her musings. He'd already mounted his dark bay gelding.

Eiryenne finished tightening the girth and got on her horse, following the man as he led the way, as always. Then something occurred to her.

"If you knew they might see your magic or find the bandits' bodies, then why stop? Do you *want* them to find us?" she asked hesitantly.

"I want them to follow us instead of heading to the border," he replied. "The last thing I need is word of this getting to the Emperor. If we're lucky, I'll drop you off at the castle before they can attack again. If not … well, it will save me a return trip." He shortened the reins. "One way or another, I aim to make sure there is no one left to carry news of the Tairung Necklace to the Emperor."

He planned to hunt them down, she realized, and she found that she didn't like it. Even though they were after her, she still thought it was cruel to hunt them down and slaughter them like Danzi had done with those bandits. Knowing that the warrior mage would say such sentiment was foolish, she kept her mouth shut about it.

Besides, even if he was a powerful mage, Danzi was just one man. Bandits were one thing, but trained soldiers were another matter entirely. After all, aside from the horsemen, there were giant wolves, demons, griffins, and who knew what else to contend with. All sorts of deadly creatures were apparently part of the Empire's army, and even Danzi would have difficulty if he had to fight them all.

They rode on through a shallow pass, keeping to the rocky alpine trails. The trees were getting sparser, and there was little cover to hide in. There were a few hours of daylight left, and it looked like Danzi was planning to make the most of them.

A blind corner was coming up, formed by a mound of rock sticking up out of the mountainous earth. Danzi stopped before it, listening. Then he slowly moved Chief forward, gripping the reins in his still weakened left hand. His right hung almost idly at his side, though from experience Eiryenne knew that even empty-handed, the mage could be dangerous.

Danzi peered around the corner as he rounded it. All seemed well, so he turned to beckon Eiryenne to follow him. She gave Neil a nudge, and her stallion picked up a slow trot.

Suddenly, an enormous winged tiger swooped down out of nowhere and rammed into Danzi, sending him flying off his horse's back. He landed hard on his bad shoulder with an audible thud that made Eiryenne cringe. Surprise was written on his face; he had not expected the attack. Another sharp, rocky face rose from behind the boulder-strewn mound, not visible until one was completely around the corner. Danzi couldn't see the creature diving at him until he was already knocked from the saddle.

It was on him before he had a chance to grab his sword. Eiryenne saw the cat's sparking claws bury into his chest. His stiff leather jacket had taken the brunt of arrows and swords without giving way, but the tiger's claws sliced through it like butter. Danzi raised his hands, and fire exploded from his palms, engulfing the offending tiger in an inferno. It drew back, yowling, but didn't retreat. Its torso was larger than that of the tigers she'd seen in Hayden's book, and it had no stripes. Its fur was jet-black, and wings like an owl's rose from its shoulders. Two long, narrow fangs stretched down from its top jaw; they were so long that they couldn't even fit in its mouth.

Forcing the sabre-toothed tiger back with his fire, Danzi tried to scramble to his feet. But more beasts dove in. Three griffins and a handful of demons surrounded him. Some were caught by his fire. Others were not; they fought back with flashes of their own magic. The griffins' magic seemed to come from their wings; with each wingbeat, a wave of yellow or green light would flash out with the wind that they created, threatening to blow Danzi's fires out.

A mixture of men and wolves were coming out from the path in front of them, encircling the trapped mage. Some began to approach Eiryenne. She turned her horse around and prepared to make a run for it, but they'd already blocked off the trail from where they'd come.

Panic flooded her mind. They weren't getting out of this.

She looked back to where Danzi fought. The griffins had extinguished his fires with their wind magic and were moving in. He leaped high, higher than his legs should have carried him, landing in a crouch on a wide rocky ledge carved in the mound that rose up behind him. Then he straightened. His eyes blazed, and his face was like thunder. He seemed to radiate fury. Eiryenne was aware of a sudden build-up of energy in the air, like the charge before a lightning strike.

Then Danzi's body dissolved into a mass of white-hot flames. They engulfed his entire silhouette, burning brighter and brighter until Eiryenne could no longer make out his features. The blaze began to rise and expand, shooting up and around the plateau until its entire surface was alight. The flames began to settle into a new shape. As they started to fade, Eiryenne saw a huge, dark form in Danzi's place.

Once the white flames faded, she gasped. It was both the most magnificent and most terrible creature she'd ever seen. Crimson scales lined his skin like jewels, each shimmering with different shades of red and adorned with a touch of gold. His proportions were something like a tiger's, with a neck more the length of a horse's, only thicker. He had large, rectangular-shaped jaws and small ridges of pointed scales above his amber eyes. Two shining horns that seemed to be fashioned out of burnished gold crowned either side of his head, each with a pair of smaller ones beneath them. Great wings hung from his shoulders, and thick layers of orange leather stretched between red ribbings. Rows of flat orange plates lined his belly, starting at his throat and going all the way to his tail. Each powerful limb ended with four enormous gleaming claws, white with a silver sheen.

The dragon, for it could only be a dragon, seemed to pull all the light in the valley toward him. It settled and condensed along his scales, making a thousand small fires spring to life upon his hide. Yellow and orange lights, all predominated by that rich red flare, flashed up and down his brilliant scales with each breath he took.

The griffins paused only for a moment. Then, uttering a collective screech, they moved in. The dragon unfurled his wings and leaped into the air above them, a great flood of red and orange fire rolling out from between his jaws and incinerating two of them.

The third griffin angled his wings and flew away, trying to get behind him as the sabre-toothed tiger moved in, the demons on its heels. They bombarded the dragon from all sides. Two blasts of fire from his paws took out some of the demons. The tiger he met head-on. It swiped at him with its claws, but the effect now was far less than it had been on the human, and it barely breached his scales. The dragon's talons, on the other hand, made deep gouges across the tiger's side, slicing easily through flesh and bone. The big cat let out another yowl of pain and tried to bite the dragon's left wing, the one he was favouring. His fangs missed their mark by an inch as the dragon turned in the air and bathed the rest of the demons harrying him in fire. One of them managed to latch onto his tail, but with a sharp jerk he sent the beast plummeting toward the rocks.

Now the griffin dove at his back, its razor-sharp beak primed and biting winds sailing out from beneath its wings. The dragon sensed its approach and turned, propelling himself upward with a single beat of his wings. The griffin banked sharply to avoid him, but its wing still clipped his outstretched paw. Claws wreathed in fire wreaked havoc on the griffin's appendage, and it, too, began to fall.

That was when the tiger struck. With a sweep of its wings it charged the dragon, sinking its enormous teeth into his already wounded shoulder. Then it tried to withdraw, but the dragon turned, and arching his neck to reach his foe, struck with his jaws. He fastened them around the tiger's torso, and with one bite he was through its chest, blood and guts spilling out onto its fur. Life left its eyes as it dropped heavily back to the earth.

The demons now mobbed him in earnest, some fastening to his tail and biting his wings while others attacked with blasts of their own magic. A ring of fire rolled out from the dragon's sides, as flames washed over his entire body and splashed onto the offending demons. They let go instantly, screeching as flames caught their heads and paws, burning off entire limbs on contact.

His airborne enemies finished off, the red dragon angled his wings and swooped toward the ground, where the men and wolves waited, along with the wounded griffin. He killed the griffin first with a bite to the neck before turning on the horsemen. The soldiers' horses were showing the whites of their eyes in panic, and the riders themselves were pale with fear. It took all their control and discipline to whip their terrified mounts toward the dragon, hurling swords and spears that bounced off his scales and shooting arrows that burned to ashes even before they reached him. The wolves attacked him as well, but their luck was little better. With slashes of his talons and snaps of his jaws, the dragon destroyed them all, ploughing through man, horse, and wolf as if they weren't even there.

His work done, the red dragon now turned toward Eiryenne and her horse.

The girl was transfixed. She stared with open-mouthed wonder, unable to take her eyes off this magnificent, savage creature. Her mind was torn between fear and awe. Neil turned rigid beneath her, apparently frozen in terror.

The dragon walked up to them, stopping when he saw that her horse was on the verge of bolting. He moved with as much grace on the ground as he did in the air, moving smoothly from paw to paw. Both his wings were now tucked in at his sides, but his left one hung loosely, blood running down the webbing. There was a set of deep scratches in his chest, also bleeding. His muzzle was splashed with his enemies' blood, with some splatter reaching the row of plated scales between his eyes. As Eiryenne met his mesmerizing amber gaze, she felt herself sink into a familiar trance. This time it was more powerful than ever.

Then the dragon blinked and released her. He turned his head to look down the trail.

"We should probably go look for Chief," he said in Danzi's voice. It was somehow deeper and more guttural than before, rumbling with newfound volume. "He bolted after I fell, but I doubt he's gone far." Then he looked down at her horse, who had tensed his legs, ready to flee from this strange creature. "Relax, Neil. It's me." The white fire surrounded him again, except now Eiryenne could see that it was not completely white, but rather a very light, pale yellow. The dragon's silhouette dissolved and shrank back down. When the fire cleared, the blonde man with a pointed beard and amber eyes stood before her again. He was clad in the same clothes as before, though they were splattered with fresh blood — mostly not his own. More blood dripped from his fingers and mouth from when they had been claws and fangs. The gold tinge in his beard and sword were muted by a scarlet cast.

Eiryenne finally found her own voice. "D-Danzi?"

"Hmm?"

"You're a ... a ..." she whispered.

"A dragon, yes," he replied matter-of-factly. "What of it?" Blood dripped down from his mouth and coated his hands, and there was a fresh puncture wound in his shoulder, as well as bloody slashes across his chest.

"You c-c-changed," she stuttered.

"I'm a shape-shifter," Danzi said. "It's fairly common."

"Wait, so you're a man who can change into a dragon?"

Danzi narrowed his eyes. "No. I am a *dragon*. A dragon who can take the form of a man. Humans themselves can't shape-shift. But various magical creatures often take on a human form for discretion or convenience. Everything from Dyre wolves to griffins can do it."

"Oh, your eyes—" Suddenly Danzi's slit-shaped pupils and sharp-pointed canines made a lot more sense.

"They don't change." Danzi caught her gaze and held it. "You can always tell a shape-shifter by their eyes. They reveal their owner's true nature."

Despite his matter-of-fact tone, Eiryenne's hands had tightened on the reins. Neil began to back up. "Are you going to eat me?" she squeaked.

He frowned. "Nothing has changed. I'm the same person you first met. My priorities remain as they were." He turned and began to walk down the path to where the dark bay horse had gone.

Eiryenne hesitated then followed at a distance. The magic was strange enough, but this? She could hardly wrap her head around her travelling companion suddenly turning into a giant fire-breathing beast.

She reached down and patted her horse's sweaty neck. "Brave boy," she said. "I know I would've bolted, if I were a horse." Even now, she fought the urge to turn her mount around and gallop in the opposite direction. But something kept her hands steady on the reins.

Up ahead, Danzi had found his horse, standing behind a boulder. Chief shied away from him at first, his nostrils flaring at the smells of blood and fire. But Danzi grabbed his reins and held him still then swung onto his back.

The rest of the afternoon passed by in a blur. Danzi made a brief pause to stuff some herbs onto his wounds, but they didn't stop again until the daylight was beginning to dim and Eiryenne had trouble making out their surroundings.

By the rapids of a river, near a bridge, Danzi brought Chief to a halt. Eiryenne stopped Neil behind him. The dragon mage turned his horse around so that he could look her square in the face.

"We will reach the castle shortly, so listen carefully," he said.

Eiryenne's thoughts quickly jumped from wondering whether Danzi ate humans to how she was going to get by if a regiment of soldiers attacked and the dragon wasn't with her.

"I will speak to King Balon and tell him what you carry. What he does after that is up to him, but you should still use your common sense. Keep the necklace hidden from view and tell no one of its purpose. Don't let anyone touch it, unless you are certain that Balon is either passing it onto another weaker mage or having it destroyed. And keep practicing your magic every day, as many times as you can handle. This is not over until that necklace is gone, and you must be able to protect it yourself until that moment comes."

"What do you think the king will do?" she asked, hoping that he'd just happen to have a spare trainee mage available to take it on from her.

"I don't know," he said. "If he makes the wrong decision you should run."

And with those encouraging words, he turned Chief around and they stepped onto the bridge. Their horse's hooves made dull, echoing thuds on the wood. It was an unusual sound after having spent so much time riding in the country. After the bridge, they rounded the bend of the river to see the capital of Turmain laid out in the valley before them.

The buildings were big, square structures with sloping roofs and wooden doors. Eiryenne gaped at them. She'd never seen houses of this size, and so many of them, all closely packed together. Hard-packed dirt roads wove in and out of the rows of buildings. A larger one ran down the centre of the town, leading up to an enormous castle of stone and mortar. There were two large towers on either side of the outer wall, both manned by guards.

Another thing that struck her was the sheer number of people. They were everywhere, ducking in and out of market stalls, running and riding up and down the roads, and gathering around their houses.

Danzi didn't seem too impressed. To Eiryenne it was the largest, grandest settlement she'd ever seen. But by his standards, it was small and run-down, its poor state reflecting the nation's bad economy.

He led the way down the crowded street, unconcerned by the people that he was almost running over with his horse. Eiryenne followed more carefully, trying to avoid even coming close to stepping on anyone. She was used to riding in wide-open spaces, and the hustle and bustle on this street was overwhelming.

They soon came to the castle itself. A trench filled with water was dug around its perimeter. There was a drawbridge over the moat that led to the closed gate. Here the travellers stopped, and Danzi banged loudly on the metal and wood doors.

In a gap between the bricks, a wooden slot opened, and a guardsman's voice rang out. "We don't take visitors at this hour. Come back in the morning."

"We are here to see King Balon on urgent business," said the dragon mage. "Tell him that Danzi Daggoras is here with a matter that cannot wait."

The slot closed. In a few minutes, the massive doors swung open. Danzi and Eiryenne rode into the courtyard, their horses' hoofbeats ringing out loudly on the cobblestones.

A raven-haired man dressed with a servant's simplicity walked up to them and bowed. "Master Daggoras, welcome. I'm afraid the king is out on a ride at the moment. But I'm sure Magister Jeram will be more than happy to listen to your news."

Just then another man wearing grey and yellow silk, came out from a door to the side.

"What is this?" he barked. "Visitors, this late? What happened, did someone's oats spoil again? I tell you, I have no time to deal with these peasants' affairs!"

The servant who'd spoken to Danzi now walked up to him and whispered in his ear. "It's Daggoras."

The nobleman paled and fell silent. Then he appeared to try to compose himself and approached the riders with a tight smile. "Well, it's certainly been some time since we've had the … pleasure of your company," he said to Danzi. "What brings you here?"

"I need to speak to Balon," the dragon mage replied. He slid off his horse, and Eiryenne did the same. "Today."

"He's not here," Jeram said. "You can tell me your concerns, and I will pass them on to him as soon as he arrives."

"That won't do," Danzi said. He studied Jeram coolly. "We will wait, then, until he returns."

The magister sighed. "Very well. He should be back later tonight. You can hand your horses over to Nadin. He will get them settled in the stables." He paused, looking over at Eiryenne. "In the meantime, you and your friend can wait in some of our rooms. She looks like she could do with some fresh clothes and a bath. Anything else, well, just let me know." He paused then lowered his voice. "Please tell me you're not going to kill anyone this time."

"It is not on my immediate agenda," replied Danzi, his expression as inscrutable as ever.

They were afraid, Eiryenne realized. These people weren't being polite out of kindness; they were doing it out of fear. She wondered what kind of response she'd have gotten if she came here without him.

A servant came to escort her to her room. Danzi headed in the opposite direction. It was clear he thought his job was done; he'd gotten her this far, and now there was nothing left for him to do but speak to the king and hand this mess over to someone else.

The room they gave to Eiryenne must have been a token of their fear and respect for her mentor, because it was enormous, many times the size of the biggest room she'd seen in her village's houses. A fancy woolly rug lined the stone floor, and there was a large bed next to the window. A fresh set of clothes lay on it: a turquoise tunic and vest, a well-made pale brown jacket, and a pair of tan breeches, complete with dark leather boots.

A noble or more experienced traveller would have undoubtedly taken note of the creases and stains in the material and the poor quality of the stitching, but to Eiryenne the clothes were utterly glamorous.

She'd already started taking off her own threadbare jacket when she noticed something in the corner of the room. It was a hollow shape made of a hard, white material and filled with warm, soapy water.

Eiryenne hesitated, thinking that she'd look like a fool if the king summoned her and she was busy soaking in the bathtub. Then again, she didn't know when an opportunity like this would present itself again, so she stripped off the rest of her clothes and got in. She didn't remember the last time she'd bathed; in the summer, she took occasional dips in the river by the village. But now that it was autumn, the water had already cooled too much to wash in it comfortably.

It was strange to see all the grime come off her skin, revealing clear, pale patches that grew until the dirt was almost all gone. Following Danzi's advice, she hadn't taken the necklace off. Now she turned it over in her fingers, admiring how the stones shone even more brightly beneath a film of water. Despite now knowing how deadly it was, she still found herself entranced by its beauty. It was easy to let her gaze wonder down those sparkling veins of blue until she lost herself in the contours of the gems.

***

"The king is back," Jeram said. "He will see you now."

"About time," grumbled Danzi, getting up from where he'd been sitting.

"Shall I fetch the girl?"

"No," the fire mage said. "That won't be necessary."

Jeram fell back as Danzi walked into the throne room. It was a long, ornately decorated room with the king sitting in front of the back wall. Danzi strode over, stopping in front of the throne without bowing.

"Balon," he said with a nod.

"Daggoras," the king said curtly. He was lanky, with long, dark hair and a scarred, weathered face. He was dressed in blue robes of fine silk, and there was a jewelled dagger on his belt. Three gold rings rested on his fingers. "What's your reason for barging in this time?" he demanded, glaring at Danzi down his hooked nose.

"What I have to say is for your ears alone," said Danzi. He glanced around at the royal guards.

"Leave us," barked the king.

The head guardsman hesitated. "But Your Majesty, you want us to leave you alone with a—"

"Trust me, if Daggoras wanted to assassinate me, he would have done it already," snapped Balon. "He has little concern for witnesses. Now go."

The guard bowed then led his men out of the room, followed by the other nobles that had stood behind Balon's throne.

The king turned back to Danzi. "You better not be wasting my time."

The dragon mage met his gaze and held it. "You know of the Tairung Necklace?"

"Tairung? I've heard bits and pieces of the story," Balon said. "Some cursed necklace that can raise an undead army. Naught but stories, obviously. Don't tell me you came here to say that there is such a thing."

"The first time we met, you thought dragons were just stories," Danzi reminded him. "The necklace is very real. In fact, it's in your castle right now."

"What?" bellowed the king. "You dare to take advantage of my hospitality and bring a token of destruction into my home without even telling me? Just who do you think you are?"

Danzi narrowed his eyes. "Don't pretend like you have a choice," he said, his voice quiet but dangerous. "You know very well who I am. You've seen what I can do. King or not, do not try to fool yourself into thinking you are on equal standing with *me*, human."

Balon fumed silently for a moment before speaking again. "So where is it? And what the bloody hell do you want me to do with it?"

"The necklace was kept in your country for years, hidden. Now the Emperor is seeking it again. The only reason his soldiers aren't swarming your castle walls now is because its evil is somewhat contained when it is worn by a weak mage. The girl I brought, Eiryenne, is its current holder. I did half the work by bringing her here. As king of Turmain, I expect you to deal with issues that affect your nation. This is one of them."

"But you're a bloody dragon, for Kantgo's sake! Can you not just breathe fire on it and be done with the thing?"

"No," said Danzi. "Destroying it is beyond me."

"And why do you expect that I can?"

"You know what will happen to Turmain should you fail," said the dragon mage. "I have other matters to deal with."

The king paused, his brow furrowed and his frown deepening. "No," he said finally. "I want no part in this. Take the wretched thing and go elsewhere."

Danzi scowled. "I will not. You're the one that has a duty to this land. You are a king, and it's about time you started acting like one."

"You dare to speak like that to me? That necklace is an ancient evil. You've brought a curse upon us all," hollered Balon. "I don't care if you have to go to the ends of the Empire. *I order you* to get it off my lands."

"Foolish human," Danzi snarled, a violent spark flashing in his eyes. "I am bound by no one's orders." And with those words, blinding yellow-white flames rose up to cover his body. Within a split second, a huge red dragon towered over Balon.

"Guards," screamed the king. "Guards, take him."

Men began to rush into the throne room.

Danzi opened his jaws, pointing his muzzle skyward. A blast of fire struck the ceiling, ripping through stone and mortar until there was a dragon-sized hole through which a patch of the starry sky could be seen.

"You are lucky," said the dragon, "that this requires you to remain alive." He unfurled his wings and jumped into the air. "Deal with the necklace or lose your kingdom. Your choice." One flap of his wings and he was through the hole, ignoring the shouts of the guards that he left below him.

The magister was one of the last people to inch into the throne room in the wake of the dragon's flight. He peered about, noting the destruction of the ceiling and the lack of casualties.

"Well," he muttered to himself. "Could be worse. I always thought this place could use a skylight."

Chapter 7 ~ Castle Grounded

Eiryenne was standing by the window in her new clothes when she felt the ground shake. Opening it, she saw the dragon fly out of the smoking hole that he'd made. Apparently, his talk with the king had not gone well.

At night, his scales were dimmed to a deep, dark crimson. The full moon gave silver highlights to his golden horns and gleaming talons. His flight was slightly lopsided because of his injured wing but somehow graceful, nonetheless. She watched him fly away until he was just a dark speck among the clouds. Then he was gone.

"Good riddance," said a voice from another open window below her. "I won't be sorry if I never see the likes of him again."

"Nothing but trouble, that beast is," agreed another voice. "And a dangerous one at that. We're lucky he didn't go on the attack again."

"That brute better fly far, far away."

Eiryenne frowned and closed the window.

There was a knock at her door, and Jeram came in, followed by a man in silky blue robes and a small procession of royal guards.

"Eiryenne, show His Majesty the necklace that the dragon spoke of," said Jeram.

So, this was King Balon. Eiryenne gave him a quick glance. She thought she'd be awestruck upon meeting the king, but now she realized that she had seen far more extraordinary things that day.

She hesitated, then put her hand to the chain around her neck. Danzi had said not to show it to anyone, but he also told her that it was now up to the king to decide what to do with it. She gripped the chain and lifted the necklace out from underneath her shirt, even though her instincts told her it was the last thing she should do.

Everyone in the room let out a collective gasp. Most seemed torn between inching forward and pulling back; the king did both. He backed up, then came as close to it as he dared, looking at the stones with something like awe.

"Magnificent," he whispered, his hand beginning to move forward despite himself. Eiryenne saw this and slipped the necklace back under her shirt.

Balon snapped out of his trance and tried to compose himself. He nodded to Jeram and the guards, and they left her room. She heard voices in the hall.

Knowing that it was important to find out what decision the king was going to make, Eiryenne quietly walked over to the door and put her ear to it, trying not to think about what they'd do if she was caught.

"Lock her in there," the king said. "She does not leave the room, understand?"

"Of course, Your Majesty," said Jeram.

"Send for our best mage. If this necklace can really raise a forsaken army, then I'd like to have Taugoff on hand when I decide to use it."

Cold fear gripped Eiryenne's heart. This was exactly what she didn't want to happen.

Footsteps came down the hall toward the men, and a new voice reached her ears.

"Your Majesty, the Bremian ambassador is getting ready to leave, but two of his guards' horses are down with colic."

The king sighed irritably. "Very well, give them a pair from our stable." He paused. "Wait, no. Use Daggoras's mounts. It's not like he's coming back for them."

"Yes, Your Majesty."

There were more footsteps as the entire group dispersed.

Eiryenne waited until the sounds faded then tried the handle. It was locked. She banged on it, but no one answered. Running to the window, she opened it and looked around. It was too high to jump from.

She sat on her bed, kneading her forehead and feeling helpless.

The king was going to try to use Tairung's army. That made the entire journey she took to get here utterly pointless.

And worst of all, they were taking her horse.

Sounds from the courtyard made her look up. She looked out and saw Neil and Chief both bearing riders in a green uniform that held long, sharp spears. In front of them were a handful of other horsemen, but Eiryenne only had eyes for Neil. The young stallion pranced and snorted, refusing to cooperate with his new rider. She flinched as the man riding him took a whip to the seal bay's flank and dug his spurs into Neil's sides.

Gathering whatever courage she could find, she stuck her head out the window. She'd already lost her home and the people she knew. Surely, she couldn't be losing her faithful mount as well.

"Stop," she yelled. "That's my horse. You're stealing my horse. Neil!"

Neil turned upon hearing her voice, but his rider yanked his head back toward the gate.

Down in the courtyard, one of Balon's guards looked up. "Shut up, girl," he said. "Or we'll bolt your window shut, too."

She backed away from the window, stifling a sob.

***

The days after that passed by in a blur. Nervous-looking servants stuck a plate of food inside her door twice a day. Aside from that, the occupants of the castle didn't interact with her.

She paced around the room during the day, sometimes sitting on the windowsill and watching people move about the courtyard below. As far as imprisonments went, she supposed she had lucked out. After all, this was better than being tossed into a small cell in the dungeon. If not for the king's delay in speaking to Danzi, she supposed that was where she'd be. But as it were, they were reluctant to move her.

They feared her, she realized. Or at least they feared what hung around her neck. The servants who brought her food had a look of panic in their eyes, as if opening her door invited a curse.

And for all she knew about Tairung, perhaps it did.

She knew that Danzi had told her to run away if Balon made a bad choice. But she was given no opportunities to do so. The servants who fed her were always accompanied by guards, and they never left the door open for more than a second or two to put dishes in or take them out.

She decided it would have to be up to her magic, so she continued to practice every morning, going through the exercises Danzi showed her. Though there was no sure way to test her barriers, she was able to start thickening them and holding them for a few seconds longer. Her attack spells, however, continued to elude progress. Even after clearing her mind, she had trouble doing much more than taking a chip out of the bedframe or tearing a piece of fabric.

Eventually, even the luxurious room became small. Day in and day out, she was trapped inside. She missed the open country. She also missed her horse dearly; she'd become quite attached to Neil after their journey together. And in a strange way, she also wished that Danzi was still here. Locked doors and high windows would never be a problem for him. Bloodthirsty dragon he might be, but so far, he'd had a solution for every obstacle they'd encountered.

Boredom soon bid that she start to experiment with her magic. She cast her mind back to Hayden's storybook and the things that it said mages could do—destroy, create, conceal, and move things. One of the first that she tried was levitation. Sending out a plume of her light, she wrapped it around a piece of cloth that had fallen off her old breeches. Concentrating, she thought of birds and flight and winds, trying to instil the thought into the fabric. Slowly, it began to rise until it hovered a few inches off the table. Then Eiryenne brought thoughts of the dragon's flight into her magic, and the spell changed. The fabric bent almost double before going up a little more and then plummeting to the floor.

She blinked. This was not as straightforward as she thought.

Some of her other ideas were far less successful. Try as she might, she couldn't get a pair of wings to grow on her back or turn herself invisible.

As she lay back on her bed that night, she thought of what else she might be able to do to sharpen her skills and pass the time. So far, the spells that would come in most handy for an escape weren't working. When the king's mage came, there would be trouble. She had to be ready.

Eiryenne thought back to the time when she'd healed the finch, remembering how she'd scanned his body with her magic to find his faults. Perhaps she could also scan other things. Doors, for instance.

She put her hand on the heavy slab of oak, trying to ease her mind down into its wooden fibres and trickle into its lock. Instead, she became aware of a spider crouched at its bottom. It was just a tiny pinprick, a dot of life that her magic touched.

She thought for a moment. If living things were what her powers were drawn to, perhaps she'd have better luck with that group of soldiers coming down the hall. She concentrated on the thud of their boots until it seemed like the noise was coming from inside her own head. A small tendril of light, bluer than purple, snaked underneath the door.

One of the men gasped. "Oh god, what is that? It's got my foot. Help me!"

There was a clatter of dishes and the sound of rapidly retreating footsteps.

Someone gave a light chuckle outside her room. "The little mage is getting bored."

The door opened. It must have been the servant that was caught in her spell, because a guard shoved her food into her room. He was about to close it when the woman who'd laughed at her spell spoke again, and he let the door linger open for a second. Eiryenne didn't see the speaker or catch what was said, but she saw her opportunity. She focused on a small piece of wood that lay on the ground, one that she'd chipped from her bedframe. Sending out a stream of magic, she nudged it into the side of the door just as it closed.

Waiting until the sounds of the soldier died away, she walked up to the door. It hadn't swung shut all the way because of the wooden chip, so the knob turned. Her palms felt sweaty and her lips quivered as she started to open the door. Then she paused, her shoulders beginning to shake as well. She'd never be able to get past the guards. They might throw her into the dungeon this time or decide that she was too much trouble and kill her. After all, Balon was planning to use the necklace. He probably wouldn't need her anymore once his mage came.

She took a breath, steadying herself. One thing was certain: she would not be avoiding an ill fate by staying in this room, only putting it off. Out there, at least, there was a chance. A small one, but a chance, nonetheless. She had to try.

Suddenly there were more footsteps. Eiryenne froze. They were coming up to her room.

Remembering how her magic had sent the servant scurrying, she tried again, casting out a thread of her power underneath the door, trying to snag the men's feet.

This time her magic was met with a solid wall of resistance that quenched the light instantly and forced her to her knees.

Her door swung open. In walked a tall woman in blinding yellow robes with a young boy on her heels. Magister Jeram followed, along with a handful of royal guards.

The older woman shook a finger at her. "Naughty girl," she said. Eiryenne recognized the voice that had laughed at her first attempt to spell the guards. This woman must have been at her door the whole time, waiting and watching, getting a measure of Eiryenne's power.

"What do you think, Taugoff?" asked Jeram.

"She's a mage all right," said the woman. "But young and weak."

"Show her the necklace," ordered the magister.

Eiryenne hesitated.

The woman called Taugoff crouched down in front of her. "Do it, girl, or I will force you to." Pale magenta light began to shine around her hands. Looking into Taugoff's eyes, Eiryenne realized with a start that she was not human. Her pupils, rather than being round, were horizontal ellipses. She didn't seem to have to blink, either.

"What are you?" she whispered, looking from him to the young man beside him.

"Observant child," Taugoff said, her tone low. "All the others think that's the result of a backfired spell. But considering the company they found you in, I'm not surprised." Her mouth curled downward with disdain. "Now, show us Tairung's masterpiece."

Eiryenne lifted the necklace out from her shirt, and as always, the atmosphere changed. Its effect seemed to be even more pronounced this time. Taugoff's expression shifted, her face becoming hollow and hungry. Eiryenne saw her grip the rug that she crouched on to stop her hands from reaching out.

Her apprentice had no such self-control. The boy's face contorted into a diabolical grin, and he lunged toward Eiryenne, dark green light flickering around his arms.

Without even thinking, she called on the barrier spell, and a wall of magic rose up to intercept the boy. He broke through it as if it were made of hay and went for her throat. She grabbed his arms, trying to keep the necklace out of his grip. But he was too strong. One of his fingers brushed the blue-black stones.

Next thing she knew, Taugoff was hauling the young man off her. "Stupid boy," she yelled. "If you blindly give in to its temptation, the necklace will consume you."

"But it *can* be controlled?" Jeram frowned. He looked worried; it was taking four guards to hold off Taugoff's apprentice. The young man was still madly struggling, arms outstretched in the necklace's direction. His hands began to glow again, but Taugoff quickly cast two circles of magenta light around the boy's wrists, and his magic faded.

"With the right spells and enough power, yes," answered the older mage. She gestured for Eiryenne to hide the necklace again. Once it was out of sight, she walked over and grabbed her apprentice by the shoulders. "We are going to do this, but we are going to do it *right*."

The boy stopped struggling. "I–I'm sorry, master," he mumbled, looking at his boots. "I don't know what came over me."

"Tairung's essence will bring out the evil in all those who gaze upon it," said Taugoff. "Whatever greed, whatever anger, anything like that inside you— t will grab a hold of it and never let go." She got up and gestured for the boy to follow her. "We will start preparing the spell now, Jeram. When I call, bring the girl down to the main hall. It's about time we gave this struggling country a proper army."

"If she's a mage, shouldn't we—" Jeram began.

"No," Taugoff said. "Just lock the door properly this time. She doesn't have the skills to get out."

They all exited the room, leaving Eiryenne to her thoughts. She crawled to her bed and collapsed onto it.

She didn't know what kind of creature those two mages were, but it was clear that both were much stronger than her. She didn't stand a chance; it was over. They'd try to summon Tairung's army, and then who knew what would happen. Something told her that the necklace's power was not as easily contained as Taugoff said. In any case, the Emperor would feel Tairung's call, and this land would fall into chaos. She wondered whether she'd even live to die in that war, or if Taugoff would kill her once she took the necklace.

Anxiety clouded her mind as the thought of her imminent death and all those she'd caused began to overwhelm her. She rode through the panic attack as best as she could, praying that it would be over before she was summoned.

Once it had run its course, she tried to relax and meditate while she awaited her fate. *Think*, she told herself. *There must be something. Anything.*

It looked like the only thing left to her would be to wait until they came to get her from the room, then, on the way to the main hall, take off the necklace and throw it somewhere. If the Emperor was going to find it anyway, she might as well give herself a chance to escape. Hopefully, the guards would take their eyes off her when they went to retrieve it, and she could escape while it burned out their minds.

She ran her fingers over the stones, feeling a pang of regret that she had to throw them away. She had to do it, of course. It was better than trying to do something as stupid as *using* the necklace. If she struggled to control her own meagre magic, then she would be undoubtedly overwhelmed by the all the evil powers that Tairung held. That was out of the question.

There were footsteps in the hall. Knowing that one way or another, she was not coming back to this room, Eiryenne grabbed her pack and slung it over her shoulder, along with her bow. The hunting knife she put on her belt. If the guards noticed, they didn't comment on it. They led her silently through the hall and down a narrow, winding staircase. There were windows in the wall on this level, opening out to another courtyard to the right.

Now was as good a moment as any. Slowly, so that the guards wouldn't notice, Eiryenne began to lift her hand toward her neck.

A thunderous explosion shook the castle. Then two more, so powerful that they knocked the girl and the guards off their feet. With another boom, part of the wall in front of them was blown away. Eiryenne scrambled to get up, taking advantage of the noise and confusion to bolt down a passageway to her left. She heard footsteps and shouts in pursuit, with intermittent explosions still ringing in her ears. The girl ran as fast as she could, sprinting down the stone corridor and dodging through crowds of panicked servants. Her next turn brought her into a large room that had part of its ceiling and wall caved in.

Voices rang out behind her. It was too late to turn back, so she ran over the spilled bricks and boulders to the back of the room, hoping to find a door or crack that she could squeeze through.

There were none.

She turned to see four sweaty guards in tunics and armour running into the room, their swords drawn. Beginning to panic, she desperately cast her eyes around the room for anything that she could use.

As the guards approached her, their steps slow and wary, Eiryenne got an idea. They were passing right by the hole in the ceiling, next to the mound of huge bricks and rocks that had been knocked out of it. Summoning as much magic as she could, she thrust it at the biggest stone, hoping to knock it down onto their heads.

It didn't even budge.

The men had stopped when they saw her use her powers, but now they advanced again, jeering at her.

She ignored them and looked at the rocky pile again, hoping for another idea. She realized she didn't know how to think in a fight; all her thoughts turned to fear, and she would blindly reach for the first thing to come to mind.

Danzi didn't fight like that. She thought back to how he'd fought off the bandits, never losing his cool, every stroke of his sword calculated and defined. Maybe she didn't have that kind of skill at her disposal, but she could learn something from his tactical approach.

She made herself take a deep breath, even though her lungs were resisting. Then she looked at the pile again. She didn't have much strength, but perhaps if she managed to nudge the right rock, it would make the others come tumbling down. Her vision closed in on a pebble that precariously propped up a head-sized stone. Taking another breath, she sent the last of her magic into it as the first of the guards reached her.

He struck her across the shoulder with his sword just as the pebble gave way, making the rock it held back tumble down. That rock hit a larger brick, which hit an even bigger one, until a small avalanche came crashing down onto the guards' heads. When the dust cleared, they were buried deep beneath the rubble except for the closest one, who'd struck at her. She was horrified to see a sharp slab of rock embedded deep within his skull, which was leaking a mixture of blood and a strange, clear liquid.

Eiryenne scrambled over the rocks, running back the way she'd come until she found another corridor. In the background, people were screaming, and the building continued to shake.

Had Danzi realized he'd made a mistake in bringing her here?

Indeed, as she burst out into a courtyard, there were dark shapes circling the castle. But they weren't dragons. Griffins, demons, and other winged beasts swarmed the building, bombarding it with great blasts of their magic. The Empire's silver insignia gleamed around their necks.

There were answering flashes of magenta and green as Taugoff and her apprentice tried to fight back. They didn't know it, but they were helping Eiryenne; every time one of the creatures turned away from them and tried to fly toward the girl, they got caught in one of the mages' spells.

She didn't stick around to watch. After sprinting down a new maze of corridors, she finally burst through a door that led out of the castle. She joined the throngs of fleeing servants, nobles, and townspeople. In their panic, no one looked twice at her.

Then she heard screams. A winged tiger had broken free of the castle's battle and was swooping down upon the crowd. The street was narrower than the span of his wings, so he was forced to land to try to get to Eiryenne on foot. With each sweep of his head, he impaled a new body on his monstrous fangs and threw it out of the way. He swatted people aside, his claws ripping people open to the bone.

Turning away from the chilling sight, Eiryenne forced her shaking legs to move. After she had made her way down through the city, she picked a side street that led out of the capital and ran up it. Once the buildings gave way to hills and trees, she began to feel better, but she still ran. She knew that she had to get as far away from the castle as possible, because within a certain distance, the Emperor's henchmen would still be able to sense her.

A large wolf leaped out of the shadows at her, a mad glint in its eye. She veered to the side but couldn't avoid those snapping jaws. Its teeth buried in her flesh. She screamed as the animal chomped away at her collarbone. Then there was a sickly snap, and pain shot up her arm.

Blinded by panic and pain, she fumbled for the knife at her belt. After a few long seconds her fingers closed around it, and she plunged it into the wolf's eye. It yelped and released her, running around the clearing and shaking its head.

She didn't wait to see if it would get the knife out. Eiryenne stumbled to her feet, biting her lip to keep herself from screaming. She started to run again, clutching her wounded side. Her fingers failed to stem the flow of blood.

Then she looked up, and her heart skipped a beat. Above her flew an entire flock of griffins. The one at their head, a dark-coloured beast with burgundy-tipped feathers, seemed to be looking right at her. But they didn't deviate from their course; to Eiryenne's relief, the flock kept on their northward heading, ignoring her.

Only later did she realize she'd seen no silver insignia around their necks.

Her brain was too preoccupied to give this much thought. Her thighs were starting to burn, but she ignored them. This time she used her fear as her fuel, and adrenaline numbed the pain that was burning deep within the slash on her shoulder. She ran until her feet felt like they would fall off and her torso felt like it would explode from the agony. And even then, she kept running. Branches tore at her face and rocks threatened to trip her as she ran, her pace slowing by the second.

Finally, her aching legs simply gave out. She fell onto her face, blood loss and exhaustion catching up to her at last. The earth felt damp and cool beneath her cheek, and then she knew no more.

Chapter 8 ~ Facing Demons

Darkness. She was falling through darkness. Her body glimmered a purplish blue, but everything else was in shadow. Then the stones around her neck began to glow, surrounded by black and blue fire, which extended out until the flames were biting her flesh. She tried to cry out but found she didn't have the breath to do so. The dark silver chain on which the stones hung was tightening, forcing every breath she made to be shallower than the last. She struggled, trying to grab hold of the chain and pull it away from her skin. But the fire only jumped onto her hands, turning them to blackened stumps before her eyes. And the chain itself didn't stop at choking her. It continued to contract, cutting through the flesh of her neck while the flames continued to burn her body.

She gave a muffled scream that soon turned to a gurgled moan as the chain sliced through her windpipe and blood spilled into her throat. With a final jerk, the necklace snapped through her spine and decapitated her completely. Her body burned to the ground while her head continued to fall. Then it hit something hard and continued to move, rolling along a sloped, hard surface. Corpses flashed before her eyes. She recognized them: Hayden, Tina, her aunt, her parents. She saw them all in graphic detail. Hayden's pale, lifeless face gazed blankly at her while a crow pecked out his eyes and then reached into the empty sockets to grab a chunk of his brain. Tina lay butchered and quartered like a pig; the soldiers that had killed her were chopping up her body and hanging bloody strips to cook over a fire.

Then she saw her parents, dead but waving to her from the depths of a roaring fire.

"Eiryenne," they screamed. "Help us!"

"I can't," she sobbed, tears running down her cheeks and collecting at the end of her neck. "What can I do? You're dead!"

"It's your fault," Tina said. She got up with only half her body parts attached. "Damn you, Eiryenne, it's because of you that I ended up like this."

"I'm sorry," she whispered. Her own face was paler than the corpses'.

Suddenly the necklace appeared around the stump of her neck. It became heavy. It was as if the weight of the world hung from around her neck. She looked at the bloodstained stones and saw shadows moving within them, passing from one vein of shining blue to the other. Ghostly shapes rose out of the rock to scream at her, their voices dripping with hatred and agony. Then a thread of black light moved out from the largest stone.

The view changed, and she was at Balon's castle again, which now stood next to her village. Her head was stuck on a pike next to a pile of bodies. In front of her, the demons and beasts of the Empire continued their slaughter, killing entire families as she watched.

"Stop it," she screamed. "Stop It!"

The stream of darkness coming from her necklace grew and solidified until it took on the rough shape of a horse. But when she looked closer, she saw that it was like no horse she'd ever seen. It towered above her. Its pelt jet-black was swirled with grey markings. Its thick, wild mane stood on end. Its hooves were split in half and contorted into pairs of monstrous claws. A single twisted, crooked black horn rose from its forehead. The tip was missing, and black ooze dripped from the hole. Shifting shadows cloaked the beast, sometimes appearing to take the form of one monster or another before sinking back into its hide.

"They're right, you know," said the creature. Its voice was deep and gravely and layered with other, fainter voices. There was madness in its eyes. "They would all be alive if it weren't for you. The blame for their deaths stains your soul, and their spirits will haunt you until your dying day."

Eiryenne shuddered, hating the truth in his words, and found that she had a body again. She clutched her arms around her torso and looked up at the beast that was tormenting her.

"Tairung," she whispered, realizing.

"Free me, girl," hissed the creature. "Release my spirit from those stones, and I'll spare your pitiful life when I rule these lands once again."

Eiryenne opened her mouth, but no sound came out. Her tongue was paralysed with fear. She wanted to get away from this horrible place, get rid of this terrible burden and go hide in some distant corner. But if she released Tairung, she knew that just make more people die?

The deranged unicorn took a step closer. Red saliva dripped from his fangs. His muzzle was grotesquely twisted and disfigured, a parody of what any equine was supposed to look like. "If you don't break the seal, then you will never be free of me," he rasped, a thousand demonic voices echoing his words. "There's nowhere you can hide where my essence won't be felt. You will bring death and doom to anyone and everyone you meet. Every town you come to will be ravaged by the forces that are drawn to my aura. You will be running for the rest of your short, pitiful life — a futile struggle that will come to an end very soon."

Tairung stepped even closer until Eiryenne could smell his putrid breath. "I deal with demons, child. Including those who cross the line between this world and the next. Who knows, if you were to oblige, I might even see to the return of your parents." He paused. "But if not ..." Suddenly Eiryenne was frozen to the spot and he slowly, meticulously sliced off her legs with his horn. "There are a thousand ways for you to die, each more excruciating than the next. And I can kill you a thousand times in here before my demon brothers finally finish off your real body. By then you will be begging for oblivion."

Black fire shot out of his horn. It struck her right sleeve and began eating away her arm. Eiryenne screamed until her throat was raw, her panic leaving no rational thoughts as she watched the flames eat away first flesh, then bone.

***

She opened her eyes to see orange fire searing her neck and shoulder and sizzling with agony. The menacing, dancing flames embodied everything that she feared and hated in this world. Panicking, she screamed and jerked away her mind simply overwhelmed by terror as her phobia of fire kicked in with full strength.

The flames vanished. Then someone clamped a hand over her mouth and nose, shoving a bunch of small leaves under her nostrils. Eiryenne clawed madly at the hand, trying to get it off, but it didn't budge.

The leaves under her nose had a strange but not unpleasant smell. It was heavy and slightly sweet, with a hint of spice. And as she breathed it in, her racing heart began to slow. The incense filled her lungs and made her head feel heavy, gradually calming her frantic thoughts. Her quick, shallow breaths deepened as the panic ebbed out of her body, along with the pain from her wounds. She relaxed her grip and stopped trying to throw the hand from her face. She took another breath, and let it out slowly, enjoying this newfound calm. Then she looked up.

Danzi was crouched next to her, one hand pressing the herbal leaves to her nose, the other gripping her wounded shoulder. Sunlight streamed through his hair, turning it to gold. There was fresh blood on the sharp point of his beard and more on the leather-like fabric of his clothes.

Eiryenne sighed with relief, taking in another lungful of the wonderfully smelling leaves. A few more deep breaths and she felt like she was floating, Danzi's face drifting in and out of focus along with the branches she could see behind his head.

He slid his hand out from underneath Eiryenne's, letting her hold the leaves to her nose herself. Then he placed his other hand on her exposed collar bone.

She watched as fire rose up from his fingertips and filled her wound. Through her herbal daze she could feel the pain renew. But she also felt the flames knitting together torn strands of her muscle and fusing shattered pieces of bone. Danzi was healing her. And he was doing it the only way he could — with fire.

She looked at the flames, watching the red melt into the orange, and saw the yellow that lined its edges. And since the delightful daze that the herbs put her into barred her from feeling fear, instead she looked at the fire with wonder. It was beautiful. She watched the tongues of fire dance between Danzi's hand and her flesh, she felt a heavy burden lift from her shoulders. She looked at the fire; she accepted it. She accepted it for all it could bring: warmth, healing, power. As she lay back and closed her eyes, she knew that she was no longer afraid of fire.

When it was done, she sat up and groaned, rubbing her shoulder and side. They were still caked with blood. But when she rubbed away the bloody crust, beneath it there were only a few faint scars.

"Oww," she said, slurring slightly. "What did you do to my arm?"

"I fixed it," Danzi said.

"I didn't know that healing was always so painful."

"It will be if I do it," he replied. "A dragon's magic is meant to destroy things, not heal them. Healing goes against my nature. So, it will always hurt when I heal someone."

She rubbed her neck. Her collar bone felt as if it were on fire. Which, really, it had been. Then she looked down at the leaves that had calmed her. Perhaps a few more breaths of that would take the edge off the pain—

But Danzi grabbed her wrist when she tried to reach for them. "That is the Valhern Herb," he said. This was undoubtedly another trick he'd learned from his herbalist friend. "It will calm your mind, but you should use it only when you really need to. It is very easy to become addicted to it."

"Addicted?"

"You'll need more and more just to function normally. Eventually, you'd consume such vast quantities that it would kill you." He let go of her wrist and stood back. Strangely enough, the rips in his jacket from the winged tiger's claws had disappeared.

"Oh."

Danzi scooped up the small, wrinkled leaves and put them into a small cloth bag before handing it to her. "If you can use it wisely, however, you should take some, and keep it on you. We won't be able to afford any more panic attacks where we're going."

Eiryenne barely heard him. "Tairung," she whispered, "I dreamt of Tairung. Could he really reach me?"

Danzi nodded with a frown. "I think it's surprising that you've gone this long without him trying to tap into your mind. As long as you ignore him, he shouldn't be a problem."

"He showed me what happened to Tina…"

"Not everything he says will be the truth. I saw Tina this morning when I flew over Rosfiord," Danzi said.

Eiryenne gasped. "She's okay?"

"She has some injuries, but she'll live." He paused. "Now, tell me what went on at the castle."

She told him what had happened with Balon, and his plans for the necklace, before going into how she'd escaped.

"You knew he might do this," she said. "Why did you leave me there?"

"When the fate of their land hangs in the balance, some men rise to the occasion. Others, well, you saw what happened," he said. "But whichever would be the case with Balon, I had other business to see to in the meantime. I did do some investigating, however, and I now have an idea of how we should go about destroying Tairung's relic once and for all."

"You planned for this?" she asked. He'd left her at the castle on purpose, knowing what would happen, while he went hunting for answers.

"It was a possibility," Danzi said. "And I like to be prepared for all possibilities."

She thought about this for a moment. Then she got to her feet.

"So where are we going?" she asked.

"The Empire."

Eiryenne dropped her bow, her mouth agape. "We're heading into *the Empire*?" Now that seemed like a sure-fire way to die, she thought.

Danzi nodded. "I can fly over Gosrun and Bremia, but we'll have to go on foot from there. My true form will be recognized too easily; we'll need to find some horses before crossing the Empire's borders."

"Neil and Chief were taken by Bremian ambassadors," she said, feeling slightly hopeful. "Maybe we will come across them." She looked at Danzi. "Will we?"

"We might," he said. "Now gather your things. We're moving out."

She tied her bow to her pack and swung it over her shoulders. Her hand went to her belt before she remembered that the knife sheath was empty; she'd lodged her blade in a wolf's head.

Travelling into the Empire seemed like a bad idea, but she was sure that if there was an easier way, Danzi would have found it.

"Ready," she said. "Wait, are we walking there or—"

Her words caught in her throat as yellow-white fire surrounded Danzi's form and he transformed back into his real shape. The red dragon towered over her; his shining scarlet scales a stark contrast against the azure sky.

Well, he *had* said something about flying.

Eiryenne eyed the row of sharp spines that ran along the dragon's back. They started by his horns and went all the way to the tip of his tail. There wasn't any space for her to sit. She was about to ask how this was going to work when Danzi scooped her up in one of his front paws. It was large enough to go all the way around her middle, and Eiryenne gasped as the points of those deadly talons came uncomfortably close. But they were more dextrous than they looked and none of them snagged her skin. The first three claws and the digits ran parallel to one another, but the last one, closest to the inside, jutted out at an angle. This arrangement let the dragon grip things without necessarily having to skewer them on his claws. Just like people, dragons had thumbs.

Danzi lifted his paw until she was off the ground completely then used his other three legs to jump into the air.

Eiryenne gasped as they lurched away from the ground. The dragon opened his wings and began to beat them, rising higher and higher. She experienced a strange feeling of weightlessness, as if they were falling, only up instead of down. But once she realized that Danzi was not going to drop her, wonder replaced the fear. The dragon soared high above the treetops, still rising. The height both chilled and enthralled her. The forest turned into a quilt of small, bobbing dots of autumnal colours. The ridges became thin lines of darkness and the fields were yellow patches, broken up by tiny grey lines that were rivers. It was as if the entire world was stretched out below them, and she could see all of it from this exhilarating new perspective.

Currents of wind buffeted her, and each flap of Danzi's wings resulted in a motion that rocked her upper body back and forth. After a sudden jolt that felt like it would snap her neck, she decided that she needed to stabilize herself somehow, so she used her arms to brace herself against the dragon's muscular forearm. Just like his claws, Danzi's scales were rock-hard and warm to the touch. It was as if his fire always burned just beneath their surface.

She lost track of time, watching the landscape flow away beneath them. They passed small mountain chains and canyons, looking no larger than strewn pebbles and ditches.

The webbing on the dragon's wings was slightly translucent in its thinnest places; when the sun was at its brightest, she could see light shining through the membrane, giving it an orange glow. Danzi was still listing to the left because of his injured wing, but he didn't stop to rest it. She could see the crusted-over wounds where the tiger's fangs had punctured him.

"Doesn't your wing hurt?" she asked, not sure whether he'd hear her over the wind.

"It does," he replied without turning his head. "But we still need to get to the border quickly." He gave his wings another flap. "Pain is only a limitation of the mind."

They soared on. Now and again Eiryenne would spot roads and tiny figures travelling on them. Her heart skipped a beat every time they passed travellers on horseback, but Danzi didn't slow. It had been a while since the ambassadors had ridden from the castle, she reasoned with herself. Maybe they had just enough time to get near the border. More than anything she wanted to see Neil again. If they were going to ride into the jaws of death, she wanted to go on the back of her friend.

"Where are we now?" she asked.

"We're well into Bremia now," the dragon said. "Soon I will start looking for mounts. I'd rather not fly within view of the border."

At this height Danzi must have looked no bigger than a large bird to the minuscule shapes on the roads. He dipped slightly lower, and Eiryenne could see that his head was angled downward; he was scanning the travellers.

"These won't do," he mumbled. "Half are ponies, and the rest are those flimsy parade horses."

Eiryenne squinted down, too. The horsemen below them were no larger than ants. How he could make out any details was beyond her.

They flew on until more dark dots came up on the road. Danzi circled and began to descend. "I think we found those ambassadors you were talking about."

The descent was terrifying. Eiryenne felt like the pit of her stomach had fallen out and even imagined that she was starting to slip through Danzi's claws. But she forced herself to focus; Neil might be here. As they drew closer, the black dots grew larger until they took on the shapes of bodies. And they were indeed clothed in the green uniforms that Eiryenne had seen the ambassador's guards wear.

Without warning, Danzi opened his claws. She didn't even have time to scream, because the earth was only five feet away, and he dropped her into a big pile of leaves. She scrambled to her feet, dizzy. The ground seemed to shift beneath her feet.

"Warn me," she muttered. "Warn me next time before you do that."

"So that you can beguile me to set you down lower? No." Danzi shifted back into his human form and walked among the corpses while Eiryenne stayed at the edges of the road. "Bandits," he said. "Looks like they've done our work for us." He bent over one of the guards.

The girl looked away. She'd seen enough corpses in her dream to last a lifetime. Instead, she thought of where the horses could have gone. The bandits may have taken most of them, but surely a couple had escaped.

There was an empty pail lying in the bushes. It must have fallen out of one of the ambassador's packs. She picked it up then turned and stepped into the trees. There were hoofprints there amongst the fallen leaves. Putting her fingers to her lips, she whistled the way she did at Hayden's stables whenever it was time to feed the horses.

Taking a breath, she whistled again, this time adding her usual call. "Neil, Horace, Beck, dinner time!" She rattled the empty pail like she had rattled their feed buckets, hoping that Neil still remembered the call.

There was an answering whinny from the trees. Then a horse emerged, stepping somewhat hesitantly over rocks and branches. His body was a pale, chocolate brown while his legs and mane were black. Tan patches were splashed across his muzzle and flank along with a good deal of mud.

"Neil," she squeaked, running over to throw her arms around her horse. He nickered and mouthed her shirt, as if asking where the food was. She stepped back and looked him over. Apart from a few scratches on his legs and whip marks on his flanks, he was in good shape.

She ran her hands over his muzzle, breathing in his sweet, horsey aroma and telling him how glad she was to see him again. Then she heard a snap from behind Neil. Looking over his shoulder, she saw Chief and a bedraggled-looking grey mare also approaching, more hesitantly than the young stallion had.

"Chief," She beckoned. "Come on, you know me. It's all right."

He inched forward then snorted and walked over until he was nosing her palm. She grabbed his bridle before he could wander off again. The sudden movement spooked the grey mare, and she took off into the trees.

Holding on to Chief with one hand and Neil with the other, Eiryenne walked back out to the road. Danzi saw them and nodded his approval. He took Chief's reins from her with one hand. In his other he held a thin, short sword and a small dagger, both stained with blood. Evidently, he'd stripped the items from the corpses.

"Here," he said. "You'll need these."

Eiryenne hesitated. Robbing the dead seemed wrong. Not to mention all that sticky, half-dried blood.

"What do I need them for?" she asked. "I'm a mage, not a warrior, and a weak mage at that."

"Take them," Danzi insisted. It was more of an order this time. "Wash off the blood if it bothers you."

With a sigh, she took them, trying to avoid touching the bloodier parts. The sword was small but heavier than it looked. There were a few pieces of old cloth in the pockets of her jacket, and she took one of these out, using it to wipe off as much of the blood as she could. She buckled the sword onto her belt, along with the dagger, slipping off her old knife sheath while she was at it. The new weight felt strange, awkward. She swayed to the left as she walked. This would take some getting used to.

Danzi checked Chief's saddle bags. Both his and Neil's were filled with fresh supplies courtesy of the Bremian ambassadors. Soon they were on the road again. Neil's saddle and gently rocking gait seemed very comfortable to Eiryenne after her bone-jarring flight with the dragon. Still, now that they were on the ground, it occurred to her just how little of the landscape they saw from here.

The winding road climbed up into a chain of dark, towering mountains. Mirror-like ice coated their peaks, and a chilling wind blew through their passes. Danzi chose a path that would take them around one of the smaller mountains. But *small* in terms of mountains was still huge to Eiryenne. Suddenly, she wished they were flying again; Danzi could fly over this entire mountain chain in the blink of an eye. The horses' speed slowed to a snail's pace once they began to ascend the challenging alpine path.

When the ledge widened enough that the two horses could walk abreast, Danzi drew up next to Eiryenne.

"This is one of the less-guarded routes," he said. "But we may still be watched. If anyone questions you, say you are a peasant going to Hurdenbrak to visit relatives."

She nodded, her lips too numb with cold to form words. Down in the valleys there might be an autumn chill, but here the temperatures were plummeting well below freezing. Her breath formed mist in front of her face, and little ice crystals were forming on her cheeks and eyelashes. There was no escaping the biting wind that whipped her face; the cold seemed to seep into her very bones and threaten to turn them to ice. Even though she had new clothes from the castle, they were not meant for winter.

She wished she'd at least gotten some gloves. Her hands were numb, her fingers starting take on a bluish cast. The reins slipped through her frozen digits. But Neil didn't stray; there was nowhere for him to go. To their right was a solid wall of rock; to their left was a harrowing drop, straight down for over a hundred feet to the base of the mountain. Neil was cold, too. His winter coat had not yet grown in completely, and he walked with his head down, braced against the relentless wind.

Eiryenne thought that since dragons were creatures of fire, the cold would be even harder on Danzi than it was on her. But instead it was the exact opposite; the temperature didn't seem to bother him at all. Ice barely had a chance to start building on his beard before it melted right off, and there was no sign of frostbite on his hands. While Eiryenne was hunched over, her shoulders arched against the wind and trying to avert her face from it, Danzi rode as he always did: shoulders square, back straight, his eyes as clear as usual.

The alpine path twisted to the right, forming a sharp incline before levelling out again. Their horses stumbled to find footing on the icy slope. Chief went first, slipping and sliding as he scrambled to the top. Neil followed. He walked carefully over the first few patches of slippery rocks and was nearly at the top when his hooves struck ice and slipped out from under him. He fell to his knees and tumbled off the left side of the path, starting to fall down the side of the mountain.

Eiryenne grabbed him around the neck, hoping that Danzi would be able to transform and snatch her from the air before they hit the ground. It didn't get so far. Neil jerked to a halt almost as soon as he'd started to fall. He hung there, almost vertically suspended over the drop. His rider dared a glance behind them.

Danzi was holding on to Neil's croup with both hands. He pulled and quickly lifted the horse back onto solid ground without any apparent effort.

"We still have a ways to go," he said. "Pay attention to where you're going."

She nodded, barely hearing him. The cold was starting to fog up her brain. As they continued, she didn't even try holding on to the reins anymore. Neil, also shaken by his near-death experience, stayed close behind Chief. Perhaps he was also trying to hide from the wind behind the bigger horse. It didn't seem to help much, and Eiryenne continued to shiver as the cold seemed to grip her very soul and tried to turn the blood in her veins to ice. She'd never been this cold, not even in the worst winters at her village. Her shivering intensified until it turned into full-body convulsions.

Then Danzi slowed down until he was next to Eiryenne and put a hand on her shoulder. Tingling warmth spread from the point of contact, banishing the cold from her body and the ice from her blood until she felt warm and alert from the top of her head to the tips of her toes. The colour came back into her skin, and her fingers started to move and feel again.

"Thanks," she said, opening and closing her hands. Then she picked the reins back up.

Danzi reached out to touch Neil's neck, and frost started to melt from the horse's fur as his ears perked up and his movements became less rigid.

"Warming spell?" she asked. Now that he had taken his hand away, the flow of warmth ceased. But the heat that remained continued to circulate in her body, only seeping out slowly from the cold.

"Not quite," he said. "Just dragon fire."

"Dragon fire?"

"My magic takes on the shape of fire, as you know," he replied. "As it always circulates within me, I can use it to keep myself warm even in conditions like this. I just extended a bit of it to you and your horse as well."

"But if it's fire magic, why doesn't it burn?" she asked.

"Fire doesn't always burn."

Chapter 9 ~ The Empire

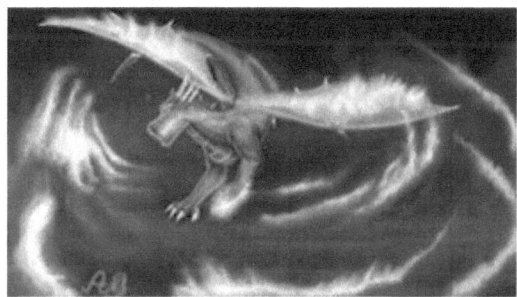

Once they crossed the mountain chain, a new landscape lay stretched out before them. It was filled with towering, jagged cliffs that seemed to scrape the sky, forests so dense and tall that they put the Turmain trees to shame and raging rivers that wound through a network of lakes.

"Welcome to the Vekarnian Empire," said Danzi.

While they'd passed through the countryside of the other three small nations without encountering much besides birds and soldiers, here the very air bustled with activity. Flocks of strange creatures flew overhead, and a mixture of horsemen and beasts patrolled the roads.

They had just ridden to the juncture of where the alpine trail met one of the lower roads when a strange rider approached Danzi and Eiryenne. He was roughly the shape of a man, with an enormous, round head and a disproportionately huge stomach. His face looked like it had been squashed in by a club, and his skin was a sickly shade of green with sharp protuberances. His horse was covered in muddy brown scales, and there were horns curling back over its ears. The horse's head had two sets of bloodshot eyes, and its cavernous mouth stretched the length of its jaws.

"Ogre," Danzi muttered in response to Eiryenne's questioning glance. "Riding a swamp kirin."

Next to the ogre was another rider, this one a regular man on a normal warhorse. Both man and ogre were clad in the Empire's black and silver, though the extent of the ogre's uniform was a black loincloth. Its silver insignia lay against its bare chest.

"Halt," called the man. "What is your purpose here?"

Eiryenne saw Danzi start to reach for his sword. Realizing his intent, she forced herself to speak.

"Good afternoon, noble guards," she said. "We are just humble peasants on our way to see relatives in Hurdenbrak. If you would let us pass, good sirs, it would be much appreciated. We don't want to be late for the family feast."

The guardsman narrowed his eyes. "Names and professions?"

Behind him, Eiryenne could see a flock of griffins flying in formation. They were too far to notice the arrivals, but if they did, the duo would be in trouble. They had to avoid attracting more attention.

"I am Amira," she said. She quickly pretended that she was weaving a story and spoke the first details that came to mind. "I tend to chickens and fix needlework. And this is Uncle Dagy, the horse trader. We lost the horses he was moving because of bandits in Bremia."

Danzi moved his sleeve to cover the gems and gold on his sword hilt.

The guard was nodding. "Very well. The road to Hurdenbrak is that way," he said, pointing to the path that forked to the left.

The ogre sniffed the air loudly. "Him," He pointed to Danzi. "He smells funny."

Eiryenne thought fast. *It's just like a story*, she thought. *Play the role.* So, she gave the ogre a look of casual annoyance. "Really, you are going to pick on my uncle just because of the ridiculous perfumes he wears? Might not such esteemed guards as yourselves be better suited to putting your talents into the pursuit of bandits? They were close to the border, you know. Might have even followed us in here."

The man nodded. "We'll keep an eye out. C'mon, Och." He and the ogre trotted off.

Once they were out of earshot, Danzi turned to her with a frown. "Uncle Dagy? *Perfume?*"

She just shrugged, suppressing a giggle.

Then a new thought crossed her mind. "Why didn't they sense the necklace?"

"Not sure," said the dragon mage. "They are probably just new recruits without enough evil in their minds."

They crossed the road and entered the forest. The trees here were enormous, wider than she was tall, and they seemed to be infinitely high. Trunks lined either side of the path they were taking, stretching skyward like pillars in nature's giant cathedral. Their crisscrossing branches high above, still dotted with bright orange and yellow leaves, were more beautiful than any roof of stained glass.

The entire spectacle made Eiryenne realize that the forests she'd seen in Turmain were no more than scattered groups of sparse, small trees compared to this.

As their horses walked through the woods, the sounds of their feet were completely muffled by the leaf litter. Pine needles were crushed beneath their unshod hooves releasing a wafting aroma that mixed with the smells of wood and earth.

Several times Eiryenne thought she saw motion in the trees. But when she turned to look closer, there was nothing.

If ogres patrolled the roads, then what manner of evil might lurk within these trees?

"Danzi," she said quietly. "What kind of animals live here?"

"Let's see, we've got everything from Dyre wolves to kirin, forest nymphs to takoras and blysmets." Then he added, "Nothing I can't kill if it bothers us."

They made camp in those woods, surrounded by towering trees and shifting shadows. Danzi insisted on having a magic lesson. He went through all their usual exercises again, observing the slight progress she'd made in his absence.

"Magic is only half the fight," he said when they were done. "You will start to learn the rest tomorrow."

***

After a night of blissfully dreamless sleep, Eiryenne woke to the sounds of unfamiliar birds. She could make out shrill whistles, followed by a trills and deeper caws, as multitudes of strange birds welcomed the morning.

When she opened her eyes, she got a slight shock to see Danzi stretched out across the clearing in his true form, dozing in the early morning sun. The man she was getting used to, but the dragon still unnerved her.

Danzi lay on his belly, his mighty head resting on crossed forepaws. The golden rays of dawn set his scales afire when it touched them. It was like an entire picture that had been painted in the tones of fire: the red dragon lay on a pile of yellow, orange, and red leaves, though they looked dull compared to his brilliant scales. There were marks in the dirt and leaves a bit farther from him, signs of a scuffle during the night.

His sides rose and fell evenly. He was asleep. Eiryenne took this opportunity to study him more carefully. He really was nothing like the dragons in Hayden's storybook. There was no serpent-like neck or narrow, winding body. The caption had described dragons as giant lizards, but in fact there was nothing lizard-like about the beast that lay before her. His build resembled that of a large mammalian predator. He had the power of a tiger, the grace of a horse, and the fire that made him uniquely the creature that he was.

Danzi opened an eye. Eiryenne quickly closed hers, pretending to be asleep. She peered out from beneath her eyelids as the dragon rose and stretched, powerful muscles rippling beneath his shoulder scales. He then walked around the nearby trees, his nostrils flared. His limbs were built upright like a lion's rather than out to the side like a crocodile's, and his gait had had none of that silly side-to-side motion that lizards performed. He moved lightly from one stride to the next with a unique grace that Eiryenne had never seen in either in animals or humans.

He must have spotted some prey because the dragon froze. He looked like a statue carved of ruby and finished with gold. Dappled light from above played across his scales and reflected off his yellow eyes. As he stood there, Eiryenne drank in every detail of the image before her, and she realized something. When she'd looked at the dragon caricatures in the storybook, she'd been struck by the inherent *wrongness* of the creatures. Their necks were too long, and their heads were the wrong shape. But now that she gazed upon Danzi, the great beast spun of red gold and fire, there was not a thing she would change.

She was looking at nature's perfection: the perfect predator, the ultimate balance between power and grace.

She wondered how much of the other storybook's other entries were true. It had depicted Dyre wolves with three heads, for instance. But Danzi had told her that the wolves that pursued them alongside the soldiers were indeed Dyre wolves. They looked like regular wolves, but two to three times as large. They were also intelligent, Danzi had said, but had no magic aside from being able to shape-shift.

The dragon stood there for a few moments before taking a slow, meticulous step forward, followed by another, and another. Then, in the blink of an eye, he sprang. There was a yelp and a crunch, then silence. Twice more he hunted down the hapless inhabitants of the forest and snapped them up before trotting back to the camp.

Eiryenne made her breakfast from the supplies in the horses' saddlebags. Neil was still asleep, but Chief spooked and tried to bolt when he saw Danzi approach. The girl rose from her seat to calm him.

"Easy, boy," she said, rubbing his nose. "You're a dragon's horse now. You better get used to this."

Neil woke up as well, but by then Danzi had already shifted back into his human form, and the young stallion looked around blankly, trying to find what had scared Chief so badly.

"You're quite different," she said quietly, "than the dragons I read about. The ones in my storybook had big long necks and only two legs."

"Ah, those would be wyverns," said Danzi. "Humans always mix us up. Why, though, is beyond me. Wyverns are very different from dragons. They are smaller and are unable to shape-shift. They hardly have any magic at all, actually they're easy to dominate. Even for humans."

Eiryenne thought back to Hayden's tales of dragon riders. "So, people can ride them?"

Danzi nodded. "Sometimes."

"Then the book was actually talking about wyvern riders, not dragon riders?" she asked.

The dragon mage's expression darkened quite suddenly. "No," he said sharply. "There are no *dragon riders*. That is nonsense. It is an insult to my species that humans even allow such idiotic ideas to circulate."

Eiryenne finished the rest of her breakfast in a nervous silence. She'd obviously insulted Danzi, even though it was by accident. And now that she knew what he was capable of, having him angry with her was downright terrifying. After she finished eating, she continued to sit there, gazing at the trees and the birds that flitted among their branches.

After a while, Danzi spoke again. "Now," he said. "I told you that there are two parts to combat. We will now work on the physical aspect. I will teach you to fight, both with a sword and hand-to-hand."

"Are you serious?" she said. "I'm no warrior."

"We will be heading deep into enemy territory," Danzi said sternly. "Even I cannot be everywhere at once. The better you are at holding your own in battle, the safer the necklace will be. Now face me."

Hesitantly, she put down her water skin and did as he said.

"Have you ever punched anything in your life?"

She shook her head.

Danzi sighed. "I thought not." He showed her several different punches and kicks and had her try to copy the movements.

She made a first and tried to punch the air like he'd showed her, but she ended up overreaching and almost falling forward onto her face.

"Mind your stance," he said. "Too narrow and you will be easy to unbalance. Too wide and you won't be able to move enough. And keep your wrist straight. Try again."

Again and again she punched the air, trying to follow Danzi's suggestions. He had her alternate with the left hand and with the right before switching to kicks. Those didn't go much better.

"You're just starting," he said. "I will be drilling these movements into your muscle memory. Only then will you be ready to use them in a fight. Now, draw your sword."

She lifted the blade. It seemed to weigh a ton in her tired, aching arms.

Danzi drew his sword also and walked over to stand next to her. The first movement he demonstrated was a high, short vertical cut. Eiryenne had trouble keeping the sword from slipping from her fingers as she copied it. The sword felt heavy and awkward in her grasp. Then Danzi took a step and brought his blade across in a wide, curving arc. This time Eiryenne's sword did fly out of her hand as her momentum carried her arms too far. Still, Danzi had her retrieve the sword and repeat the motions until her arm muscles burned fiercely.

"Enough for now," he said finally. "Let's move out."

Her fatigue made it hard to lift Neil's saddle, but eventually she got the horse tacked up and finally swung onto his back.

They rode through the forest all day. Time and time again, Eiryenne thought that she saw something moving in the trees.

"Would soldiers be following us in here?" she asked.

Danzi shook his head. "We're taking a route through the more lawless parts of the Empire. Bandits and other criminals run amok here, but not soldiers."

That didn't make her feel much better.

***

When the light began to wane, Danzi led them out of the trees and onto a narrow dirt road. There were low mountains on the horizon. Up ahead, Eiryenne could see the outlines of buildings. They were coming to a city.

"Are we going in there?" she asked. "I thought we were trying to avoid everyone."

"I have some business in Loturg," said Danzi. "We won't be staying long."

There were no guards to greet them as the two riders entered the city. The buildings here were big and old, made of dirt and crumbling stone. By the size of them, Eiryenne guessed that this had once been a prosperous city. But the squalor she saw on the streets told her that bountiful times were long gone. Every person that passed them had hollow, hungry eyes and sunken cheeks. Their clothes were dirty and tattered, the rips sometimes big enough to reveal skin stretched tightly over protruding ribs.

These people were starving, Eiryenne realized. She was shocked to see the once-grand stone houses packed to the brim with hungry families trying to avoid the cold. Those who had no roof over their heads lay at the edges of the streets. Some weren't breathing.

"What happened here?" she whispered.

"The Empire doesn't take care of its people," Danzi explained. "The Emperor puts all his gold into his armies. He pulls whatever he can from the land and them abandons it. The river here was poisoned years ago by the corpses and spells he dumped into it, and the crops have been failing for many seasons. He will occasionally have his soldiers come to cities like this, to take up any able-bodied men and women for his troops and execute anyone who makes a complaint, along with their relatives. Hunger and disease breed here like vermin. And nothing ever changes." There was no emotion in his voice as he spoke or any in his face as he looked into the eyes of the abused. "They are born into poverty and controlled by fear. And that is how their lives end as well."

A little girl ran up to Neil.

"You have such a pretty horse," she said, stroking Neil's muzzle with grubby fingers.

"Thank you," said Eiryenne. Then she looked closer and saw a big cut running the length of the girl's cheek. "Oh my, what happened to your face?"

"Them soldiers did it," said the girl. "They took my da and whacked me when I cried. They took my horse, too. He looked just like yours. What's his name?"

"Hannah," came a shout from the side, and a thin woman came running over to scoop up the child. "Stay away from them, Hannah. I told you not to talk to strangers."

"But I'm hungry, Ma. And that horsy looked so much like Jack, I just had to say hello," the girl protested. She looked back over at Eiryenne with imploring eyes. "You don't have a spare bit of bread, do you? We haven't eaten since last week," she said.

"Hannah, that's rude. You know they won't give anything to you," scolded her mother, beginning to carry her away. "They're all alike, those Empire folks."

"Wait," Eiryenne called. Her heart went out to this small, troubled family. She reached into her saddlebag and pulled out a small parcel, handing it to the astonished woman. "There's some bread in there, and a bit of dried meat."

The woman's jaw dropped. She accepted the parcel with shaking fingers. "Th-thank you," she murmured before stepping back into the shadow of the buildings. Suddenly there were shouts as other people who'd seen the food dove in after her, trying to pry it from her grasp.

"Hey," Eiryenne yelled, but another group was had now surrounded her horse, clawing at the straps of her saddlebags.

"Get back," growled Danzi. He drew his sword and whirled it about, striking away some of the beggars with the flat of his blade. The rest of them backed off, eyeing him nervously as he hoisted his sword high that everyone could see it clearly. The blade flickered with flames. "The next person to get within five feet of us gets their fingers burned off," he continued. "Do you understand?"

The crowd of townsfolk parted, clearing a way down the street for them. Eiryenne kept Neil close behind Chief, trying not to look at the dozens of hungry eyes following them.

"Don't you see how pointless that was?" the dragon mage said. "You will get nowhere by trying to feed just one or two people. Provender them, and a thousand more will come clamouring your way."

They stopped at an old building on the edge of town. Danzi got off his horse, and Eiryenne followed suit, tying their mounts to a rail in front of the building. There were several other horses tied there, mangy-looking animals with wild eyes.

She followed him through the doors. There were tables scattered throughout the room. Men sat at some of them, drinking out of big tankards and laughing.

A silence fell over the pub when Danzi and Eiryenne walked in. Most of the men were looking at him with fear, a few with scorn. A couple of younger ones near the door got to their feet and crowded the dragon mage.

"And what're you doin' here, old man?" one of them drawled.

"Looking for Kafer," Danzi said. "Now get out of my way."

"You better turn around and get the hell outta here," said the second. He took a step and quick as a flash struck out with an ugly-looking dagger.

Danzi's hand morphed into a dragon paw, and he caught the blade in his claws then tossed it away. The man backed away, and in a quick blur of fire Danzi's hand turned human again.

"Kafer don't take no visitors—" His sentence was cut off when Danzi hit him in the chest open-handed and sent him flying into the wall.

"Wait here," the fire mage said to Eiryenne and strode toward a nervous-looking, pale blonde man that sat close to the counter.

The man Danzi had thrown into the walls was trying to sit up, groaning loudly and clutching his ribs.

"Stupid! Don't ya know who that is, Raban?" said a voice off to Eiryenne's right. "That's Danzi Daggoras, and you should be thankin' the heavens that you got off with just a couple o' broken bones."

Eiryenne turned. The speaker was a clean-shaven man dressed in a faded purple tunic and black breeches. He gave her a broad smile. "Hello, there," he said brightly. "What's your name, lassie? I'm guessing it's your first time here."

"Um … I'm Eiryenne," she said hesitantly. "And yes, it is."

"I'm Rol. Come take a seat," he said, drawing up a chair. "Your friend looks like 'e needs a few minutes to settle things over there."

She looked over to see half the men surrounding Kafer already knocked to the ground. Danzi had grabbed him roughly by the shoulders and was shaking him. "We had a deal," he growled. "So where is it?"

"I lost it," said Kafer. "I'm sorry, it's gone. Ahh!" He cried out as Danzi smashed him into the table.

"Would you like a drink?" asked Rol matter-of-factly, as if he saw this kind of carnage every day.

"Er, sure," Eiryenne said. She took the glass that Rol handed to her and fiddled with it. "This happen around here often?"

"Whenever Danzi comes, it's a given," chuckled Rol. "I'm not sure what kind of adventure he's dragged you on, but I can only hope you came on it by choice."

"Well, sort of."

Rol took a sip from his tankard. "So, where are you from?" he asked innocently.

Eiryenne was about to answer but hesitated.

"Oh, come on," Rol said with a grin. "Old grumpy-guts over there can't be much fun to talk to." He turned to observe Danzi hitting Kafer in the face.

She chuckled. "All right, I'm from Turmain."

"Turmain. That's a long ways away," said the man. "You must miss your family."

"I don't have one."

"Oh, I'm sorry," Rol said, looking earnestly sympathetic. "I didn't mean to pry. Tell me instead about how you managed to survive that kind of company." He nodded toward Danzi. "What's the secret? Are dragons really that ticklish?"

"Rol, it is not wise to joke about the likes of *him*," said a man from a neighbouring table. He looked shaken. "Daggoras is a cruel murderer," he spat. "Chaos shadows the red dragon's path. He brings death everywhere he goes. He also happens to be one of the most powerful mages in Shotang. I mean, have you *heard* of the kinds of things he's done? I heard he once killed a thousand men with a single spell! And burned an entire fortress to the ground with only—"

"Whatever," Rol said, waving his hand. He looked back at Eiryenne. "Now, on a more important topic, can you tell me whether the ale over in Turmain is as bad as it is in the Empire?" He took another sip of his drink and grimaced comically.

"I don't know, I haven't tried it," she said, looking down at her cup. She was about to raise it to her lips when she heard a strangled groan. "Rol?" she looked up. Rol was being held in a headlock by a man who'd moved in from a table in the back.

The stranger tightened his grip, and there was a crack. Rol fell to the ground motionless.

"Don't drink that," he said, pointing to Eiryenne's glass. "I saw him put something in it."

"What? But he acted so friendly," she retorted, looking at the man in confusion.

"Not everyone who wants to kill you will tell you to your face," said the man. His voice was smooth, not as deep or rough as Danzi's, but with a similar cadence. He had a slender build and was dressed in a blue tunic with a navy-blue vest. There was some silver embroidery at his sleeves, and a pair of long daggers hung on his belt. "In fact," he continued, "sometimes the killers will be the nicer ones. I'm sure Danzi hasn't been very conversational during your travels. But he's gotten you this far, hasn't he?"

His face was partly covered by shadow, but Eiryenne could make out short, neatly combed black hair and a thin beard. "Who are you?" she asked. "Are you going to try to kill me, too?"

"My name's Lianos," said the stranger. "And, if I was going to kill you, would I have stopped you from drinking poison and done away with your would-be assassin?" He took Rol's seat, kicking the body out of the way.

"I … I suppose not," she stammered. Then she glanced back to where Danzi continued to pummel Kafer, who was by now little more than a bloody pulp. She shuddered. "Did he really kill a thousand men with one spell?"

"I doubt anyone could count that many corpses in a reasonable amount of time," said Lianos. His lilting voice was pleasant to her ears. "And whatever the case, I think you would be wiser to judge Danzi not by what he's done but by what he is doing now." He glanced to the side just as Danzi knocked out one of Kafer's teeth. "Er, well maybe not *right* now."

Eiryenne sighed. Maybe Lianos had a point. Danzi had never tried to be nice to her like Rol, but he kept her alive. He opposed the Empire when few others would dare to. He couldn't be all that bad.

Her thoughts were interrupted by the sound of footsteps. Danzi was walking over to them, tankard in his left hand. With his right, he was slipping a large stone key into his pocket.

"Got what you came for?" asked Lianos, getting up. The other man nodded, and Lianos led them to a table in the back, where he'd been sitting.

"Well, I wasn't expecting to see you here, Lianos," Danzi said, sitting down. "I didn't think you worked this area."

"These days I work almost every area," said Lianos. "The Emperor is closing in on the camp. Hurraine has me running all kinds of jobs in the joint effort to thwart him."

"Hrrmm." Danzi gave off a sound that was half grunt and half growl.

"Wait, you also work against the Emperor? There are more of you doing this?" asked Eiryenne.

Lianos looked at Danzi, who sighed. "Go ahead. Tell her."

The man put down his drink and leaned forward on the table. His face caught the light, and with a shock Eiryenne saw that his blue eyes had the same slitted pupils as Danzi's.

"A few hundred years ago," Lianos began. "There was a warrior who despised the Empire and wanted to bring a halt to all its nefarious activities. He gathered what allies he could and waged war on Varcroft, the Emperor. The movement is known as the Resistance. Ever since then, we've been working on putting the Emperor out of business. Right now, he's trying to find our base so he can strike the hidden camp and destroy us. Our current leader, Hurraine, is trying to avoid this. That's why I'm here."

Danzi continued to sip his drink, staring into the bottom of the tankard.

"Did they poison your drink, too?" Lianos asked him.

"Yes. They never do learn, do they?" he replied with a slight chuckle. "Cheers." They brought their tankards together with a light ring of glass, and both took another swig. "This is probably the third time I've been here, yet they still think that a common poison will work on dragons."

Then Lianos said something else to him, but Eiryenne could no longer understand. He spoke using strange, raucous words that sounded both harsh and elegant. Danzi replied in kind.

"What language is that?" she asked before she could stop herself.

"Draconic," Lianos said. Then he turned back to Danzi, and they resumed their cryptic conversation.

All things considered, it is strange to see you keeping such company, Lianos said in Draconic. *Tell me, what brings you two to these lands?*

She is wearing the necklace of Tairung, what do you expect? Danzi replied. *You've heard of it. Take it off or kill her and the Emperor's forces will be down here instantly. Of course I won't stand to have it fall back into his hands.*

Ah, I see. Lianos nodded.

I'm taking the girl to Boyevin Cavern so we can destroy the necklace.

You'll be heading deep into the Empire, then.

Yes. But it's a risk I'm willing to take, said Danzi.

What are your plans after that? asked Lianos.

You mean the girl? Leave her behind or get rid of her. It's all the same to me. We will see how things play out. By the time we get to that Cavern, there's no telling what will happen.

Hmm. Lianos looked thoughtful. *But why bother teaching her magic and combat if you are only using her to ferry the necklace?*

It is precisely because *I'm using her to ferry the necklace that I am teaching her to defend herself. I can't be everywhere at once, so the better she can fend off attackers, the better her chance of reaching the Cavern alive. Or at least getting close to it. The Emperor has a lot of his men out there. If she is killed before we get to the Cavern, I'll have to bring the necklace there myself with half the army on my tail.*

Yes, that would be problematic.

Danzi took a sip from his tankard. *Her powers won't grow enough to change the reach of the necklace significantly, so as far as I see, the more skilled she gets at magic, the better.*

Lianos nodded. *How is she doing so far?*

Not too well, even for someone that's never had instruction. She also shows an inclination toward healing. Not that that'll help us much. Wounds serious enough to slow me down are still beyond her capacity.

You know, Lianos said, *healers aren't that common. The Resistance could always use some new ones. The choice is yours, obviously — but think about that.* He switched back to Common. "My mission takes me in the opposite direction, so good luck on your quest," he said. "Nasty bite, by the way. Was that a smilodon?" He pointed to the puncture wounds on Danzi's shoulder. They were crusted over but still hadn't healed.

"Among other things," said the dragon mage. "You mind?"

"No problem." Lianos reached over and put his hand on Danzi's shoulder. Blue fire flickered around his fingers. More tongues of flame appeared in the slashes on Danzi's chest. When Lianos was done, the wounds had disappeared, leaving intact, only somewhat reddened skin.

He stood up, and Danzi and Eiryenne followed him to the door. Once outside, they saw that a street urchin was rummaging through Neil's saddlebags. He turned to run when he saw them coming, but Danzi had grabbed him by the collar before he could get far. He lifted him off his feet and shook him. The boy dropped the food that he was carrying.

"He tried to take the horse, too," commented Lianos. He picked up Neil's untied reins. "Lucky your mount didn't wander off."

Eiryenne looked at the terrified boy that hung in Danzi's grip. She knew what it was like to be hungry enough to steal. So, taking a breath to steady herself, she walked over to Danzi. "Let him go," she said quietly. "Please. He's just hungry. I would've done the same." She paused, deciding to change tactics. "Come on. He's not worth the effort."

The dragon mage shrugged and threw the boy to the ground. Eiryenne dug a small piece of bread out of her saddle bags and gave it to him. He grabbed it and took off.

"You're wasting your time," Danzi said roughly, getting on Chief.

Lianos handed Eiryenne Neil's reins. "Don't mind him," he said. "This world could always do with a bit more kindness."

She mounted her horse and turned back to say goodbye to him, but the man was already gone.

"Who is he?" she asked Danzi.

"My brother."

Chapter 10 ~ The Theory of Magic

The locals continued to stay clear of the two riders. But as Danzi and Eiryenne turned to exit the city, a dirty little boy ran out to stand in front of their horses.

"Excuse me," he said. "Is it true? Are you two really mages?"

"What of it?" Danzi said gruffly. "You're in our way, boy."

The child quailed beneath Danzi's fearsome gaze. But he stood his ground. "I've heard that mages can heal. Please, my sister is dying. Won't you help?" His voice quivered, and his lips shook. He was obviously terrified.

Danzi had his horse walk forward until he was towering directly over the boy. "I said you're in our way. And healing is not the only thing that mages can do."

"I know that you can strike me down where I stand, sir," the little boy said. His voice was shaking, and his cheeks were streaked with dried tears. "But I had to try. I promised them I'd take care of her." Starting to weep, he slowly backed away from the horses.

"What's wrong with your sister?" Eiryenne asked gently. She appreciated the little boy's bravery, knowing first-hand how intimidating an effect the dragon mage could have.

"I don't know. She's been sleeping for days. I can't get her to wake up," he wailed. "She's havin' trouble breathing."

"Show me," said Eiryenne.

"Have you learned nothing from your earlier exploits here?" Danzi sounded exasperated. "You can't make a difference on this level. You are fighting these things on a grander scale by preventing the necklace from falling into the wrong hands."

"I can make a difference for this one person," she told him. "Besides, I need the practice. Healing's the only thing I've been decent at so far, and I've yet to try it on people."

She expected him to object again, but instead he just shrugged. "Very well," he said, looking thoughtful. "It's time to see what grade of healer you really are."

The boy led them down a narrow alley. Eiryenne followed him on foot, while Danzi brought up the rear, leading their horses and giving fierce looks to anyone who came too close.

"Here she is," the child said, stopping at a small alcove. Inside it, covered in rags, lay a skeleton-thin girl. Her skin was a sickly shade of green, and her breathing was ragged.

Eiryenne got down on her knees, putting a hesitant hand on the girl's forehead. She was drenched in sweat, in the final throes of a deadly fever. "This is bad," Eiryenne muttered. "Where are your parents?"

The boy wiped his face. "My dad said some things about the Emperor. Bad things. He said that we shouldn't be forced to drink poisoned water and starve to death while he feeds and equips his army. They put him to the gallows. Mum, too. Me and Sakah almost got caught."

"They'd execute *children?*" she gasped.

The boy nodded sorrowfully. "They done it to my other sisters and my brother, and we got nowhere else to go."

Eiryenne shook her head and turned her attention back to her patient. She put both hands on the girl, letting her magic flow through the child's body, trying to find what was wrong. But compared to the finch she'd healed, the human body was unbelievably complex. She found herself getting tangled in strange energy rhythms and contorted organs.

"A lot in there, isn't there?" said Danzi from behind her. "Try looking at it as one whole picture. See if you can find the single element that is unbalancing everything else. Sometimes it's that simple."

Eiryenne took a breath and let her awareness of the girl spread until she was aware of her entire body. There were feelings of wrongness coming from her gut and throat. But the most powerful came from her lungs. Eiryenne zoned in on them. Her magic painted the image in her mind: there was a deep crack running through the left lung. Blood and mucus dripped through it. Something else was clogging up her airways. So Eiryenne reached for more power and concentrated on clearing out that gunk. Blue light with purple streaks spilled out from her hands, sinking into the girl's chest until it poured into her lungs. Eiryenne thought of a stiff brush, the kind she used to clean out the horses' manes and formed her magic into a brush-shaped wedge that she used to scrub at the girl's lungs.

Then it occurred to her that she should probably close that cut first. Too caught up in the spell to realize her growing fatigue, she tried to send in another burst of light. That was when darkness filled her vision, and she collapsed.

***

The familiar clip-clop of hooves was the first thing that greeted her, along with a bumpy swaying motion. Eiryenne opened her eyes to find herself tied to Neil's back again. She reached for the quick-release knot that Danzi usually put at her shoulder and sat up, feeling groggy.

"What … what happened?" she said. The city was gone. They were riding through trees once again.

"You used too much magic," said Danzi. He handed Neil's reins over to her. "And you passed out. I put you on Neil and rode out of the city, where we were met by a group of Imperial soldiers."

"I slept through an *attack*?"

"When you use up all your energy, your body shuts down to recuperate. You'll sleep like the dead."

"And the girl I was healing?"

"You gave her a chance."

They stopped at a clearing, surrounded by enormous trees. After she ate, Danzi put her through her paces once again, ignoring her complaints about fatigue.

"You must build up your endurance," he said. "The enemy will not wait until you are rested to attack you."

She forced her aching muscles to move and carried out the movements as best as she could. When it came to sword practice, however, she couldn't stop the weapon from sliding out of her tired fingers, no matter how hard she tried to hold on to it.

Since her magic had still not returned in full, Danzi skipped their magic lesson and let her retire for the evening.

The next morning, she woke to find the dragon mage up at the crack of dawn, as always. He was on his feet on the far side of the clearing, performing slow, deliberate motions that almost looked like a dance. First, he stretched out his hand forward, then continued the motion, bringing it about in an arc until his fingers brushed the ground. He then took a step and repeated it with on the other side, his hands flowing like water. Slowly, his movements intensified, until he was doing outright jabs and swings.

He turned and saw her watching him. "Morning stretches," he explained. "Want to try?"

It was harder than it looked. Eiryenne stumbled off balance more than once while trying to copy Danzi and found that her joints protested being bent in such strange directions so early in the morning. He told her that like everything, it would become better with practice and repetition.

Indeed, as the days wore on, the warm-up came more easily to her. Her muscles were also getting used to the punches and kicks, and Danzi soon had her hitting his open hand in mock sparring sessions, calling on the movements he wanted her to do in different, unpredictable orders.

"Faster," he'd bark. "Left jab! Right kick! Turn!" He soon started putting in a few blows of his own for her to block or avoid. At first, she was terrified of being hit, until she saw that he did no more than tap her with his knuckles when she didn't block his punches in time. He went on to show her how to break out of various grips and holds; if someone had you in a headlock, for example, give an elbow to the ribs, a heel to their shins and twist out of their grip. He told her to use her assailant's weight against them, showing her how to attack against their centre of gravity and unbalance them.

Danzi worked her hard. Every morning, there was a gruelling amount of push-ups, exercises, and sparring to do in addition to her evening magic lessons.

She sometimes complained of fatigue or tried to slow down, but Danzi wouldn't let her stop. "Discipline your mind," he'd snap. "You can't give in to weakness." He would make her continue whatever exercise she was on, often until she was literally dropping from exhaustion.

As she became accustomed to pushing her body to its limits, she found it easier to push herself further with her magic as well. And slowly but surely, her spells were improving.

With hours of backbreaking practice, the sword, too, was becoming more familiar in her grip. She learned to keep it balanced in her hands as she twirled and cut, stabbed and slashed, all under Danzi's critical eye.

One day, he drew his own sword and told her to face him. "Now," he said. "We spar."

She gulped and tightened her fingers around her sword. Danzi attacked first, sweeping toward her with a large, vertical swing. She quickly raised her sword to block it, and the force of the impact almost knocked it out of her hands.

"It would be better to block that with the flat of the blade," he said, pausing. "Otherwise …." He turned his blade slightly, and it slid down the edge of hers until it reached the hilt and would have sliced off her fingers if he did not stop. "See? Now try that again."

He came at her once more, and this time she blocked him squarely with the flat of her blade. Danzi then turned his sword and aimed a cut at her shoulders. This one she blocked, too, but just barely. His subsequent blows were faster, until Eiryenne was sweating and having trouble catching up. Between parries, she tried to fit in a swipe of her own, but Danzi blocked it even before she had brought the sword halfway.

She didn't raise her blade in time for Danzi's next attack, and the force of it caught her off guard. The sword went flying from her hand. She closed her eyes and braced herself, breathing hard.

There was a light touch of cold steel against her cheek. She looked up. Danzi had the flat of his blade against her face. He looked puzzled.

"What are you still so scared of?" Danzi asked. He took his sword away. "You *know* that killing you would be counterproductive to my purposes."

She shook her head wordlessly. After seeing people losing life and limb to that blade, she found it hard to be on its business end, even if she knew it was just a sparring match.

Danzi sighed and sheathed his sword. "I'll make a warrior out of you yet," he muttered.

They rode from one grassy hill to another that day, skirting the edges of the forest. There was a small mountain in the background that appeared to be Danzi's objective. Eiryenne wondered again about where they were going and what he was planning to do with the necklace. He hadn't mentioned it, and she hadn't worked up the nerve to ask him. But she decided that she was tired of being kept in the dark; she resolved to ask him the next day. For now, she decided to start asking some questions on a more benign subject, but one that had intrigued her ever since she found out she was a mage.

"Danzi," she said. "I have some questions."

"About what?"

"Magic."

He shrugged. "Go ahead. I suppose the more you know, the better prepared you will be."

"How come not all humans have magic? Is it the same for dragons?"

"Dragons are magical by nature," he said. "Just like elves and griffins. They all have magic. Whether they know how to use it, that's a different story. Humans, on the other hand … some have it, some don't. Magic in humans is uncommon. It's also hereditary. If an entire mage clan is wiped out there wouldn't, in theory, be any more human mages in that region." He looked thoughtful.

Well, so far so good. He seemed to be in a talkative mood. So Eiryenne continued. "So how come not all mages shoot flames like you do?"

"Some mages have an elemental inclination. Mine is fire," Danzi said.

"Do I have one? What causes it?"

"No. It is usually determined by species. Dragons have an inclination toward fire, for example, while griffin magic takes the form of wind, as you've seen. Humans and elves usually don't have any."

"Does it make you more powerful?"

"A mage can either be weak or strong and be an elemental; it is not proportionate to strength. An elemental mage will have a certain advantage over certain elemental mages, while being at a disadvantage to others. For example, I would have an advantage over a druid, whose magic is woven within trees. And a water-based mage would have an advantage over me. But whether that advantage is enough to win a battle all depends on the strength of the mages in question. If a novice water mage were to challenge me, it would make no difference. But if there happened to be one with whom I was evenly matched, the elemental advantage might be enough to tip the scales."

"I see. So even though your magic looks like fire, you can still do most of the same spells as a non-elemental mage?" she asked.

"Everyone is slightly different," said Danzi. "Mages, whether elemental or not, will all have a tendency to be better at some spells than others."

"What's it depend on?"

"Full of questions today, aren't you?" He smirked slightly and leaned back in the saddle. "A mage's tendencies can be determined by their elemental powers and species. For example, dragons are usually creatures of power and destruction. Thus, the nature of my magic is volatile and destructive, dictating that I am particularly skilled at direct offensive spells. I prefer shooting flames at people, since it comes naturally to me and usually works. With some practice, I've also learned more indirect spells: barriers, enchantments, and the like." He paused. "Still, there is a lot of variation within species. Healing spells come naturally to you, yet healers among humans aren't that common, unlike, say, unicorns. You will need to work a bit harder on your offensive spells. You can still do it well; you will just need more practice. I am living proof that you can still learn magic that goes against your inclination, if you practice enough."

"And what would that be, for you?" she asked.

"Well, think about it."

"Hmm." she thought for a moment. "Healing?"

"Yes. It requires the utmost precision and control, and with my magic, it's very difficult. But I managed to learn it, though being healed by a dragon does come with a few drawbacks. The person I'm healing will always feel like they're being burned, not replenished. It's still a crude, rough magic, no matter how carefully I apply it." He paused. "I also cannot heal myself. But that is not so uncommon, since for some reason healing your own body is much more difficult than healing someone else. It is easier to take external energy to repair the problem."

"Hmm." They sat in silence for a few minutes as Eiryenne processed all she was learning about magic. It was such an unusual, fascinating thing. She watched the sunlight reflecting off the ruby on the hilt of Danzi's sword. "I have another question," she said after a minute.

"Very well."

"Why do you use a sword? Why not just fling handfuls of fire and be done with it?"

"My magic is hard to control, precisely when I am in human form. This sword focuses my fire, letting me direct it exactly how I want it."

"Hard to control? But I've seen you use magic with your hands before without a problem."

"Let's put it this way. I can fire a bolt of flames from my hands and still take down my target. But if the amount of magic is large, everyone within twenty feet of me will also be burned to a crisp. The sword prevents that."

"Oh."

***

Around noon, the riders were assaulted by a group of Imperial soldiers, a mix of men, ogres, and other strange creatures that Eiryenne couldn't identify. Danzi fought them off without a problem, and they moved on, riding until the light started to fade and they were within half a mile of the mountain.

Danzi got off his horse. "There's something I need to check," he told her. "Take the horses and move slowly toward the mountain until I return." He handed her Chief's reins and walked to the edge of the trees. Then he transformed, and the magnificent red dragon leaped into the air, flying low over the trees and heading for the mountain's summit.

His scales were blood-red in the low evening light. Danzi pumped his wings, glad to be flying without listing to one side now that Lianos had fixed his shoulder. He kept to the shadow of the mountain, scanning the ground for anyone who might spot him.

The trees dwindled away beneath him. He angled his wings to catch a thermal and rode it to the top of the mountain. Landing on a rocky ledge beside a cave, Danzi poked his snout into its dimly lit depths. The dark did not hinder his eyes in the slightest. Everything was as clear and crisp as it was in bright sunlight, just darker and the colours less saturated.

"I know you're in there, Yostreb," Danzi said, his deep voice echoing on the cavern walls. "I see you. Come on out, you old feathered brute. I want a word."

"Is that Daggoras I hear?" came an answering squawk. The creature at the back of the cave stirred and got to its feet. "Have you come to light my tail on fire again?"

Danzi stepped back from the cave, giving the beast room to exit and stand on the ledge next to him. Yostreb was a griffin but twice the size of the ones he'd fought in Turmain. He was of a different, more ancient breed. They were dying off, these Spectral Griffins. As Yostreb emerged from his cave, he looked up at Danzi with his one good eye. His feathers were a glossy grey, his beak a tinted blue. Numerous scars had cleared patches of skin on his neck; his skin drooped with age and was mottled with wrinkles.

"What do you want?" asked the old griffin.

"Information," the dragon answered. "I know you still keep an eye on the Empire's movements. Where has Emperor Varcroft been sending his troops?"

Yostreb gave a resigned sigh. "Oh, you know, the usual. He's been snooping around up north again, except this time Tartaway had enough and officially declared war."

As the griffin continued to speak, Danzi glanced down to the base of the mountain. Eiryenne was slowly making her way across the glade and coming closer. Danzi estimated that she was about nine hundred feet away.

"He's also been looking around for that Resistance camp," continued Yostreb. "He swept through Turmain and couldn't find anything, so now he's aiming at Stroinke."

The griffin babbled on, but Danzi was keeping his eyes on Eiryenne while he listened. Four hundred feet … three hundred …

Yostreb suddenly fell silent. His head snapped to the left. "Oh, what is that?" he mumbled. "Could it be?" He spread his wings, ignoring Danzi.

It was never good to ignore a dragon.

***

Eiryenne made her way slowly toward the mountain. She wasn't sure why Danzi was having her do this, but she supposed he had a good reason. He always had one.

Suddenly, a screech rang out from the summit. Eiryenne stopped. There was another loud squawk.

If that was a griffin's rallying call, she was in trouble. She turned the horses around and took off.

She was halfway down to the road when she heard wingbeats above her. Danzi glided over her head and landed in the clearing. There were grey feathers on his muzzle.

"I told you to stay at the mountain," he said. Even on his dragon face, Eiryenne recognized a frown. He shifted back into human form and got on Chief again.

"There was a noise," she said. "I thought it meant trouble."

"No, it was the sound of me strangling trouble," he said. "I wanted to find out what the exact range of the necklace is, and it turned out to be about three hundred feet. Remember that distance."

She nodded.

They soon made camp by a small stream. After meditating, Danzi started their usual magic lessons. Once she finished her usual spells, he had her try to make her magic flow into something invisibly. He demonstrated this by making a leaf a few metres away burst spontaneously into flame, even though Eiryenne had seen no transfer of magic.

"The key is to move your energy quickly and subtly," he said. "Make it jump to the object you are concentrating on by bridging the space with your mind."

Eiryenne gave this a shot, but it only resulted in a blob of light forming in her hands then jumping over to the leaf she was aiming at.

"You're overthinking it," Danzi said. "Don't think, just react!" He threw a rock at Neil.

Caught completely off guard, Eiryenne sent out her magic without trying to control it. She didn't think about the path from her hands to the rock, she just thought about blasting it out of the air before it could hit her horse.

A thin spray of light appeared around the rock, making it shift course slightly, but not quite enough. Danzi's orange fire turned the rock into ash before it hit Neil.

"See?"

Eiryenne shook her head. "Don't do that again."

"You might not always like my methods, but they work," he said. Then he pointed to a stump by the river. "Aim for that next."

"Don't I need any words? I've always heard that mages must utter something to cast magic more easily," said Eiryenne.

"Words can be used, but they are not necessary," said Danzi. "There *are* mages who spend their entire training memorizing long, complex incantations and learning how to apply their magic to their words. That's not how I do it. I cast magic with my mind and manipulate spells through instinct. This is the way I am teaching you. It is harder to master, but once you've got it, you will have an advantage over mages who cast only through words."

"How so?"

"Think about it. If you are up against another mage and you both cast a spell at the same time, you can concentrate faster than he will finish speaking his incantation," Danzi said.

"Well, I think I've got a bit of a grasp of how to cast out my energy directly," she said. "But what about more complex things? Like putting an enchantment on something?" Hayden's book had mentioned those; supposedly, enchantments were spells that took effect on a thing or person after a period of time without the mage even having to be present. She wondered if they were real.

"To successfully enchant an object, you must make sure that your strength is not only great enough to sustain the spell on it, but also enough to make the spell affect whoever your target is. Otherwise, the person picking up the enchanted object can break the spell." He paused. "But as for how you do it … as you grow more and more familiar with the kinds of mental motions and concentrations you need to do particular things with your magic, you can start combining and manipulating them to create the spell you want. We'll get to enchantments eventually. However, I also won't cast out words entirely. Even I use them sometimes, when the spell in question is very complex and rather unfamiliar to me."

"What language do mages use for these incantations?"

"Any language will work if applied properly. You could even use Common. But most mages prefer something else so not everyone can understand it. I typically use Draconic. But humans usually cannot pronounce it correctly, so I'd suggest going with Elvish instead."

"Will you teach me?"

"No. You have yet to master this thought-based stage of training. Words would only weaken you, and enchantments we will work on later. Now, go make that stump dance."

It was hard, but by the end of the evening she could make wisps of her magic spontaneously appear on the stump and shake it slightly. Danzi then had her try to combine this with some of her other spells, a barrier, perhaps, but with this she had no success.

Their session left her exhausted, and she was glad when Danzi finally called a halt and she slumped into her blanket.

***

Her daily exhaustion usually meant deep, dreamless sleep, but that night Tairung stalked her once again.

"You think you're safe, don't you?" he drawled. "You think that dragon can take on anyone in the Empire?" He chuckled evilly. "Believe me, even he has his limits. And it will be interesting to see what you'll do when you no longer have his protection."

"Go away," she muttered, trying to tear her gaze away from his mad eyes but finding herself unable to do so. "Go sit in your stones until we destroy them."

Tairung laughed. "Has Danzi told you his plan? Even if he succeeds, neither of you are making it out of there alive. But no matter." He paused, looking around him. "Daggoras will not be a problem after tomorrow. I enter the dreams of the men who seek you just as easily as I enter yours. I have called them, told them where you are, and who you're with. They will come for you very soon, and you will watch Danzi drown in his own blood shortly before you die in yours."

Chapter 11 ~ The Limits of Fire

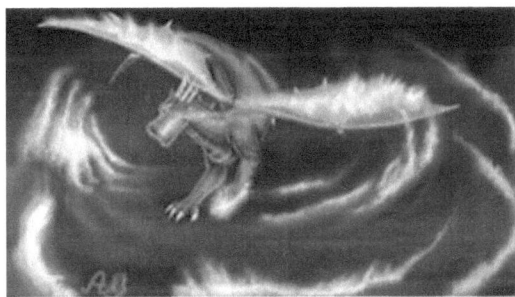

The next day started ordinarily enough. Danzi dismissed Eiryenne's concerns about the dream, saying that there was no way to tell whether Tairung was just manipulating her emotions. In any case, he'd keep an eye out, as he always did.

After their warm-up, however, Danzi skipped the hand-to-hand combat and went straight to the sword work. Following that, they settled by the stream for some meditation.

"Today I'll try to teach you two new skills," Danzi said after a few minutes. "The first of these is the ability to sense another's magic. It can be useful to detect enemy mages before they start to engage with you. To do this, you must extend your awareness out to your environment and the people in it. Close your eyes."

Eiryenne closed them, continuing to breathe deeply and keeping her mind clear. She took in the sounds and smells around her, from the gurgling of the stream to the branches shifting in the wind, and birds calling in the distance.

"Now focus on me," he said.

Eiryenne let her mind follow the sound of his voice, concentrating on the presence she felt in front of her. They exhaled in unison. Danzi took another breath, and the sound seemed like it was much clearer than before. There was a faint, rhythmic thudding in the background as Eiryenne focused her magic. She thought of Danzi and all he was—unlikely protector, maker of fire, a scent of leather and ash. She remembered the way his fire flickered around him and how it felt when it hummed over her own skin.

"That's right. Find the fire. Reach for it."

She felt her own magic being met by a thread of flames. She grabbed hold of it with her awareness and followed it back to its source. Suddenly, she became aware of an entire network of fire, twisting and turning, fuelling muscles that could move faster than any human and hit harder than a horse. They flowed around the dragon mage's heart as it continued to pump, sending blood and fire throughout his body. That was the noise she was hearing: his heartbeat.

"Tune into the magic. Then open your eyes."

She could see him sitting there in her mind's eye. She pictured how the fire she felt must look. Then she opened her eyes.

To her surprise, she could now see his fire magic. It ran down his arms like a molten river, pooling in his hands. His face was a latticework of tiny flames, with two bright yellow ones behind his eyes. The fire flowed down through his chest and was brightest around his torso.

She looked down at her own hands. They were threaded with purple and blue.

"Got it?" he said. "Hold it. Now break your concentration."

She thought of Tairung and the glow she saw faded.

"Wow, that was amazing. Do all mages see like that?" she asked.

"Most of them will be able to call upon the ability at will, but not all of them will have it switched on all the time. Now," he paused. "Another feature of magic is that it can be universal. Simply put, it is possible to use another mage's power. I think I showed you this when we first met."

She nodded, remembering how he had pulled a strand of magic out of her before she even knew she had any.

"Some mages will be able to resist spells that pull their power from them, but it is still a handy thing to know how to do." He got up and moved closer so that they were just an arm's length apart. "Hold out your hand."

Eiryenne tried not to jump when he reached out and poured a handful of flames into her palm. They didn't burn her; they just made her skin tingle and her bones hum in that strange way that dragon magic did.

"Right now, I am keeping that fire in your hand. When I withdraw my concentration from them, you will have to take over. Ready?"

She nodded and found that she was aware of the dragon mage releasing his hold over the magic in her palm. She put tendrils of her own magic around it, trying to keep it in place. After a few tries, she was successfully able to keep it from slipping through her fingers.

"Not bad," he muttered. "This might be another of the few things you have a knack for."

Danzi spent the rest of the session having her manipulate his fire and practice locking onto his magic. Though the dragon fire was hard to control, when she managed to direct it correctly in an offensive spell, it obliterated the branch she was aiming at. When they were done, Eiryenne found that, unlike after most of their lessons, she was not at all tired. Though that shouldn't have been so surprising; she wasn't using much of her own magic.

After a quick breakfast, they saddled the horses and moved out. They hadn't ridden for more than a few hours when Danzi held up his hand and stopped.

"There," he said, pointing toward the sky.

Eiryenne looked up, but whatever Danzi was pointing at was right next to the sun, and she couldn't glance up there for more than a second before her eyes started to water.

Danzi had spotted some griffins flying wide circles high above. They were too far away for Eiryenne to make out, but Danzi's keen eyes quickly determined that these four were scanning the ground, looking for something. They were too distant to be within range of the necklace, but to be safe Danzi and Eiryenne brought their horses deeper into the trees.

The wind was shifting, and the dragon mage sniffed the air. "We have company," he said. "Just humans, by the smell of it. Shouldn't be a problem. But I'll have to try not to use too much magic. I'd rather avoid having those griffins spot us. They could be scouting for a much larger force." He drew his sword and gestured for Eiryenne to do the same.

She switched Neil's reins to her left hand so that she could hold her sword with her right and took a deep breath. No matter how many times they were ambushed, she couldn't help her prebattle nerves. Today in particular a sense of dread hung over her shoulders. She thought she heard Tairung cackling in the back of her head.

The horsemen hit them at the next group of oak trees. A dozen or so burst out from the bush, brandishing swords. Even though Eiryenne had been expecting them, she still felt a jolt of cold, raw fear.

Danzi hacked through the first man to rush him, killing him with a single stroke of his sword. He then whirled Chief about to confront the men that were trying to flank him.

Two of them were keeping back, Eiryenne noticed. They were watching the battle with cold, calculating eyes, barely blinking as they saw their comrades being slain.

She soon had no time to think about that as one of the soldiers skirted around Danzi and went after her. Normally, the dragon mage would have burned him to the ground before he could reach her, but Danzi's decision not to use magic was becoming evident as the man galloped at her unhindered.

Remember your training, she told herself. *This is exactly why Danzi taught you how to fight.*

She forced her frozen muscles to move and kicked Neil forward as she ducked beneath the soldier's swing. Then her arm snapped up as if of its own accord, and her sword struck the man's side.

He pulled his horse away, evidently surprised.

You are young. They will underestimate you, Danzi had said during one of their sparring sessions. *Use that to your advantage.*

But now another soldier had gotten by Danzi and was galloping at her back. She turned her horse and just managed to block his strike. The force of the impact felt like it would rip her arm out of its socket. She dropped her sword, almost falling out of the saddle.

So much for that.

She made a mental note to ask Danzi to include mounted combat lessons in their next training session. She'd done all of her practice on foot, so fighting from Neil's back felt strange.

Danzi was probably doing this on purpose, she told herself. He wanted to put her training to the test. Any second now, he'd decide that she'd had enough and would come galloping in to tear these men to shreds.

Eiryenne wasn't quick enough to dodge the next soldier's pass. The tip of his sword caught her ribs, cutting deep. The girl cried out and tumbled from her horse, landing hard. She groped around for her sword, dimly aware of that she was trying to summon her magic at the same time. But panic had fogged her mind. Her sword was nowhere to be seen.

One of the soldiers dismounted next to her, hoisting his weapon high. Eiryenne looked around frantically for Danzi. There he was, still fighting farther into the trees. He'd noticed her plight and was pulling his broadsword from another man's body as he put his heels to Chief's sides. Flames started to flicker at the edges of his blade.

Calm down, Eiryenne told herself. Danzi was going to blast these men to smithereens, and they'd continue on their way like nothing had happened.

Then she saw the two horsemen that were hanging back before moving in from either side. Danzi swung at them without looking. After all, they were just men; what could they do?

His swing was careless, and the soldier ducked under it, just managing to avoid having the top of his head chopped off. Eiryenne thought that he was going to try to stab Danzi, but instead he clamped something around the dragon mage's outstretched sword arm.

The flames on Danzi's sword flickered and died. An expression of shock registered on his face. He turned toward the offending soldier, but his movements were sluggish. Before he could raise his sword again, the soldier on his left shoved his other arm in toward his chest and clamped something around his other wrist.

Now Eiryenne could see what they had put on him. Manacles.

That chain was puny by a dragon's standards. It should have been no problem for Danzi. He gave it a mighty wrench, snapping his arms outward and waiting for the rain of shattered chain links. To his surprise, the chain held.

With a scowl he tried again, but his struggles were in vain.

He couldn't break it.

One of the soldiers gave him a mighty shove, knocking him from his saddle.

"No!" Eiryenne realized that the screaming was coming from her own throat. Then the soldier who had advanced upon her struck her in the head, and she lost consciousness.

***

"I'm taking it."

"No, it's mine!"

"What do you think you're doing? I want it."

There were several grunts and the sounds of a scuffle.

"Hold it. Just leave it on her until the boss comes."

"Fine."

Eiryenne opened her eyes. Things came gradually into focus. She was lying on the ground in a clearing, surrounded by trees. She blinked. No, surrounded by soldiers. Her head ached where she'd been struck, and the cut on her ribs burned something fierce.

"Bloody hell," said another voice. "Where's he *get* this stuff?"

"No wonder his jacket was so heavy."

She squinted. On a flat rock in the centre of the clearing, several items were laid out. There was a sheathed sword, broad and long with a ruby set in its gilded hilt. Next to it lay a long dagger with a leather sheath, various knives, a belt with an angled buckle, and a bunch of coins. A handful of them were small and made of copper, a few were silver, but the majority were large and flat, made of gold.

Then there was the sound of something hard striking flesh, followed by a splatter.

"Did your mother teach you to hit like that?" Danzi's voice rang out.

Eiryenne looked up, and her jaw dropped.

Across the clearing Danzi was hanging under a thick oak branch, strung up by his wrists. He'd been stripped of his cloak and jacket, revealing a dark red vest, which lay open over a crimson tunic. But his clothes were hard to make out because of all the blood. Danzi was soaked in it, from his forearms to his boots. A pool of red had formed beneath him.

Several of the men were in front of him, holding large, bloody knives. As Eiryenne watched in horror, one of them stabbed the dragon mage in the chest, leaving a new bloody cut to add to the multitude that already covered his skin.

"I'm going to ask you one more time," growled the man. "Where's the Resistance camp?"

Danzi met his gaze levelly. "Tell me, who brought you these manacles? I am puzzled as to why blundering fools like yourselves possess such a powerful magical object."

One of the men rammed him across the face with a club.

"Scurdal? Raitlin? Who was it? I can only think of a handful of mages that could make this kind of spell ... unless Varcroft has gotten some shiny new pawns to play with."

"Shut up," roared the soldier. "We're the ones that are doing the interrogating."

"Really?" The dragon mage lifted a bloodied eyebrow. He barely blinked as he was struck repeatedly. More blood splattered the grass with each blow.

Danzi's frown only deepened, his eyes glittering with malice. He couldn't wait to be out of those bonds. "Are all you grunts, so poorly versed in torture?" he asked. His mouth curled in a sneer. "They don't even give you proper tool kits these days. You really don't know what the hell you are doing with those knives."

"We'll see how cocky you are when we've strung your guts out by your head." The lead soldier plunged his knife into Danzi's stomach up to the hilt, drawing a slow, meticulous cut and twisting the knife cruelly. The others continued to do the same, gouging out chunks of the dragon mage's flesh.

Eiryenne bit her lip to keep herself from screaming.

"Didn't anyone ever tell you," Danzi said to the man who'd stuck him in the belly. "That it's not a good idea to disembowel a living dragon?"

The man had cut through the fire mage's flesh and reached his stomach. He'd just pricked the organ with his knife when suddenly, sparks flew from the wound. The man jumped back, swatting at his arm.

"What the hell's that?" he snapped. His companions backed off, too, looking alarmed.

Danzi smirked. "Just something I ate." He might not have had access to his magic, but his digestive system had a fire of its own, which both let him digest anything and gave prospective torturers burnt fingers.

"That's it," the man grumbled, kneading his singed hands. "Someone take off his fingers."

The man on his left took out a small, curved gutting knife and climbed up on a rock to reach the fire mage's hands.

"Which finger?" hissed the soldier, knife at the ready. "Index, middle, thumb."

"Well," the man with the burned fingers looked thoughtful, "maybe the index, for a start."

"I vote for middle," Danzi said, matching their hushed tones.

"Quiet," the soldier snapped. "Take his thumb."

Eiryenne looked away as the man began to saw away at Danzi's fingers. She stared at the grass, trying to absorb herself in its endlessly shifting green blades, and shut out everything else.

She tried to move, but her wrists were tied. Looking down, she saw that they were tied with rope. Rope could be cut. As Danzi had predicted, they were underestimating her.

But there were soldiers both to her right and her left. They'd notice if she tried to break free. She'd have to wait.

She shut her eyes tightly, trying to forget the awful images of the torture. It didn't work. She only saw it more clearly. And there, laughing at her horror, was Tairung. She felt his presence as though he was standing next to her in one of her nightmares.

Maybe this *was* just a nightmare. Eiryenne prayed that she was dreaming; she'd wake up on Neil's back, tied to the saddle as always. Danzi would scold her for being so slow in avoiding that soldier's blow, and they'd ride on.

But no matter how much she wished it, the scene didn't change.

"It ain't comin' off."

She dared another glance up. The men were still sawing away at Danzi's thumb. Miraculously, his digit was still there, bloodied and battered, with a deep cut all the way around the base, but intact.

"Whadda ya mean it ain't coming off?" another soldier demanded. He stalked up to the rock and pushed the other man off it. "Get outta the way. I'll show you how it's done." He took a twelve-inch dagger from his belt and moved in. But no matter how much he sawed at it, Danzi's finger refused to budge.

With a frustrated grunt, he switched to the pinkie finger and began to hack madly at it. Still no results. Now red in the face, the soldier changed his grip on his knife and moved closer, standing on the edge of the rock.

As he reached for Danzi's hand again, the dragon mage's limp fingers suddenly sprang to life and seized the soldier's sleeve.

The man tried to wrench himself out of Danzi's grip, to no avail. The fire mage's grip was like iron and couldn't be shaken. Danzi tried to manoeuvre his fingers to where he'd be able to grab the man's wrist. He almost had it when the black fabric tore, and now off-balance, the man went careening off the rock and head-first into the tree trunk.

Danzi smirked. It would take more than human-forged steel to cut a dragon's tendons.

The rest of the soldiers were chuckling as the torturer got to his feet.

"Shut up," he told them. "Just cut off his arm or something."

Danzi gave him a look. "You really think that's going to turn out any better? Let's see, you couldn't even cut off my finger, so logically you're now turning your attention to a much larger joint." He rolled his eyes.

With a snarl the man took his knife and stabbed Danzi in the chest.

Danzi waited until the soldier was glaring into his face and spat blood into the man's eyes. "I'm going to enjoy killing you," he said, his voice low and dangerous. "You have no idea who you're dealing with. I can take far more damage than any man you've ever tortured. Your arms will tire long before you can even begin to break me."

"We'll see about that," growled the soldier. They renewed their assault in frenzy, putting every sharp thing they could find to use.

Eiryenne tore her eyes away from the horrifying sight, but she could not block out the sounds of steel and wood continuing to strike flesh.

Instead, the girl tried to occupy herself by examining the objects on the stone slab. She recognized her own sword and dagger, but everything else was undoubtedly the contents of Danzi's pockets. The quantity of coins was surprising; she'd never seen so many in one place, let alone gold ones. A few rolls of parchment lay beside the coins, as well as a small, pocket-sized book with a powder-blue cover. There were also a couple of small knives, shining amulets, some gemstones, a bit of coral inlaid with crystal, and a large, engraved key made of stone—the one he'd gotten from Kafer back in Loturg. It was covered with strange brass symbols. Next to the key was a small cloth bag. One of the soldiers tried to open it, but orange fire lashed out onto his hands, and he dropped it, screaming.

"Whatever's in there, it must be pretty valuable," commented one of the soldiers. "It's the only thing apart from his medallion that we can't get our hands on."

"Doesn't matter," said his companion. "The griffins went to get Raxge. He and his mages will be here soon. They'll take care of it."

"I dunno, maybe we should've had one or two of the griffins stay," muttered the man. "We're not getting anywhere with this guy."

"He'll crack. They all do. Besides, he can't do a thing while he's got them manacles on. And the girl? Like she's anything we can't handle."

The men continued to torture Danzi. Eiryenne ventured a glance every so often, just to check that he was still alive. She felt helpless. She knew she couldn't do anything before dark.

The sun was beginning to set. The dragon mage's snide remarks were starting to fade. Eiryenne looked up at him just in time to see more blades being driven through his calves.

Danzi's jaw tightened. He looked annoyed. He looked more irritated than she'd ever seen. It must be driving him crazy that he was at the mercy of people he could kill so easily.

It seemed to take forever, but the soldiers finally decided to call it a day. A pair of them stayed up to keep watch while the rest went to sleep.

Eiryenne dug some of the calming herb out of her pocket and took deep breaths. Once she felt its effect start to take hold and numb her anxiety, she reached out with her magic. The faint feel of Danzi's fire reached her, but it was distant and clouded. Between her and the dragon fire was an icy veil, thin but firm. She moved her awareness to the heavy manacles that bound his wrists. They were filled with a strange, cold magic. Just touching them with her mind made a chill go down her spine; she shivered involuntarily.

There had to be a key of some sort. But how to find it? Eiryenne knew she wouldn't have time to search every soldier's pack. Perhaps she could find it with her magic. Maybe the key would have a touch of the same cold mage craft that was in the manacles.

Eiryenne exhaled, letting her awareness expand throughout the clearing, looking for that icy energy. She found it on her third sweep; it lay in the pockets of a soldier halfway between her and Danzi.

Her decision made, she then formed a narrow wedge out of her magic, filling it with thoughts of cutting steel and flaming swords. She drove it into the ropes around her wrists. Bit by bit, she started to cut through them, stopping every time the soldiers on watch turned in her direction.

Every minute seemed to feel like a lifetime as she peeled through the rope, strand by strand. What if it took all night? Eiryenne started to wonder what would happen if she didn't break her bonds by sunrise. Could Danzi take another day of this? Could *she*? She thought.

She bit her lip and concentrated harder, but to her chagrin the girl still couldn't make the spell cut the ropes any faster, no matter how hard she tried. Overdoing it simply made the spell spark and fizzle out of existence. Taking another breath, she recalled the magic to her fingertips and tried to force herself to be patient.

At long last, the rope fell away from her skin. She repeated the procedure with the ropes around her ankles and then got up.

She tiptoed through the camp, every snore and shuffle the sleeping soldiers made almost giving her a heart attack. She had to duck down among them a few times when the ones on watch looked her way. But the darkness worked to her advantage; they didn't see her nor notice that one of their prisoners was missing.

She soon drew even with the soldier who held the keys. He was fast asleep. Heart pounding, Eiryenne carefully opened his pocket and slipped her hand inside. As her fingers closed around ice cold metal, she knew she'd found what she was looking for. Slowly, afraid to even breathe, she pulled the key out. It was spun out of a dark, slightly translucent metal that felt like it was engraved with something, though in the dark it was hard to make out the details.

Clutching the key tightly even though it numbed her skin, she crept toward the oak tree from which Danzi hung. Deciding that she was clear of the sleeping soldiers, she quickened her step, anxious to free her companion. With a soft thump her foot came down on someone's face.

The man sat up with a confused groan as she bolted toward the tree and hid behind its trunk.

"Ugh? What was that? Hey, someone's there."

"What are you talking about—wait, the girl's gone."

Voices were coming from the clearing. The soldiers were stirring. Eiryenne would have panicked if the herb hadn't worn off yet. Instead she ran over to Danzi and climbed on a rock behind him. She reached out for one of his manacles, trying to find the keyhole by touch in the darkness.

"It's to the inside, lower down," Danzi muttered. "Same on the other side."

Her fingers finally found a small depression, and she fumbled with the key for a second or two before it slid into place. She turned it. The manacle slid open with a sharp click. Then she grabbed for the other one, trying to ignore the approaching soldiers.

"Hurry," yelled one of the men. "The key's missing. We have to find it before—"

Click.

Danzi exploded from the manacles in a whirlwind of fire, gunning toward the men with flames leaping from his arms. Eiryenne, remembering what he'd said about using his magic without his sword, hid behind the thick tree trunk.

The fire shaped Danzi's hands into dragon paws. He tore open the first man he came across then turned to catch a sword in his claws. He punched through the man's skull with his talons before releasing another wave of flames, catching half his tormentors and most of the clearing on fire. They screamed, some dropping to the ground, others trying to run. The rest continued to rush him.

From her hiding place, Eiryenne could tell that Danzi was moving much slower than normal. Unfortunately for the soldiers, slow for the dragon mage was still faster than a human. He ducked around their blows before hacking away at them with his claws, tendrils of fire rising at his command to burn the ones that escaped his grasp.

Two of the men who'd tortured Danzi had turned to run. They were almost at the edge of the clearing when the trees in front of them exploded into flames. Their legs were the next to be caught in Danzi's web of fire. As they stumbled and begged for mercy, the dragon mage swept down on them with a vengeance, ripping through the first man's arm before slicing through the second one's stomach. Blood spurted from their bodies, helpless against his sharp claws.

Danzi bent over the first man and sank his claws into his neck. "I told you I was going to enjoy killing you," he hissed. He struck the man over and over, until he was a broken mess of blood and exposed bones. His companion whimpered, trying to crawl away. Danzi pinned him to the ground with his foot before leaning over and slashing the man's chest open with his left paw. He plunged his right through the soldier's torso, not stopping until he'd gone all the way through.

"Now," he said. "Tell me where you got those manacles."

"I don't know," whispered the man. "I ... swear."

"Hrrmm." Danzi turned his talons inside the body he'd impaled on them, tearing at the man's guts. The soldier gave a strangled yell. "Don't toy with me, human. Unlike you, I know what it takes to cause real pain."

"Please, I don't know." The man's face was covered in sweat, his breathing ragged. Danzi gave his insides another wrench. "All right, all right! Corporal Hemmingway gave them to us. He said he said to put 'em on you. That's all he said. I don't know where he got his orders!"

"And the griffins?"

"The griffins were ... were part of it," the man gasped. "They were supposed to distract you, then go get someone."

"Who?"

"Mages. That's all I know!"

Danzi put his talons up to the man's neck and pressed. "*Which* mages?"

"I don't know."

"Who gave Hemmingway the manacles?" He began to slit the man's throat.

"I … I wish I knew," whispered his victim. Then his eyes rolled back in his head, and he died.

"He really didn't know," Danzi muttered to himself as he got up. He turned to look across the clearing at the corpses. "This doesn't make any sense. This doesn't make any sense!"

Eiryenne stayed behind the tree, her knuckles white as she clutched the rough trunk. She knew she ought to be glad that the men were dead.

Still, it didn't make what Danzi did to them any less terrible.

The dragon mage walked up to the stone slab and scooped up the cloth bag, putting it in a pocket inside his vest. Then he put on his jacket and started putting the rest of the items back into his pockets. Finally, he buckled on his sword belt and latched his cloak around his throat.

"Eiryenne, come get your things," he said, still panting.

She walked over to the stone slab, feeling numb as she gathered her pack and put on her sword.

"It's strange," he said, almost to himself. "Those manacles weren't easy to make. If someone went to all that effort, why leave them with human soldiers who don't even know how to torture a man properly? Trust me, I know what real torture is and that wasn't it. Why not just … why are you crying?"

Eiryenne jumped at the switch of topic. She turned to meet Danzi's gaze. His face was splattered with blood, and his eyes, visible only by the light from the smouldering corpses around them, looked savage. She shook her head wordlessly. What was done to him was horrible. But watching him brutally murdering everyone, then torturing that last man, had been almost as bad. How could she explain it to him? Danzi obviously thought they deserved it. She couldn't say she didn't agree, but that didn't make it right.

"You still have the necklace, don't you?"

She nodded.

"Then let's get out of here." He turned to walk toward where the horses were picketed in the trees.

The girl followed, trying to avoid looking at a scene resembling one of her nightmares. She almost slipped on someone's dismembered torso and looked down in shock, caught up in the horror of the violence.

That was when she thought she heard Tairung.

His voice was faint, as though he was speaking from some distance. It almost seemed like he was talking to someone else.

Against her better judgement, Eiryenne concentrated on his voice, letting her awareness slip down toward the stones that hung around her neck.

The test was successful, Tairung was saying. *The manacles work like a charm. Come get the dragon, my friends. He is wounded and weakened. He won't put up much of a fight.*

Suddenly she was looking through the mad unicorn's eyes at a legion of marching soldiers in gleaming black armour. Griffins, tigers, and wolves mingled with them. Above them all flew a large, black horse with wings sprouting out of its shoulders.

Tairung appeared to notice her. The image faded, and she was looking at the clearing again. She watched the fire mage pause to lift the manacles on the tip of his sword and then fling them into the darkness. Then he walked up to the horses and untied Chief.

Eiryenne opened her mouth to warn him about the people that Tairung was calling, but the necklace suddenly tightened around her neck, cutting off her air supply and making it impossible to breathe, let alone speak.

Nosy girl. You'll not be saying a word to him, the dark unicorn whispered in her ear. Then he chuckled. *Maybe it's even better like this. I get to watch you struggle with the knowledge that he is heading to his doom, and you can do nothing to prevent it.*

"You coming?" Danzi asked. He'd mounted Chief with some difficulty and was now waiting for her.

She nodded, walking up to Neil, untying him and swinging up onto his back without another word.

"What … what were those things?" she asked once they were away from the clearing. "Why couldn't you break them?"

"There are certain ways to bind magic," Danzi said. "Some techniques are universal, blocking the powers of all mages that fall under the spell. But these manacles were specifically engineered to bind fire magic. Not an easy feat." He smirked. "I must have really annoyed someone."

Eiryenne stared at the steady drip of blood that continued to flow off him. "Shouldn't you rest or something? Or I could try to—"

"I'm fine," he said sharply. She still couldn't see any pain registering on his face, just irritation. Still, she *could* see how stiffly he moved. He might have been a master at concealing his agony, but he would be lying if he said that his injuries didn't bother him. She realized it was pride that prevented him from stopping to wrap something around his wounds. He didn't care that he was bleeding; he was insulted. A dragon caught and tortured by humans. He was furious.

Chapter 12 ~ Fire Fall

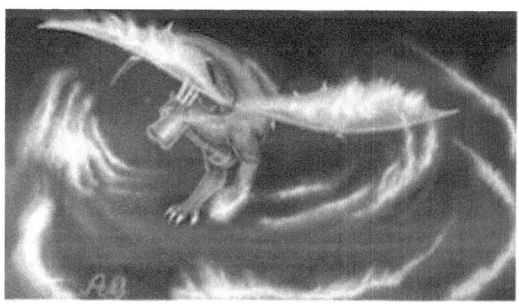

Eiryenne shook her head, trying to shake Tairung's presence from her thoughts. He was more intrusive now, gloating and sneering at what he said would be Danzi's demise. And the second she opened her mouth with the intent of warning the dragon mage, Tairung tightened the necklace until he was almost choking her, forcing the girl to be silent. After a few tries, she gave up. There was nothing she could do, she realized. They were walking right into a trap, which she knew about but could not avoid. She berated herself for listening in on the black unicorn's conversation. It would be better not to know so that this terrible feeling of suspense and dread would stop hanging over her shoulders like a heavy shawl of ice-cold iron.

They didn't get far from where they'd left the group of human soldiers when Danzi turned his head sharply, evidently hearing something that was beyond the range of her human ears. He scanned the forest behind them.

"Pursuers," he said. "We need to pick up the pace—"

The words were barely out of his mouth when dark shapes came into view beyond the trees. Danzi put his heels to his horse's sides, and Eiryenne did likewise. From their trots, the horses broke into a canter. They ran among the trees as quickly as they could. But the terrain was rougher here; their pursuers had forced them off the trail and through the bush. The horses couldn't gallop flat-out as they dodged trees and crashed through bushes.

Eiryenne dared to glance behind them. She saw the soldiers from her vision, dressed in gleaming black armour and atop great warhorses. Not all of them were men; she saw ogres and other, strangely shaped riders. A few leaped from their mounts to run through the trees. The kirin that some of them rode weren't as hampered by the trees as the horses were and quickly started to gain on their quarry.

Up ahead of her and Danzi, the trees were finally parting. There was a path there, a trail that led into a tunnel through the side of a mountain. The shaft's mouth gaped at them. A deafening screech made Eiryenne look up. In the sky was a flock of griffins, high above the tangle of branches. They'd be overhead in seconds.

Eiryenne nudged her horse into a gallop. She didn't know where the tunnel led, but if they could only get there, at least their winged pursuers would be forced to take a detour. It was far better than getting caught out in the open like this. She doubted Danzi could fly well in his condition, or he'd have shape-shifted by now.

Chief, slightly ahead of her, was almost at the cave entrance when a loud, harsh neigh rang through the air. It came from behind them. Danzi slowed his mount and looked over his shoulder. He looked shocked.

A jet-black winged horse was flying toward them. Its wild, dark mane blew about on the wind, and the feathers on its wings were edged with dark brown. There were splotches of white at two of its fetlocks, and a thin, jagged blaze shaped like lightning ran down its muzzle, interrupted by black in two places. Its burgundy eyes stared savagely at them, and there were two horns curling back over its ears. Its beastly mouth ran all the way to the back of its jaw and was open to reveal several rows of crooked teeth.

The surprise on Danzi's face turned to rage. He hauled on the reins and wheeled his horse about, almost crashing into Neil. Eiryenne had to turn Neil so sharply to avoid a collision that her horse skidded and fell to the ground, throwing her into the bushes.

For the first time since she'd known him, Eiryenne saw the dragon mage lose his composure.

"*You,*" he roared, his gaze burning with hatred and his face contorted in a furious snarl. He launched himself from the saddle and transformed, jumping into the air and flying up to meet the pegasus, his frothing jaws open and fangs gleaming. Blood ran from his wounds in great waterfalls of red, but he paid them no heed.

"Danzi," muttered the girl, trying to scramble to her feet, "what on earth are you doing?"

Anger was giving energy to Danzi's tired wings, and sparks of fire jumped over his scales as he sped toward his opponent. Flames lashed out from between his jaws.

They were ready for him. A curtain of sparking yellow and black lightning came from the pegasus's horns, casting Danzi's fire aside. Streams of red and green magic rose from the ground; there were mages among the soldiers. They wrapped around the dragon in a cocoon of light fastened by the pegasus's lightning. Danzi roared and tried to break free, but now griffins and winged tigers had come to add their magic to his bonds. Their combined strength was too much for his weakened powers. The cocoon tightened until it raked against his wings, and the black pegasus dove in, sending a burst of black lighting to hit Danzi in the chest. The web of magic quickly pinned his wings to his sides. He fell out of the sky, still snarling his outrage.

Eiryenne was running toward the cave when an ogre jumped out of the trees and tackled her to the ground. She felt her hands being roughly bound.

She groaned. Adrenaline had numbed the pain caused by her fall from Neil and the ogre's tackle, but now it came through full force. Her entire left side ached; it felt like she'd broken half the bones in her body. She was dimly aware of growling and scuffling in the background as the ogre clamped a hand around her arm and began to drag her through the trees.

Suddenly, the motion stopped. Eiryenne yelped as a club came down on the side of her face.

"You better cooperate," hissed the ogre. "Or the next one'll crush your skull."

A man with strangely pale skin, pointed ears, and coal-black hair walked up to them. He wore the black uniform of the Empire, adjusted to form flowing robes instead of a soldier's short tunic, and the insignia around his neck glinted in the sun as he leaned forward to study Eiryenne through deep-set, dark eyes.

"So, you're Danzi's little mule," he drawled. There was a jagged scar running from one side of his face to the other, crossing his crooked nose. "A weak mage. Of course. How else could he have gotten the necklace through undetected?"

Free me, warlock! Tairung's voice rang in Eiryenne's head. *I've been limited by her for long enough.*

Apparently, the warlock heard him too, because he reached out and ripped the necklace from Eiryenne's neck.

"No," she burst out, trying to stand. The ogre smacked her cheek with his club.

"Silence," he said.

She fell back to her knees, clutching her stinging face.

The warlock turned the stones over in his fingers. "Magnificent," he whispered. Then he lifted his gaze to Eiryenne. "Now, where did you get this?"

She pursed her lips.

The ogre shook her. "Answer Raxge's questions or I kill you."

"Family heirloom," she said.

"Where are you from?"

"Turmain."

"That makes sense," he muttered. "A secret strain of low-level mages, an entire lineage dedicated to protecting it. No wonder Varcroft couldn't find it." He paused. "Now. How did you find him?" He gestured to the dragon mage, who'd been shackled once more and was now chained to the rocky side of the mountain, his arms splayed out to either side.

"He found me," she said. "My village was attacked. I ran. Then I bumped into him. I've been travelling with him since."

"What was his plan for the necklace?"

"I don't know."

The ogre hit her so hard that she thought her skull would crack.

"Tell me the truth."

"Please, I don't know," Eiryenne gasped. She was starting to panic now. Her vision was blurry from a mixture of blood and tears.

"What did he want to do?"

More hits. She thought she heard something snap.

"Stop it," she panted.

"Well?"

"I … I wish I knew," she whispered, the pain causing more tears to run down her face. "Look, why don't you ask him yourself?"

Raxge glanced back at the dragon mage. "Danzi's resistance to torture is legendary. Thankfully, we've got just the man for the job." He smirked and turned away.

"If we don't need the girl anymore," said the ogre. "Can I kill her, sir?"

Raxge casually waved a hand. "Sure."

Death is too easy. Tairung now easily projected his voice so that all could hear him. *Break her spirit. Let her watch the dragon die.*

"Very well," the warlock said. He walked over to where Danzi was chained.

"Now, I'm not going to insult you by suggesting that you give up anything without a proper bit of torture," he said. "I think we both know you're too stubborn for that. And truth be told, I'd torture you anyway just to prove I could break the one they call unbreakable."

"You have no idea who you're dealing with," Danzi said.

"Actually, we do. We do quite well."

Raxge stepped out of the way so that the pegasus could walk up to Danzi. It shape-shifted, turning into a man with long, wild black hair and burning eyes. The horns remained. He stepped up to Danzi with a smirk curling at the corners of his mouth.

Upon seeing the man, Danzi lurched forward, trying to wrench free of the manacles that bound him. They were the same as the ones that had bound him before, made of cold, fire-binding metal. He was powerless to break them.

"You," he snarled. "Blackthorn, you traitorous scum. How dare you show your face to me again!"

Blackthorn chuckled and blasted him with a bolt of black and yellow magic. "Well, when I heard that they were hunting you, I couldn't pass it up. We knew you wouldn't be able to resist going after me. And I wanted to come watch your downfall … again."

Danzi lurched forward, but the manacles refused to yield. He pulled at them until they bit deep into his skin and made his wrists bleed. But he didn't seem to notice. The expression on his face had turned to murderous rage; he stared at Blackthorn with utter hatred.

"We just had to make sure that the manacles worked," Raxge said. "And that was easy enough. We *were* going to come get you from those soldiers, but you managed to escape somehow."

"Shouldn't have put a keyhole in," muttered the ogre.

"So, we called Blackthorn in. The perfect way to ensure your capture."

"Nothing but bait, as always," Danzi sneered. Blackthorn hit him.

"Now." Raxge clapped his hands. "Time to finish what those petty soldiers tried to start." He paused then sent a wisp of sickly yellow light to wrap around Danzi. "Torture spells are a finicky thing. The thing with them, as I'm sure you know, is that after long enough, the subject develops resistance to them. Now, there are seven kinds of primary spells. We know you're very well acquainted with the first six. But I daresay not even you've come across the last." He raised his hand. "Say hello to number seven."

Danzi braced himself, an involuntary shiver running along his spine.

Knifelike blades of dark yellow light encircled the dragon mage before forming a band and crashing down on him.

Danzi's face tightened as the magic ripped through him, dicing up flesh and bone, nerves and fire, life force and soul. Pain overwhelmed his iron nerves within seconds.

Eiryenne expected him to bear this torture as impassively as he had the last. But to her shock, Danzi's mask of inscrutability disintegrated and his face contorted in agony. He let out a strangled growl of pain.

It was upon him, destroying him from the inside out, mangling his insides into shapes that life should not have sustained, then putting them back only so they could be sliced open again. Along his arms and neck, his skin split and peeled back, bones broke and reformed and broke again, as every part of his body was broken and twisted beyond recognition.

His jaws, frothing with blood and saliva, opened wide in a silent scream as the invisible knives seized the network of fire and life coursing throughout him and began to tear it to pieces.

And still, the spell kept him alive, as that was the point of torture spells. They did more than just mangle the body. They transcended the boundaries of ordinary physical torture by attacking the nerves and energy pathways directly to cause pain beyond mortal limits. They kept the body of the victim in a kind of stasis while it was being damaged, containing the life energy and forcing the heart to keep beating, not allowing the brain to lose consciousness.

Pain blinded him and overwhelmed his senses. Danzi convulsed madly in the throes of death that would not come. He threw his head back and let out a howl of agony.

The sound chilled Eiryenne's heart. She watched in disbelief as the dragon mage thrashed in his bonds, the grotesque spell spilling blood from his open forearms like rivers, until the men before him stood ankle-deep in blood. She shook violently, horrified by the scene, feeling so desolately helpless, watching the mage she was starting to idolize, who represented the hopes and dreams of the future, being broken down into rotten pieces of himself.

His roars became more desperate and frequent as Raxge continued to burn him, and Blackthorn stood there and laughed.

His enemy's laughter only made it worse. Somewhere in that blinding tornado of suffering there was also rage. Danzi tried to grab hold of it, tried to concentrate, and for a few minutes he did. But it had been many years since he had to resort to these kinds of tactics, and as his lungs were peeled from his chest and chopped up into pieces, his sanity faded from his mind once more. He gave voice to his madness, letting out a sound that was more a scream than a roar, rising high on the cold mountain air and carrying across with it the essence of his suffering.

It tore through Eiryenne harder than the ogre's club, knocking the wind from her lungs and freezing her breath in her throat. She opened her mouth, but no sound came. Involuntarily, she lowered her vision to see magic. And she quickly wished she hadn't.

Danzi's fiery orange pathways of fire were strung out all over the place, being dragged from his body by the yellow spikes and twisted, turned and cut along with the flesh that sometimes accompanied them. His heart was torn from his chest; it continued to beat. It and all the other bits and pieces of him were suspended in a dim yellow bubble, holding it all together, keeping a flow of magic to him and literally pushing the blood and life energy to not cease moving.

Tairung's laughter quickly joined the cacophony. But rising above it all were Danzi's tortured roars.

Finally, Raxge's arm started to cramp. He released the spell and put Danzi's organs more or less where they'd been. The magic he left in a mess, and the wounds, of course, would not be repaired. He only needed to keep Danzi alive until the next session.

Danzi slumped forward in his bonds, breathing hard, his chest rising and falling rapidly, lungs struggling to process air. He was almost unrecognizable amidst all the blood and raw flesh.

The warlock lowered his hands, looking satisfied with himself.

"Well, I daresay no one's gotten results this good from that man for two hundred years," he said smugly. "Torture of the body is one thing. Torture of the mind is another. With the right training, both can be resisted. But both have limits. You can only tear up a man's body so much before he dies. You can only break his mind so much before he goes insane. But put the two together, add magic to the mix, and include torturing the very essence of his life and voilà." He spread his arms. "The perfect torture."

Blackthorn chuckled. "Now that was exquisite," he said. "They should have more like you."

"Ah, there were, but our friend here took them all out." He paused. "He forgot the Seventh Cohort, though. We always kept a low profile, unlike those other pompous bastards—and look where it got them."

Grinning widely, Blackthorn walked over to Danzi and kicked him.

"So weak, Daggoras," he sneered. "So powerless. You're pathetic. I expected more."

At the sound of the pegasus mage's voice, Danzi looked up with some difficulty. "I'm going to kill you," Danzi snarled, gurgling slightly because of the blood in his throat, more blood spraying out of his mouth as he spoke.

"You've already been trying to kill me for years," Blackthorn exclaimed. He leaned in until he was face-to-face with the bloodied warrior. The pegasus mage smirked. "You've hunted me for decades. And you've yet to put a single scratch on me. How many other people can say that?"

Danzi's head suddenly snapped forward. He sank both his sharp canine teeth into Blackthorn's nose. The other mage drew back with a start.

"Rectified." Danzi was the one to smirk now. He licked his lips. He'd been wanting to taste this blood very badly for a long time now. "But you know what? That only makes you the master of running away."

Blackthorn hit him across the face. Then again. Danzi growled. "Well, I've done rather well during my life on the run, don't you think?" he gestured around them. "I took a leaf from Tairung's book. New army, new powers. You, on the other hand," he leaned in more carefully this time, "I took everything from you, Danzi. Your power, your leadership, your friends. I *destroyed* you. The great Danzi Daggoras, brought to his knees. Reduced to a wandering rogue with no purpose."

The dragon mage seethed silently, gnashing his teeth.

"I took everything except for your life," he said. "And believe me," he straightened, "that will soon be rectified."

Blackthorn turned away and walked to where Danzi's possessions lay spread out on the ground. He bent over them. "And now, finally, I can claim what is rightfully mine." He tried to pick up the cloth bag, but flames burst into being to burn his hand, making him spring back with a curse.

"It was never yours," Danzi said quietly. "And it never will be."

These words seemed to have some effect. Blackthorn's face darkened visibly. He turned around and punched Danzi as hard as he could.

But the fire mage was smirking again. "It still burns you, does it not?" he whispered. "After all this time it drives you insane that it is I who still has your prize. And the most ironic thing is I never even sought it."

"Shut up." Blackthorn hit him with a spell this time. Then he turned his magic upon the cloth bag, but it still refused to yield its secrets.

Just then a small grey griffin flew into the clearing, a scroll in its talons.

"Urgent message for Colonel Raxge from his Royal Imperialness the Emperor Varcroft," he panted.

"Well, what is it?" asked the warlock.

The messenger raised his head. "The Resistance have sent out their army, sir. They aim to strike the capital."

Blackthorn's eyebrows shot up into his hair.

"The Emperor has ordered for all our southern troops to mobilize immediately and confront them," the messenger griffin continued in his light, youthful voice. He was young. But he was also scared. "Blackthorn is to go north to finish his previous mission in Tartaway. Here it is in writing." He passed the scroll to the warlock, who opened it, double-checking the seal and signature.

He sighed. "It's genuine. You're to be off soon, then."

Blackthorn looked unsettled. "No. I want to stay here and watch Daggoras die."

"Orders are orders."

He pointed to the cloth bag. "The bag has an enchantment upon it, some kind of protective barrier. Can you break this spell?"

The warlock contemplated the spell work in front of him for a few seconds. Then he shook his head. "No. We'll have to get it back to the capital and hand it to one of Varcroft's specialist mages. Scurdal should be able to do it."

"Well, I want it clear that the contents of this bag belong to me and me alone," the pegasus mage said coldly.

"Stand down, soldier," Raxge replied. "This isn't even your mission; you're part of the Tartaway siege. You've done your part here. Varcroft will decide what to do with the spoils. Now go; you've been ordered back up north."

Blackthorn frowned. "Can't I just kill him now?" he said. "I mean, look at him. It wouldn't take much." He sent a bolt of his magic into Danzi's chest, making him convulse and splatter blood.

"This man is a goldmine of information," Raxge said. "And Varcroft knows it. If I can get even some of it, I'll be rewarded beyond my wildest dreams. Or did you really think that the Necklace was the only objective?"

I heard that! Tairung sounded miffed.

Raxge looked back at Danzi. "What you see before you is three hundred years of ancient knowledge. What other person could tell you how the Ruldes fell, or where the Faraj Treasure lies, or how to kill a Firedrake? He's seen empires rise and fall, toppled some of them, too, fought almost every kind of magical creature in existence, and has had a hand in everything from the Tintos Rebellion to the Battle of Iolou Court. We may never get a chance like this again."

Blackthorn sighed. Then he turned to Danzi. "I'll be back to spit on your grave, dragon, you can count on that," he spat. Then he transformed into his pegasus shape and took to the air.

Danzi watched him go. There went his target.

Now, when will you release me from these stones? demanded Tairung. Free from Eiryenne's limiting influence, he could now speak freely to anyone there, but it was obvious this was still not enough for him.

"When I finish with Danzi."

Very well. Make it good.

"Oh, I assure you, it will be." Raxge turned to his troops. "All right, everyone prepare to move out. Except for squad five," he said. "We'll stay here to finish what we started. And you," he said to the young griffin. "Report that we'll be an hour behind but no more. Tell Varcroft we'll be along as soon as we get the last from the dragon."

Soon the soldiers departed, either flying or riding off, until it was only Raxge, two griffins, and a handful of other soldiers left.

He approached Danzi and resumed the torture spell.

"You will tell me what I want to know," he said. "Every bit of it, you understand? I'll break you until you're nothing. You're already nothing."

Danzi bared his teeth at him even as he convulsed from the spell, hitting his head hard against the rock behind him. But that was nothing compared to what he felt now. Knives of magic, harder and sharper than any mortal blade, were being driven through his bones and riveted through his skull.

"A few minutes more of this and I'll have you weeping at my feet, begging for mercy."

Danzi snarled at him, more rage than pain. He would roar, he would yell, he would thrash, but he would never beg. No, he'd go insane first.

A thousand knives resumed their play along his chest, as the pain built until he lost all coherent thought and was screaming the roars of madness. Pain was the only thing he knew, the only thing he was aware of as a thousand rocks pounded his skull and a thousand swords cut him up into little pieces and cast him into the wind. The wind that should have blown him to dust but did not.

He wanted it to end. He yearned for respite, for oblivion. It was not a thought but a simple desire, an inherent reaction of flinching away from something that hurt, the seeking of solace.

Except there was none for him. There never would be.

And in that strange state, maddened by pain, when all the world consisted of was agony, everything else felt small, insignificant, unimportant. What consequence did his life have, or anything in this wretched world, for that matter? Ending the pain was all that mattered. Until the agony got so intense that even that idea fled his head and he simply screamed and lost himself in his blind emotion once more.

"I've broken you," shouted the warlock. "I am your master, Danzellius Daggoras! Now bow before me and tell me everything you know."

An invisible hand curled his spine down, breaking it in two before snapping it back up like a string. Like a puppet.

And something deep within the dragon's soul stirred. A primeval, deep-rooted rage ebbed into his maddened consciousness, focusing it, giving him something new to concentrate on.

He was no puppet. He was no pawn.

"Bow deeper this time, that's right. Time to snap you in two. Tell me about the Risoterk and I'll end it. I said *bow*."

Danzi looked up at him through reddened eyes. "Never," he croaked. He locked onto the rage, and he raged against the pain, he raged against the dying of his fire.

Raxge frowned. "Perhaps you didn't hear what I said. Answer me!"

Anger brought sweet clarity to the turmoil in Danzi's soul and gave him new strength. The dragon's rage was his power. And like a dormant volcano renewed, fresh hatred pooled into his eyes as the ancient magma inside him was tapped.

Of course there was meaning. Of course he had power. He was Danzellius Daggoras, the red dragon, the lord of fire and master of power. With every fibre of his being and everything he ever stood for and ever would stand for, Danzi raged. And inside himself, inside what should have been a rancid carcass, he found power.

Something sparked in his eyes. And from beneath the pool of blood on his chest, through his ripped open tunic, there came a glow. A white glow, pure white. As it got brighter, it became clear that it came from the gold medallion that still hung around his neck.

"Answer me," the warlock shouted.

"I answer to *no one*," boomed the dragon mage, a true roar this time. Pure white fire appeared on his chest, spilling over onto his arms and eating away at the manacles. It was through them within seconds.

In a flash Danzi transformed. The great red dragon waded through the remnants of the warlock's spell as if it wasn't there. Then he seized him in his mighty jaws and shook him viciously from side to side, tearing him to bits. He tore half his body off then quartered what was left before taking the head and spearing it on one long, bloody fang.

The necklace was sent flying. Eiryenne tore her eyes away from the scene and struggled with her bonds for a few moments before breaking them, then running over to where it had fallen and scooping it up, looping it back around her neck. The ogre guarding her hadn't noticed; he and the other soldiers were all fighting the dragon. The blinding white fire still blazed around his silhouette, hurting her eyes.

By the time she dared to look up, all of them were still.

The dragon collapsed onto his side; his breathing ragged. The grass around him was soon flooded with blood. As Eiryenne approached, he shifted back into his human form, sprawled out on his back. The top of his shirt was still open, and the medallion lay on his chest, rising and falling with his rapid breathing. Many flames seemed to be carved into the gold, and they appeared to move before Eiryenne's eyes. Sometimes she thought she saw a dragon amidst the flames, a clear crystal in its grip. Then she blinked, and the image was gone, lost in the golden fire.

Tairung was furious. *No,* he shouted in her head. *This is ridiculous! This is just—* She felt him pause and notice the medallion. *Oh, what's that?*

"You tell me," she whispered. Eiryenne was surprised that Tairung, with all his years of experience with magical artefacts, was as puzzled by Danzi's medallion as she was.

Then the medallion's motion ceased. Danzi went still. He'd stopped breathing. Panicking, Eiryenne ran to him and dropped to her knees beside the wounded dragon mage. She put a hand on his chest and reached out with her magic. The damage was horrendous. Everywhere she looked, his flesh, bones, and organs were torn and mangled. His lungs had shut down and his heart was slowing. The network of fire running throughout his body was dimming.

"No," she whispered, horribly aware that she didn't have the strength to fix everything. There was no single cut that she could heal to save him—everything was entwined. And it was all killing him.

There was a groan from the side. Eiryenne looked up. Some of the soldiers were still alive. Her heart caught in her throat when she saw yellow light swirling around one of them and indigo around another. Those were mages. Alive, but barely. Danzi's last lesson came back to her. If she could take their magic, she might be able to get the strength to heal him.

She drew away from Danzi and walked closer to the fallen mages, stopping a few feet away. Then she focused her awareness on the first one, an elf with indigo-coloured magic. He didn't seem to notice her, and she fervently hoped that he was incapacitated enough to give up his power without a fight.

Unlike Danzi's fire, the elf's magic felt strange and alien to her mind. She reached for it, grabbing hold of it with a strand of her own purple-blue light. Then she pulled. The strand broke before it was halfway back to her. Gritting her teeth, she tried again, willing the magic to come to her with every ounce of willpower she possessed. Slowly, it began to snake toward her. She'd been lucky; the elf had been hit before he could expend a lot of his magic, so there was a substantial amount left. She kept it on the frontiers of her consciousness, finding it a struggle just to hang on to it. Then she went back to Danzi and kneeled again. She put her fingers to his chest and let her awareness spread throughout him once again.

His heart had stopped beating.

Fighting her panic, Eiryenne released some of the magic she'd collected, wrapping it around his heart and squeezing briefly. Then she released it before squeezing again several more times. His blood began to flow again, sluggishly. She sent in more magic, zapping the muscles of his heart until they began to contract by themselves. Then she cast out the elven magic toward his injuries. It was harder to control than her own magic, and much of it slipped out of her grip the second she released it from her fingertips. Grasping what she could, she worked as quickly as it let her. She began the long process of mending flesh and straightening out bones, starting with the damage around Danzi's vital organs. Soon, gashes began to close, muscle fibres knit together again, and organs became whole.

Within seconds, she'd used up all the elf's magic. But there was still so much left to do. Without getting up from her seat, she pulled at the magic from the fallen griffin and the other two mages. When it was all inside her, it started to crackle and burn, but she ignored that, channelling all the strange energy into her healing. Unlike the quick, clean job she'd done on the bird and the reasonably accurate healing that she did with the girl, this was crude work. Danzi's internal energy patterns were completely foreign, and it took an enormous amount of power just to bring two sides of a cut together. Then there was the contorted state of his network of fire and life energy—a result of the magical torture, but there was nothing she could do about that.

She noticed something strange as she continued to repair his organs. Were there some missing? She couldn't find the intestines or bladder. But no, the body's energy didn't feel incomplete, just broken. The torture spell had been self-contained.

His system was the strangest of any animal she'd come across. Stuffed inside the human-shaped torso were an enormous set of lungs and an oversized heart. The liver seemed ordinary enough, but the stomach was peculiar, made of three compartments and filling up the remainder of the body cavity, fizzing with a strange energy. As Eiryenne eased a tear in the hip joint back together, she realized that from the navel down there were no other organs—just pure muscle.

Her last drops of magic she sent into the muscle beneath his lungs, making his diaphragm contract. Then she sat back, feeling dazed.

Danzi took a breath. Then another, and another.

Eiryenne slumped back onto the grass, exhausted but enormously relieved. The fire mage was going to live. She had only managed to heal a handful of his injuries, but it was enough to keep him alive.

After resting for a few minutes, Eiryenne made herself get up. There were still things to do, and with Danzi out of commission, the task of gathering their horses and possessions was now hers. She walked over to where the soldiers had their things. She picked up Danzi's discarded jacket and started putting the rest of the items back into its pockets, trying to remember where he'd put everything the last time. She hesitated when she came to the cloth bag. But when she picked it up, no fire lashed out at her fingers. She could feel something hard and long inside. Thoughts of magical tree branches went through her head, but she resisted the urge to look inside. As she slipped it into the pocket of Danzi's vest, however, the half-open flap briefly revealed a flash of something white. She quickly pulled it shut, not daring to face the dragon's secrets.

Then the girl brought the dragon mage's jacket, vest, and cloak over to where he lay and put them on the ground next to him. She went back for his sword; she needed both hands to lift it, or rather to drag it along the ground to the rest of Danzi's things.

A noise made her look up. One of the soldiers had stumbled to his feet. He swayed as he walked, blood still pouring from his wounds. But he had an axe in his hand and a determined expression on his face.

Eiryenne looked around her. Her own sword and bow were still out where the soldiers had put them; she'd have to go around the man to get to them. Danzi showed no signs of waking up. She looked instead at the massive weapon that she still held in her hands and tried to draw it. She managed to get the blade out of the sheath but could not hold it aloft. The most she could do was drag the blade through the grass. Eiryenne could barely lift it, let alone swing it in battle.

The girl was about to throw it aside when she felt a familiar tingle in her fingers. Looking down, she realized that there was fire inside the ruby and within the gleaming blade. Dragon fire.

Instead of trying to hold the sword up, she wrapped both hands around the hilt and held it vertically, the point pressing into the earth by her feet. She drew upon the fire like she'd done during their lessons, its familiar warmth wrapping around her mind.

She'd never been good at offensive spells, and she wasn't feeling particularly angry. Instead, Eiryenne put all her pent-up emotions into the spell; her fear, her dread, her horror, and her relief all gushed out in one inscrutable burst like a scream.

A ray of flames shot out of the ruby and hit the approaching man in the gut. Dropping his axe, he clawed madly at his burning tunic before ripping it off. His entire belly was one nasty burn. Coughing, he turned and stumbled away before collapsing in a pool of melted armour and blood. Eiryenne turned away, bracing the blade on a nearby stump in order to slide it back into its sheath.

She walked back over to Danzi, leaving the sword by his cloak. Then she went back for her own things, putting on her sword and dagger then swinging her bow and pack over her shoulders.

In the back of her mind, she heard Tairung again. He seemed to be talking to someone else. She realized that the demented unicorn was calling reinforcements again. This time she did not bother trying to listen in on the conversation.

Their horses were a short walk from the clearing, tied up next to the soldiers' warhorses. Eiryenne knew she could take one of them if she wanted to, but she'd gotten too attached to Neil to want to trade mounts, even for one that was battle trained. She left the big horses alone and retied Chief and Neil closer to the clearing. She gave each horse a short groom and stuffed their saddle bags with fresh supplies from the warhorses' packs.

She then sat down away from the dragon mage, hoping that he would wake up soon. She wasn't sure what kind of backup plan Tairung had, or whether the Emperor would spare any more soldiers when he had two wars to contend with—the North and the Resistance. But somehow, she wasn't sure which call the soldiers would listen to if it came down to it: Emperor Varcroft or Tairung.

There was a soft growl. Eiryenne looked up. Danzi had opened his eyes. He lay still as he looked around, his jaw tight. Then he lifted a bloodied hand to grab on to a rock and slowly pulled himself upright. He leaned against the rock, breathing hard. Blood began to pour from his wounds again.

He gave the corpses surrounding them a long look before glancing down at his chest and noting several healed cuts. He looked at Eiryenne. "Who—?" His voice cracked, and he began to cough, spitting up some blood before trying to speak again. "Who healed me?"

"I did," she said. "Some of the mages were still alive, so I took their magic and did what I could."

Danzi lifted an eyebrow. "N-not bad," he croaked. He reached for his vest, but his hand shook when he tried to extend his arm, so Eiryenne passed it to him. He swayed as he put it on, and Eiryenne gripped his elbow to steady him.

"I'm glad you're okay," she said quietly. The idea of being stuck in this hostile land without him had been, quite frankly, terrifying.

The fire mage pulled out of her grip, almost falling over. She passed him the cloak and jacket without trying to help. Danzi, perhaps realizing that he wouldn't be able to put them on without losing his balance, laid them on the ground next to him. He then buckled on his sword belt with unsteady fingers.

"It was a trap," he muttered. "It was a bloody trap and I fell for it."

"I ... I heard Tairung calling to them," she began, expecting the necklace to tighten. It didn't. The evil unicorn realized that there was no point in stopping her from speaking of a failed plan.

"You did?"

She nodded. "Back at the other clearing, I heard him talking to someone, so I concentrated on his voice until I could hear what he was saying. He was talking to these soldiers. I saw them through his eyes. I tried to mention it, but the necklace would tighten around my throat until I couldn't breathe. I don't know why, though. He's never stopped me from speaking before."

"Hrmm, you shouldn't have dipped your awareness toward him," said Danzi. He hacked up some more blood before continuing. "He took advantage of it."

"I've been hearing him," she said absently. "I hear him speak during the day now. It used to be only in my dreams, but since yesterday that changed."

"Don't give in to him again," Danzi said. "The more focus you give him, the more power he has over you."

"At least now I can hear that he's calling reinforcements. We'll have to get out of here. Can you ride?"

"I'll have to."

Before Danzi could say another word, she got up and brought Chief over. Danzi slowly managed to stand up, bracing himself against the rock and a nearby tree stump for balance. He then gripped the saddle horn and hauled himself onto the horse's back with great effort. This time he couldn't stop his face from contorting with pain, and he gave no false pretence of pretending his wounds didn't bother him. With a groan, he draped himself forward over Chief's neck, both arms around the horse.

"People have asked me why would a dragon need to learn how to ride a horse?" he muttered. "Well, it's for times like this." Times when his own legs and wings wouldn't support him, and he had to rely on other means of transportation. Those occasions couldn't come too often, but when they did, he was thankful for his riding skills.

Eiryenne folded up Danzi's cloak and jacket then tied them to Chief's saddle behind the dragon mage. She got on Neil and took Chief's reins; Danzi seemed to be in no condition to steer the horse.

"Where are we going?" she asked.

"Through the tunnel," he said. "Then, if we are pursued, take the left fork in the road. If not, take the right. We're getting closer to the heart of the Empire now. There are few safe places between here and our destination. And the closest one is not a place I would go without good cause."

They rode through the tunnel in silence. Tairung was still chattering away in the back of Eiryenne's head, but she resisted the urge to tune in to what he was saying. If she got the details of his plan, he'd only gain enough influence to choke and silence her again.

The tunnel was wide and damp, smelling of rocks and wet earth. There was just enough light for her to see by, which was just as well, since Danzi rode with his head down against Chief's mane and might not have been able to guide them in the dark.

Dripping water was the only noise, apart from hooves ringing out against the stone. The monotonous scenery made Eiryenne's mind wander. No matter what she thought of, she kept coming back to the same thing: Tairung's voice, muffled but angry, on the edges of her awareness.

Evidently, the dark unicorn's frustration was making him careless because without even trying to listen, Eiryenne was starting to hear bits and pieces of the conversation.

What do you mean? the unicorn demanded. *No! The Resistance's army won't stand a chance against mine. Why doesn't Varcroft...very well...send who you can...yes, they're in the central mountains now. You have a squadron there? Excellent. Bring them.*

Eiryenne's view changed until she was soaring above the clouds with a griffin. There was a small army marching along below it, next to a lake shaped like the letter L. The griffin turned, and Eiryenne saw a handful of mountains in the distance. She recognized them as the ones that she and Danzi were going through right now.

She blinked, and the vision disappeared. "He's got a squad coming from the west," she burst out before Tairung could say anything. "Just like the ones that came on us the last time. They're next to an L-shaped lake, I remember going past it—" Her speech was cut off as Tairung squeezed on her throat with a vengeance.

Stupid girl, he thundered, making her wince. *You've listened in on me for the last time. I should just kill you now.*

If you could kill me, she thought, *I think you would have done it already.*

Trying to block out his voice, she instead concentrated on what Danzi was saying.

The fire mage looked grim. "That means they're close," he muttered. "Too close. They'll catch up to us within the hour." There was a loud squawk from the entrance of the tunnel. "The ones that fly will probably be here already," he added, tightening his grip on Chief's neck.

"Does this mean we take the left fork?"

He sighed. "It does."

Eiryenne squeezed Neil's sides, getting him to pick up a canter. Still leading Chief, they burst out of the tunnel and onto the road that Danzi mentioned. Above them, the squawks of griffins and cries of demons were getting louder. They had to get into the trees before their pursuers cleared the clouds above the mountain.

Galloping, the two horses sped along with quick, desperate strides. They flew up the left fork and reached the cover of the forest just as the first demon crested the mountain. The road narrowed into a trail with wide, towering trees on either side. Out of sight, but not out of reach, the riders pushed on.

Eiryenne had no idea how Danzi managed to stay on his horse, but every time she looked back, afraid to see an empty saddle, he was still there, clutching Chief's mane with grim determination. Still, each stride of the gallop made him pitch so violently that Eiryenne decided she'd tie him down the next she got the chance.

Up ahead, she could make out a large, dark shape through the trees. When they got closer, she saw that it was a building. But it was unlike any building she'd seen; surrounding it was a massive, sloping wall of yellowish tan bricks. Strange, triangular towers made of the same stone loomed above it, connected by narrow walkways that lacked railings. The entire fortress was surrounded by a dry moat with no drawbridge.

Eiryenne was about to draw their horses to a halt, when Danzi looked up and said, "A little to the left. There, now keep going."

"What?" she said. The moat was forty feet wide; far too wide for any horse to jump.

"Trust me. There's a bridge," he grunted. There was no time to stop and explain.

Eiryenne gritted her teeth but didn't slow their horses. When the animals' legs hit what looked like thin air, for a heartrending moment she thought that they were going to fall. Then planks of wood appeared out of nowhere, forming a bridge between them and the massive gate.

"Let me guess," she said once they reached the other side. "Dragons see through invisibility spells?"

Danzi nodded. He tried to push himself upright in the saddle.

"Should we knock?" she asked.

He shook his head. "No. They'll know we're here." He turned to look behind them. Their pursuers were drawing closer, riding the winds above the trees. Another few minutes and they'd spot their quarry.

Chapter 13 ~ Into the Lion's Den

A brick slid out of the wall slightly above their heads. Through it she saw what looked a man dressed in a tan leather jerkin studded with silver. He had long, rich brown hair and a scruffy beard. His broad, square face was worn and scarred. He stared down at Danzi with orange eyes that had tiny, perfectly round pupils.

"You are not welcome here, Daggoras," he growled. His voice was deep and raucous.

"I know that," replied the fire mage. "But now I have little choice. I am ferrying the Tairung Necklace. I'm sure you are aware of what that does, Hirobaven."

The man's frown deepened, crinkling his wide, flat nose. "So what? Turn around and get off our territory," he barked. "That thing will only bring us more trouble."

"We are being pursued," Danzi continued. "A squad of soldiers is following our trail as we speak. You must let us in, Hirobaven. I know your people don't harbour much goodwill toward the Empire—"

"And we don't have any toward you, either." The man cut him off. "Last warning, Daggoras. Turn and go. You are in no condition to fight us."

Danzi nudged his left leg against Chief's side so that the horse took a step sideways until he was shoulder-to-shoulder with Neil. Still gripping the mane with his left hand, the dragon mage reached over to Eiryenne with his right. He grabbed the chain around her neck in two of his fingers and lifted it until the stones rose clear of her shirt. Then he turned to Hirobaven, still gripping the necklace's chain.

"You might kill me," he said. Blood dripped from his mouth as he spoke. "But I swear that the last thing I'll do is touch these stones. And when I do, everyone the Empire over will know that the necklace is here. The Emperor will sense its beacon immediately, and your place will be overrun by his forces. He'll kill every last one of you."

Hirobaven's face darkened. "You *dare*—"

"You could avoid all this, of course, by letting us take shelter here," Danzi said. "Right now, the only people who know of its location are a small squad of soldiers coming in from the west. You should be able to handle them." He paused, waiting for the man's response.

The brick slid back into place, closing the opening through which Hirobaven spoke to them. Then there was a grinding sound, and the portcullis began to lift. Once it was clear, the doors swung open. Hirobaven and a few other people were waiting for them there. They did not look pleased.

Danzi took his reins back from Eiryenne and tried to sit straighter in his saddle. He then moved his horse forward, and she followed. They went through the gate and into a wide courtyard. The entrance to the inner building was in front of them. It was flanked by two sculptures of snarling lions, each carved from the same yellow stone as the fortress's bricks. The walls on either side were also carved with lion heads, some with manes, others without. There was an inscription beneath each one: *Rosglade, Faradnerak, Jirkam, Golenhar.*

"Danzellius." The voice came from a tall, muscular man on Hirobaven's left. He had a mane of tawny hair and thick, bushy eyebrows and was dressed in a similar outfit to Hirobaven's, except that in the place of the silver adornments was gold. "You have dared to disturb our people and threaten the peace that we have worked so hard to maintain. That is unacceptable."

"I had no choice," Danzi said. "Believe me, Kyorsaw, I would not come here unless I had no other option." His horse was fidgeting, nostrils flared and eyes wide. Danzi shortened his reins and tried to hold him still.

Neil, too, was nervous. He pranced on the spot, showing the whites of his eyes. Something about these people was making him uneasy, and Eiryenne had trouble making him stand in one place. She couldn't say that she felt any better. Whoever these people were, she and Danzi were completely at their mercy.

"Him," There was a shout from the side that almost made Neil bolt. "What's he doing here? How come you let him in?"

A young man approached their group. He looked to be in his early twenties. There was stubble on his broad chin, and his messy brown hair kicked back over his ears in wild tufts. It seemed to stand on end as he glared at Danzi with hateful, dark orange eyes.

"Calm down, Grehar." A woman broke away from the group to stand beside the young man. She put a hand on his shoulder and murmured something in his ear. Then she turned back to Danzi. There was a deep frown on her weathered, wrinkled face. "We have done a lot to distance ourselves from conflict with the Empire," she said to Danzi. "I brought my nephew here so that he, unlike his father, could live out his life in peace. And now you come here, bringing the wrath of Varcroft on your heels? I should strike you down now. We both know you haven't the strength to put up a fight."

"Do it, Aunt Mytaga," said Grehar eagerly.

"That's what I suggested in the first place," muttered Hirobaven. "But he's got the necklace. He'll call on it if we attack. Then Varcroft will send his entire army here."

"There is a group of griffins and demons approaching," called a voice from atop the outer wall. Eiryenne looked up and gasped as she saw a huge, tawny lion sitting on the wall. There was a thick mane of dark brown fur around its neck, and it had bronze-coloured eyes with tiny pupils. There were more lions atop the towers. They padded across the narrow walkways with ease.

With a start, she realized that every person in that courtyard was a lion, too. She narrowed her eyes and was shocked to see yellow and bronze magic sparking inside each one. Danzi would have a hard time getting out of here at the peak of his strength, but in his current condition he stood no chance.

"Well, Kyrorsaw, what is your decision?" asked Mytaga.

The leader's mouth curled. He sighed and turned to Hirobaven. "Take them below. Put them in the east wing." He looked at the rest of his people. "When the Empire's squad arrives, tell them you have seen nothing. If they don't believe you, kill them."

As Danzi passed by, Kyrorsaw grabbed him roughly by the arm with hands that had morphed into lion paws. The dragon mage couldn't manage to suppress a grimace as the claws slid into his wounded arm.

"Whatever the outcome, you haven't heard the last of this," the lion man told him. "I'll see you pay for your actions. *All* of them."

Hirobaven led them through a passage that sloped downward. It was tall enough to accommodate the horses, though Danzi had to stoop to fit. Eiryenne had a feeling that he would be hard pressed to get off Chief at the moment. She wasn't sure he had the strength to walk.

They passed by several lions, both in human form and in their true shape. Then they followed Hirobaven through a set of heavy doors to a large, empty stone room. There was another, smaller door at the end of it. Grehar and a few other lions followed them in, standing guard at both ends of the room.

Danzi settled himself on Chief's back as comfortably as he could and crossed his arms, determined not to pass out in front of them. Blood loss had paled his cheeks and weakened his limbs, but he was going to salvage as much of his dignity as he could.

The lion men had Eiryenne come down farther toward the small door, setting several guards between her and Danzi. She gave him a worried glance, but the dragon mage's expression was back to its usual unreadable state.

Grehar, now in his lion form, was stationed closest to the girl. He didn't have his full mane yet, but the beginnings of it had started to grow around his neck.

After a few minutes, he looked over at her. "So, what's your part in this?" he asked roughly. "Do you always run errands for the dragon?"

She shook her head, trying to take on Danzi's neutral expression and not let Grehar see how much he and the other lions intimidated her. "No. I was caught up in all this by accident."

"Accident?" he scoffed.

"The necklace was handed down to me by my parents and Danzi found me after the Emperor rediscovered it. He's been dragging me along ever since." Since the lions clearly weren't fond of the dragon, she decided that it would be her safest bet to try to appear as distanced from him as possible.

Grehar looked like he didn't believe her. "Your parents let you run around a dangerous country with a cursed necklace and a maniacal dragon?" he said. "Heck of a family that must be."

She blinked. "My parents died a long time ago. They were killed by Imperial forces that were after the necklace."

"Oh." The young lion looked away. Suddenly he looked less angry.

"Why do you hate Danzi so much?" she asked.

"My father died because of him," Grehar muttered. His expression darkened.

"I'm sorry to hear that," she said. "But whatever happened, I don't think that now is the time to take it up with him."

"You mean you don't know the story?" he asked, looking surprised. Eiryenne shook her head, so he continued. "My father, Golenhar, was the founder of the Resistance. The movement had a lot of success before Danzi came along and screwed everything up, eventually resulting in my father being killed."

"So, they've even found a way to pin Golenhar's death on me, too?" Danzi's voice came from the other end of the room. "Are those the lies that they've been feeding you?"

"I was *there*," retorted Grehar.

"You were a mere cub," Danzi said. "Grehar, I don't deny that I've made mistakes. But Golenhar's death was not one of them. He died on the battlefield at the hands of the enemy."

"Silence," barked Hirobaven.

Danzi shrugged, but he didn't speak again.

Some time went by before a new lion entered. This one was a wiry, cream-coloured female with light grey eyes.

"They're here," the lioness said, speaking with Mytaga's voice.

"And?" asked Hirobaven.

Mytaga shook her head. She looked miffed. "They have the dragon's scent. Our pride is fighting them as we speak. Kyrorsaw says to take our *guests* out the back passage."

Hirobaven sighed. Then, in a blur of bronze light, his body shifted to that of a lion with a thick, rich brown mane and orange eyes. His fur had more yellow in it than Grehar's, and tufts of creamy brown lined his chin. "Very well," he said. He turned to the other lions, who had also shape-shifted upon hearing the news. "Grehar, Rytoglade, come with me. The rest of you, go assist Kyrorsaw."

Most of the lions padded out of the room, leaving the riders alone with Grehar, Hirobaven, and a coppery coloured lioness.

"This way," Hirobaven said, going to the small door in the back of the room. He put his paw on it and huffed something under his breath. With a soft whoosh, the doors glided open. He entered the passage. Danzi and Eiryenne followed, flanked by the other lions.

The corridor was wide enough for two lions to walk abreast, but the horses had to go in single file. The cold earth was hard-packed beneath them, and there were no lights to illuminate the way. Lions saw well in the dark; they didn't need torches. Eiryenne kept her horse from bumping into the walls by following Chief as closely as she could, keeping a hand on the big horse's tail.

After about twenty minutes, she could see light up ahead. The passage began to slope upward until they were level with the ground and exited into the forest through a hatch.

The two adult lions didn't linger; they turned and disappeared back down the passageway without a word.

Grehar remained. He stretched idly, and Eiryenne could see hooked claws briefly come out of their sheaths to grip the earth. Was he waiting for them to be alone so he could try to avenge his father's alleged killer?

Danzi didn't seem to be intimidated. He leaned casually forward in the saddle. Some of the blood had begun to dry, but fresh trickles continued to come from his open wounds. He looked weary.

"Tell me, Grehar," he said. "What kinds of things does the Emperor make your pride do to let you keep a fortress on his lands?"

The young lion scowled. "We pay his taxes. We let him inspect our fort and station his soldiers in it. The only reason they were gone now is because they were called off to some war. We also let him take the warriors that he wants to use for his own army or perform tasks in wartime when he requires it. Kyrorsaw told you we did a lot to keep the peace. Now all that is in jeopardy because of you." His ears flattened back against his head, and his lip began to curl.

"That doesn't sound like peace. That sounds like servitude," Danzi said. "Your father would be so disappointed in you, Grehar. Cowering at the beck and call of the very man he made his life's purpose to defeat—"

"Shut up," Grehar snarled. "You're a liar and a murderer. Don't you dare—"

"You're the one that's been lied to," Danzi replied firmly. He tightened his reins to keep his spooked horse from bolting. "Golenhar believed in *freedom*. He would rather die fighting for it than to remain in bondage and support those illusions." He paused, appearing to look away in thought. But his eyes were meticulously scanning the forest floor. "Do you remember his armour?"

"What?" Grehar blinked at the sudden change of topic. "Yes, it was gold. All of it, the plates, his weapons, everything. They buried it all with him."

Danzi's gaze flicked back to the young lion. "Really? Have you read his will?"

Grehar looked at the ground. "Yes."

Danzi's eyes briefly flitted to something on the ground while the young lion looked away—he had spotted a thin loop of rope lying beneath the leaves. Then he reached for his belt, taking the dagger that was fastened there and unbuckling it. Grehar watched him, puzzled. The dagger was about ten inches long, and its sheath was thick leather. More leather was wrapped around the handle.

Then Danzi grabbed a fold at the edge of the sheath and pulled. The leather fell away in his hands, revealing a metal scabbard that gleamed golden in the sun. Danzi unwrapped the handle, revealing an engraved golden hilt.

Grehar's jaw dropped. "Oh," he breathed. "That's … that's really his, isn't it?" Then he frowned. "What did you do, rob his grave?"

It was Danzi's turn to frown. "No," he said angrily. "I would not do that. Golenhar was an honourable leader, and I respected him. He left it to me in his will. *The dagger will go to the next Tarangil,* he wrote. *To be kept in his care until my son proves himself worthy of it.* What, did you really think I'd let Hurraine have it?"

"Either that or you took off with it," grumbled the young lion. His eyes never left the dagger. "Give it to me. It should be mine now." He took a step forward.

Danzi held his ground. "Golenhar left that decision for me to make. Or will you go against his wishes?" Eiryenne saw him glance at the ground as the young lion hesitated then continued to advance. He started to back up his horse in a semicircle.

"You forfeited that responsibility when you messed everything up," cried out the lion. He unsheathed his claws and took another step forward, preparing to pounce. His eyes were fixed on the dagger. "And then you ran. You ran like the coward you are."

"No," Danzi said, rewrapping the golden dagger in its leather skin. "I was exiled. Then I went off to find vengeance." He paused. "You gave up your chance to have this dagger when you turned your back on your father's cause and chose to live a life of submission. Don't accuse *me* of being the coward."

Grehar leaped forward. He reached Danzi in two bounds. That was when a rope noose tightened on his right hind leg and hoisted him up into the air.

"Ogre snare," Danzi said when Eiryenne looked at him questioningly. No wonder he'd been combing the ground. "Won't hold him for long. Let's go."

They put their heels to their horses' sides and galloped off, leaving the trapped lion hanging in the air, yowling.

They sped through the forest, dodging trees and jumping ditches. After cresting a particularly tall ridge, Danzi stopped. He lay across Chief's neck, breathing hard. He'd kept his composure in front of the lions, but the truth was he was still wiped out from the torture.

Eiryenne looked back at the fortress in the distance. She could see shapes circling it and fighting. There were griffins tussling in the air with winged lions. She blinked. Since when did lions have wings?

Other soldiers had surrounded the fort, but they were being held off by lions on foot. A small group split off from them and turned in Eiryenne's direction. They scanned the hills, shielding their eyes from the sun.

With a jolt, she realized that Tairung was calling to them, telling them their quarry's location.

"We have to keep going," she said. "Tairung's telling them where we are. A small group is already in pursuit."

Danzi rubbed blood from his eyes. His scalp was slick with red. "Then we ride," he said heavily and squeezed Chief's sides without attempting to straighten in the saddle.

They picked their way across the ridge and clambered onto the next one, following it for the next few miles. Then Danzi led them on a mountain path that went higher into the foothills. His breathing got more ragged the farther they went, and he began to lean precariously to one side or another. But he still didn't fall off and vehemently rejected Eiryenne's offer to tie him to the saddle. Several times Eiryenne looked over her shoulder to see soldiers in the distance, both on foot and in the air.

If they didn't find a new shelter soon, she didn't know what they'd do.

They cantered along a narrow alpine trail, climbing the first few foothills. There were bigger mountains ahead, with high, jagged peaks covered with snow. She hoped they weren't going up there; the horses were already beginning to tire, and those peaks were a long climb away.

Danzi made a sharp turn into a narrow, almost invisible cleft. Chief stumbled as he scampered over the uneven rock, almost knocking his rider out of the saddle. But Danzi clung on tenaciously. When they were through the cleft, Eiryenne saw a small, rocky basin, just wide enough for their horses to stand in. It was strewn with broken boulders and sharp chips of rock. If that was their hiding place, she didn't see how it would do much good.

The dragon mage halted his horse at the end of the hollow, facing a sheer mountain face. He pushed himself upright in the saddle, his other hand hovering over his sword. Eiryenne saw tendrils of fire being drawn up from the ruby and into his hand. Then he reached backward and pulled more fire out of his jacket, which was still strapped behind his saddle. Eiryenne focused on it and saw the fire trickling out of small pockets of magic. She thought back to the gems she'd seen.

"You can store your magic in stones?" she asked.

He nodded, continuing to siphon off more power until the stones dimmed and faded from her vision.

She heard the cries of griffins. "They're coming. Hurry!"

Danzi scowled. "I know. I hear them. You're not helping." Then he turned to face the rocks again. He let go of the reins and raised both hands, which were burning with fire. Then he began to chant in Draconic, the harsh words echoing in Eiryenne's ears. The fire rose from his hands and swirled around him before forming strange symbols on the rock and sinking into it. Eiryenne heard a distant thud and the sound of rushing water.

Danzi's chant intensified. A fresh wave of fire surrounded the rocky face, burning in a semicircle surrounded by blazing hieroglyphics. New symbols formed on the wall as he spoke, until the circle was complete. He shouted the final word, and there were three more consecutive thuds, followed by a ground-shaking scrape. Then the rock in front of them split in half and opened to reveal the entrance to a cave. Danzi walked Chief through it, with Eiryenne following closely behind.

Chief tripped over a stalagmite and scrambled to find his footing on the rocky cavern floor. He slipped and slid. Danzi was thrown from his back, falling with a dull thud into a cluster of stalagmites. One of them impaled his leg; another pierced his thigh.

The crack behind them sealed, and their surroundings were plunged into darkness.

There were no sounds but the horses' soft breathing and Danzi's ragged panting as he disentangled his flesh from the sharp rock. Then there was a brief flash of light as he transformed, followed by the scraping of scales on rock. Eiryenne called an orb of magic to her fingers to see what was going on.

They were standing in a wide, flat cavern, lined by stalagmites. The dragon had dragged himself over to the far side of the cave.

"Leave the horses here," he said. "They won't be able to get around the inner cavern."

She slid off Neil and let him wander the cave along with Chief before going up to stand next to Danzi. He put a paw on the cavern's stone wall. Fire blazed around it, and with a blinding flash a crack opened down the middle of the rock. Hot air blasted out of it, almost knocking Eiryenne off her feet.

Danzi stumbled through the crack, and she followed, bracing herself against the rocks. They were warm, she realized. Then the dragon took another weary stride and disappeared into the shadows. Puzzled, she took a step after him, only to find that she was stepping out over empty air. The ground seemed to reach up and swallow her, and she shot downward. She didn't even have time to scream. Hot currents of air buffeted her face as she fell, scalding her cheeks. Her orb of light went out like a candle.

Then she felt the presence of a new kind of magic. The lower she fell, the stronger it became, until it wrapped strangely fuzzy tendrils around her body. Her fall began to slow. Finally, she came to a halt. The girl looked down. She was floating over a pair of giant, glowing green crystals.

Then the magic pushed her over to one side and released her. She fell a few feet onto the stony floor.

Rubbing her head, she sat up. It was unbearably hot. Sweat was already beginning to pour down her face. The crystals that had caught her were the only thing in her surroundings that she could see; everything else was in pitch blackness.

She could hear the sounds of dragon claws on stone.

"Danzi?" she called. "Where are we?"

"One moment," came his reply. Then he called out, *"Raikuro!"*

Lights suddenly flashed into being, illuminating the enormous cavern. Eiryenne's jaw dropped.

Chapter 14 ~ Cave of Wonders

The entire cavern was filled with huge, gleaming white crystals. A faceted, iridescent layer of uneven crystal lined the floor and huge crystalline pillars rose up to reach the ceiling. The more jagged floes resembled huge chunks of glass, spun in all possible shapes. Some of the crystals shone with Danzi's familiar red-orange fire, while others twinkled with other shades of magic: green, yellow, gold, blue.

She marvelled at their beauty and was just thinking that the sight could not get any more incredible when she spotted the treasure. Gold was piled within a bowl of crystal the size of a small meadow. There were coins and cups, jewelled swords and gilded spears. Trinkets far beyond her wildest dreams lay there, leaning against magnificent crystals that reflected the multicoloured light deep within their semitransparent depths.

"Oh, my goodness," she whispered, looking around in awe. "This is ...t his is just *incredible*. What is this place? Where did those crystals come from? Who found all that treasure?"

"I did," replied the red dragon. He was clambering over the crystals toward a flat, raised crystalline plateau in the centre of the cavern.

"Is this your home?"

"Not really. More of a storage space."

Eiryenne opened her mouth to ask something else, but she suddenly became aware of Tairung shouting inside her head.

We're in here, he yelled. *Come on, get them already. I tire of this human vessel!*

"Tairung's trying to call the soldiers here," she said, still unable to tear her eyes away from the wonders of the cave. "Are they going to get in? Will we have to run again?" She'd only gotten here, but the thought of leaving this magical place so soon saddened her.

"If they can get me in here," Danzi muttered, collapsing onto the plateau and closing his eyes with a resigned sigh. "Then they can have me."

Reloden? Ignus? Why isn't anyone answering, Tairung screamed.

"Oh, so it looks like they can't hear you from here, can they?" Eiryenne said with a smirk.

The dragon realized who she was talking to. "The barriers surrounding this cave are the best I could forge," he said. "Not even Tairung can break through."

"Wait, so doesn't that mean that we could just leave the necklace here and be done with it?" she asked.

"No. There are a lot of other magical artefacts here. Left to his own devices and without his power contained by a mage, I'm sure Tairung would eventually be able to harness them and send a signal to the outside world."

Eiryenne wiped the sweat off her face. The heat was pressing down on her like the weight of a thousand pounds of earth. She took off her jacket, but that still didn't help. If she didn't do something, she had the feeling the heat would slowly kill her. This place was obviously not meant for human visitors.

"Danzi, do you know any cooling spells?" she asked. "This heat is just cooking me alive."

The dragon opened an amber eye. "Oh. I forgot about that. But dragon fire isn't good for cooling, even if I had any more to spare. Let's see. Go behind that big sword-shaped crystal … there is a blue amulet there. Put it on and give it the command *svorash.* That's Elvish for *cold.* It should do the trick."

Eiryenne picked her way across the crystals, which had turned from beautiful sculptures to the earth's menacing teeth, snagging at her feet as the heat sought to consume her. She was almost suffocating on the hot air by the time she made it to the crystal and the mound of silver treasure behind it. The blue stood out easily, and she took the amulet with shaking fingers.

"Sv-svorash," she whispered. Instantly, a cooling sensation trickled from the amulet in her hands like a brook of cold water, spreading along her limbs until the oppressive heat faded from her body.

She tied its fine silver chain across her wrist, next to the leather band with her glass bead. Behind another row of crystals that flickered with white light, she saw a wall made of thick, milky white rock threaded with red veins. In front of it a smaller mound of crystal with a flat top served as a makeshift desk. Coming closer, she saw rolls of parchment hanging off its edge, locked in a watertight skin along with writing utensils. On the wall hung a map of the Empire and neighbouring lands, drawn on a heavy paper that she guessed was waterproof, because it and everything else in the cave was wet.

Coming closer, she peered up at the map. It was covered with scribbles and lines, crossed-out words and arrows. It must have been drawn up a long time ago because the original black ink showed borders very different from those of the present countries. There were no borders, just dotted lines separating out some chunks of the region. Also, in black was a crossed-out title written in bold dark letters: "Shotang."

Over the black ink were different layers of annotations, each done in a different colour, first blue, then red, then orange, and so on. With each colour, the borders changed. Symbols like small triangles and spheres were also drawn on the map, surrounded by some arrows. Cities and land features such as mountains were also labelled.

Eiryenne found that as she concentrated on a specific ink colour, that layer would stand out and the rest would dim, making it easier to see. The latest set of edits, done in dark brown, showed the current borders of the Empire, stretching from the shores of the Reyud Strait in the west and over to the Asanteh Mountains in the east. Beyond the mountains lay Gosrun and Bremia, dwarfed by their enormous western neighbour. Next to them was Turmain, even smaller. To the south of the Empire was a patchwork of small, unfamiliar countries, and to the north stretched mountainous Tartaway.

Across the Reyud Strait there was another continent. It was covered in violent scribbles and set after set of crossed-out names. The original title, however, remained uncrossed: "Remfuria."

Eiryenne walked back to where she'd left Danzi. She wanted to ask him just how old the map was. In watching the different layers of ink, had she been observing the changing tides of history?

But when she reached him, she saw that the dragon was fast asleep. He needed the rest, so Eiryenne found a flat spot on the floor and amused herself by gazing at all the treasures. When her eyelids, too, began to droop, she put her jacket beneath her head and fell asleep, despite the hardness of the crystal beneath her back.

***

It was hard to tell the passage of time in the cave, but Eiryenne judged that Danzi slept for several days. While the dragon rested, she got up every so often to go exploring. Each time she set out, it seemed like the cave had something new to show her. And it was wonderful to know that for once, Tairung's evil pull would not be a problem. They were safe here in this crystal haven; the outside world and all its problems could wait. So Eiryenne lost herself in the endless marvels of the crystals and the soft, golden glow of the treasure as it poured through her hands. She avoided anything that had the slightest hint of magic, since there was no telling what kinds of things Danzi had collected over the years. But much of it was just good old-fashioned gold.

She found that she could return to the outer cavern by going back to the green crystals beneath the chasm; their curious magic boosted her up the shaft and set her down at the top. Eiryenne had been concerned for the horses, but they seemed to be doing well. A warm spring ran through their outer cavern, and edible moss grew along its sides. She took off their saddles and bridles before giving them each a good rub-down. The saddlebags, and the supplies they contained, she brought back to the crystal cave.

A good portion of the cavern was too steep or slippery to climb, and she found out the hard way that some of the crystals were razor-sharp.

But that didn't bother her. She stuck to the routes she could manage. The cave's sheer size meant that she was not likely to get bored, even with the passable sections.

When Danzi finally woke up, she expected him to be ravenous. Perhaps he was, but the one thing the cave didn't have was food. So, he shifted into human form and gobbled down a double ration from their supplies.

Eiryenne was brimming with questions about the cave. "How'd you find it?" she asked eagerly. "Why was everything wet when we came in? What kinds of protections did you put on it? How often do you visit?"

"These crystals grew under water," Danzi explained. He looked better after his long nap; the colour was starting to return to his cheeks, and he moved around a little easier. "When I first came across this place, it was filled with near-boiling water, heated by the earth's inner fires. I figured out a way to drain the water during my stays. It was a perfect hideout for me; the heat, rough terrain, and toxins made it already inhospitable to most visitors but didn't bother a dragon at all."

Eiryenne's enthusiasm disappeared. "Toxins?"

"In the water, yes. Anyone foolish enough to drink from one of the crystal pools would die within minutes," he said. "Since you are still alive, I assume that you've been drinking from the waterskins in our saddle bags."

She nodded. The pools were too hot to drink from.

Danzi laid his heavy leather jacket across his knees and drew a finger over one of the large rips in it. He must have been channelling magic from the crystals, because sparks of blue and yellow appeared on the material, melding the two sides of the tear. He continued going over it until all the breaks were gone.

At first Eiryenne was puzzled as to why he was paying this much attention to a tattered jacket. Then she remembered the way it had stopped an arrow when she first saw Danzi fight, and the few times since then that a soldier had been lucky enough to land a blow on him, their sword or axe would fail to cut through the fabric.

"That's not ordinary leather, is it?" she said. "Is it enchanted?"

"No. It's just made from a byage's hide. It'll stop most human blades and arrows. Takes something both sharp and magical to get through." He rubbed his shoulder. "It'll stop the edge, not the blunt force, mind you. But blunt force I can usually handle. Dragon bones are strong, even in this form. It's the skin that tears open too easily."

"So, it's like…armour. Leather armour instead of metal." She found it strange that Danzi wore this leather instead of some kind of metal, if he needed armour.

"Don't look so surprised. People have been using leather and fabric armour for a long time. If it's strong and thick enough, it can stop a blade or arrow. Even nowadays, padded jackets are used by men-at-arms and some of the poorer knights instead of metal."

"But you have enough treasure to get a suit of golden armour."

Danzi blinked. "That's not the point."

Eiryenne shrugged. Then she thought back to the map she'd seen. "I saw the map over in the corner. Is it old?"

"If by *old* you mean a few centuries, then yes," he replied.

Eiryenne raised an eyebrow. "Did *you* make all those edits?"

"Most of them. Why are you so shocked? Dragons live for hundreds of years."

She still found it hard to wrap her head around that. "Okay, so why do you have a base so deep inside the Empire? Wouldn't it be hard to ferry gold in here right under the Emperor's nose?"

"This wasn't always the Empire," Danzi said. He shifted to his dragon shape then stretched and lay down so that there was a large blue crystal flecked with gold beneath his paws.

"What was it like?" she asked quietly. "Before?"

"These lands were wild. They had no rulers. Different peoples fought for territory, which was split up between the dominant species. There was still conflict, and there was still death, but in those days warriors and clans lived and died by the strength of their own swords, not by how much of their lives they gave up to the Emperor." Danzi looked pensive. "This entire region was known as Shotang. Some people still call it that, despite all the changes that have taken place. When I first flew over the Tangard Valley, Loturg was not there. A river ran through that pass, cold and glacial, straight from the tops of the mountains. There were kelpies and dolphins in the water. A herd of unicorns often passed through that way. It was said that if you drank from the river after they passed it you would be cured of poison."

Eiryenne thought back to the run-down, poison-ridden city of beggars that they had passed through. She found it hard to imagine the landscape any differently.

She looked at Danzi to say something else, but movement beneath his paws caught her attention. She looked down, and to her surprise, an image was forming on the crystal upon which he leaned. She saw trees and hills in their full summer green; the river that made its way through the forest was sky blue and icy cold. Winged lions and griffins lazily coasted the breeze, ignoring one another. And then she caught side of some distant, horse-shaped figures.

Danzi noticed her staring. He drew away from the crystal, and the image disappeared.

"There is a natural magic in some of these crystals," he said. "This is one of them. It will show what you are picturing in your mind. This I knew, but I wasn't aware that others could see it, too."

"Why not?" she said. "People imagine things all the time, and those crystals are everywhere." She paused. "Oh, wait. You mean you haven't—"

"Brought anyone down here? No," he said. Danzi turned his head until she was looking directly into the red dragon's piercing eyes. "Few know about the existence of this place. And I aim to keep it that way. Understood?"

She nodded solemnly. After all, who would she tell?

***

That night she was woken by the sound of thumping. Sitting up, she saw Danzi's tail twitch and thrash, hitting the crystals behind him. He'd slipped halfway off his rock, and there were several deep gouges in the crystal beside his paws. The dragon was still asleep, his motions constrained to his dreams.

Danzi's horns were brushing a speckled blue crystal. Eiryenne could see flashes of colour and light going across it, but she was too far away to make out the image.

She hesitated. This seemed too much like eavesdropping. But now that she was looking at the crystal, she found it hard to look anywhere else. Quietly moving closer, she made out what looked like a blackened, dense forest.

At first the picture was mute, but once she put her hands on it, she could hear everything.

Danzi was dreaming that he ran after Blackthorn. He leaped and roared, pumping his wings, but the black pegasus never got any closer. He continued to taunt Danzi while getting farther and farther away. The dragon snarled with frustration and raked his claws across the earth in front of him.

Then both pegasus and dark forest disappeared, and she saw Danzi running through summer woods that blazed with colour and flowers. He stopped next to a deep, calm pool, looking surprised. Looking closer, Eiryenne saw that instead of reflecting the surrounding woods, the pool showed a different kind of scene. It showed a woman from the shoulders up, with low, sloping blue hills in the background. She had pale skin and long, fair hair. Her dark brown eyes were large and kind, surveying Danzi with a kind of sad wistfulness.

The dragon shifted back into his human form and fell to his knees in front of the pool.

"I saw Blackthorn," he said, still breathing quickly after his run. "Freya, I saw Blackthorn a few days ago and I still couldn't kill him." He banged his fist on the bank, making the image in the water ripple.

"Your anger clouds your focus," the woman he called Freya replied.

"But it's his fault. He has to pay," the dragon mage growled. "Everything I lost *that* day was because of him."

"And what you gained?"

Danzi frowned. "You know I would have rather not gained it." He rubbed his forehead. "And when I was caught a few days ago, Blackthorn almost took it. I almost lost it."

The woman tilted her head. "Danzi, do you think I would have entrusted you with my gift if I didn't think you could look after it?"

He sighed. "I suppose not." Danzi was silent for a few moments, watching the calm surface of the pool. "Why are you stuck in the water? This is a dream; you should be able to do what you like."

Freya shook her head. "There is a presence nearby, a dark one. It limits my influence."

"Ah. That would be Tairung," he said. "I'm taking the necklace to be destroyed before the Emperor can get his hands on it. Its holder is nearby."

Freya nodded. "Don't be too hard on that girl. She's doing all she can. You should be thanking her for saving your life."

"She did what she had to," Danzi said with a shrug. "She knew she wouldn't get anywhere without me."

"Be that as it may, but you're starting to forget."

"Forget what?"

"That sometimes, just sometimes, people do things for you from the goodness of their hearts," Freya said. "But you still don't know what to make of it when that happens."

"She had her reasons, just as I have mine," the fire mage said roughly. "And as soon as I'm done with her and Tairung, I'm going after Blackthorn. I'll rip him apart and—"

Freya sighed. "You've changed, Danzi. You've become more like the dragon I first met in Remfuria, not the one I was so proud to fight alongside in Shotang."

Danzi looked away. "Can you blame me?" he asked softly.

"I don't blame you for *anything*," she replied. "Please remember that. Just promise me you'll consider Lianos's suggestion."

"I was already considering it," he said.

Freya smiled sadly. "Well, I think I've run out of time. Goodbye, my friend. I will try to visit you again someday." She drew two fingers across her forehead in a salute. Danzi returned it. Then the entire image rippled, and her reflection disappeared. The pool now showed Danzi's reflection and the trees that surrounded him. With a sigh, the fire mage lay back across the grass next to the water. Then that scene, too, dissolved, and the crystal went dark. Danzi had now entered dreamless sleep.

Eiryenne crawled back to her sleeping spot. She had no idea what to make of *that*.

Rearranging her jacket to make a more comfortable pillow, she shifted the horse blanket she slept on, dragging it away from an uncomfortably sharp crystal that jabbed at her side. Then she lay down and closed her eyes, unaware that the edge of her arm was touching a blue crystal flecked with gold.

***

It seemed like she had barely closed her eyes before she was opening them to see herself standing in the middle of a barren swamp, with Tairung staring her in the face.

"What do you want?" she demanded. "Why can't you just leave me alone and let me have a good night's sleep!"

"Enjoy it while you can," he said, grinning evilly. "The peace won't last long, not with the kind of company you keep. You know Danzi is just using you."

"Neither of us have a choice," she retorted.

"Even if you survive my destruction, do you really think he'll bother with you after that? No, he'll just leave you to the soldiers while he flies off to ruin someone else's life."

"I don't … I don't really believe that," Eiryenne said, as though trying to convince herself. "He'll do the right thing. I know he will."

"Oh, I think Danzi's definition of *right* is quite a bit different from yours. Once your usefulness runs its course, he'll throw you away like the trash you are. You see, Eiryenne," said the black unicorn, "there is evil in everyone. And there's a whole lot more in your precious guardian than you could ever imagine. He and I are not so different. Come, I will show you."

The scene blurred, and it seemed to Eiryenne as if they were moving quickly, very quickly. The speed made her dizzy.

"Useful crystals, are they not?" Tairung's voice echoed all around her. "*Showing* dreams is not all they do."

Once her vision cleared, she saw a rocky cliff. Danzi was standing on it in human form, his arms crossed, looking grimly at the black unicorn that had materialized in front of him. He didn't seem to notice Eiryenne.

"Ah, Danzellius," Tairung said. "You, whose heart was as black as mine, why do you not give in to the temptation of this power?"

Danzi frowned at him. "Because I have another goal."

"Acting noble now, are you?" Tairung said. "You can't erase the past, Danzi. You were a mass murderer then, and you are still one now."

"Except I've switched to killing people who deserve it," growled the dragon mage.

"In any case, you already had your chance," said the demented unicorn. "As I recall, it was you who broke into the Vault and became the first in seven hundred years to hold up the Necklace and blow the dust off its stones."

"Yes, but you should remember what I did after that," Danzi said. "I didn't want *your* demonic strength or *your* dark army. I came there to find something that would channel and amplify *my* power." His eyes narrowed. "I had a goal then, as I do now. And when I have a cause, I am not easily shaken from it. That is why I tossed away your necklace, just as why I don't take it now. My mission today is to take down the Emperor and his allies. And nothing can distract me from it. That is the difference between us."

Tairung took a step closer. "Perhaps you are just afraid that you couldn't control my power," he snorted. "You're afraid that I would take over."

"I am not." Danzi's frown deepened. "No demon can possess a dragon's soul."

"Well, they said the same thing about unicorns, now, didn't they?" chuckled Tairung, edging closer.

"The difference is that you *let* them in."

The dark unicorn cocked his head. He seemed to be examining Danzi. "Perhaps your soul can't be possessed," he said after a little while. "But your spirit *can* be tainted."

"Not while I have this," replied the dragon mage, whipping a long, narrow object out of his jacket that shone with a blinding white light. "Now be gone. I tire of your banter." The light brightened, and Tairung shrank away from its radiance.

"Of all the talismans I expected you to possess, that was the last," he muttered. Then he dissolved into thin air.

***

Eiryenne walked carefully along the crystal ledge. She'd yet to try this route, a swath of yellow crystal with green undertones that went around the mound of sparkling quartz the dragon often rested on. Though Danzi hadn't said anything about any part of the cave being out of bounds, Eiryenne had still felt a little hesitant about going up it while he was on his mound. But now, he was over by his crystalline desk, studying his map with a pensive look on his muzzle. Eiryenne made her way to the back of the mound, slipping between faceted crystals growing from the ground like a forest made of tinted glass. This path seemed to lead through to a deeper part of the cave, though with all the crystals it was easy to get turned around. For once, however, Eiryenne knew that getting lost would earn her nothing more than a dragon's annoyance.

She saw something out of the corner of her eye: a vaguely human-shaped figure. For a second she thought that there was someone else down there with them, but when she turned, she saw that it was only a suit of armour draped over a crystalline stalagmite. She walked over to it. Was this someone who'd tried to steal the dragon's treasure?

The armour was made of thick, square bronze plates and red chain mail. Both had begun to rust over. Eiryenne turned the weathered metal over in her hands. It must have seen a lot of battles. Beside it, even deeper in the depths of the crystal cave, partially hidden by a mound of dark crystal, there was another suit of armour. This one looked to be even older; it was covered in rust and blemishes, the metal almost unrecognizable. She could just make out a row of narrow red shoulder plates accented with gold.

Eiryenne gave it another look before turning away. She rounded a stunning projection of glimmering, pure white rock that jutted out at odd angles and was crowned with a larger growth of dark blue. As she ducked under it, she saw a small alcove, naturally formed where the white crystal met the blue. The shelf, unsurprisingly, was filled with treasure. She spotted a curved sword with a translucent, crystalline blade and an engraved silver goblet next to a thick golden chain that hummed with power. There was also a piece of shiny white rock shaped somewhat like a bird.

Then a flash of crimson caught her eye. Looking closer, she saw something red and shiny in the shadows of the alcove. It seemed to be some kind of statue. The item radiated no magic, so Eiryenne scooped it out and held it in the light from the crystals.

It was a statue of a dragon carved from brilliant red crystal. It glowed from the inside as it caught the cave's light, illuminating all the details. Eiryenne ran her fingers over the scales, admiring the craftsmanship. They were each carved meticulously into the crystal, along with spines and wings. And as she looked at its muzzle, she realized it looked familiar. Squinting, she looked closer into the statue's eyes. She might have only seen one dragon, but she was pretty sure it was this one.

Whoever carved this was skilled. They'd captured Danzi almost perfectly, from the tip of his scaly nose to the ends of his curved claws and the unmistakable, proud carriage of his head. Only one thing wasn't accurate, Eiryenne saw as she looked into the crystal dragon's face. His jaws were slightly parted, but the corners of his mouth were snaking upward in a grin rather than a snarl. And though there was pride in his eyes, there was also joy. It was an expression she had yet to see on the real Danzi.

Carefully putting the statue back, Eiryenne resumed her exploration. Every item here had a story. She only wished she could persuade Danzi to tell her some of them.

***

With each day, the dragon was getting stronger, shaking off the damage from his torture. He began to move more easily around the cave, climbing the crystals that were too jagged or slippery for Eiryenne. The network of fire beneath his scales was straightening out, rekindling, getting brighter. Soon his wounds, too, began to heal. It was evident that he wanted to have his full strength for the last leg of their journey.

One day, as Danzi lounged on the top of a giant crystal, he turned to the girl, who was playing with some golden coins below. She, too, was healing. The cut across her ribs was almost closed, and the bruises on her face were starting to fade.

"Tomorrow we leave," he said. "Be ready. We're close to the end now."

"Are you ever going to tell me what our destination is?" she burst out, Tairung's warnings ringing in her head. "Or what … what happens after?"

Danzi got up. He walked down the row of crystals, stopping when he got to a large blue-flecked one. "We are going to a place called Boyevin Cavern," he said, putting his paw on the crystal. An image appeared there, showing a large, gaping hole in blackened earth. Rocks were strewed around its edges. "Watch carefully, so you know where to go if we get split up." The view moved to the alpine trail that was outside Danzi's cave before sweeping forward over the mountains, by what looked like a military camp, and to another trail that dead-ended a few hundred feet from the cavern's entrance.

Eiryenne was silent for a moment. Then she looked up at the dragon, his crimson scales a stunning contrast with the white and blue crystals around him. "What's at the cavern?"

"Not what, *who*. The Firedrake."

"What's a Firedrake?" She felt Tairung wince at the word. "And how come it can destroy the necklace when no one else can?"

"Firedrakes, are, by nature, anti-magical. They feed on magical creatures," he said. "They are resistant to almost all forms of magic; they destroy it on contact. They are the only creatures who can prey on dragons—even our magic has no effect, and our claws cannot pierce their rock-like hides."

"Then what are you going to do?"

"I will throw the necklace down its throat. The beast's saliva will strip the primary protective spells from the stones and then I'll use a spell to send them both into the abyss."

"But you just said dragon magic doesn't work on a Firedrake," she said, still confused.

"Who says I'll be using dragon magic?"

***

During their last night in the cave, Eiryenne was restless. She wanted to go and look around one last time, but Danzi dimmed the crystal lanterns before going to sleep so there was not enough light to navigate safely. The last thing she wanted was to slip and fall onto a jagged piece of quartz.

Instead, she looked at what she could see from her vantage point. The cave was bathed in darkness, with lone crystals catching the dim light and looming out of the shadows. Danzi himself fit right in here, his gem-like scales and glossy claws reflecting the soft light as well as the treasure did.

The dragon shifted slightly in his sleep, the tip of his tail moving over to rest on a piece of speckled blue crystal. Eiryenne crawled over so that she could watch his dreams.

This time, there was no black pegasus in Danzi's dream. Instead, it featured a grassy field of tall, waving grass. Through it ran what had to be a unicorn, though it couldn't be more different from Tairung. Its horn was whole, a shining, silvery stretch of tightly spiralled ivory. Its glossy coat was pearly white. It moved with the utmost grace, every stride of its gallop carefree and effortless. The unicorn's mane flowed in the wind, and the nostrils on its velvety muzzle were stretched wide, taking in big snorts of air. There was a forest, lush and green, at the edge of the field. Beyond it were the tops of distant mountains.

Just like the other crystal images Eiryenne had seen, everything was slightly different from how the place would have looked to her in reality. She supposed that the scene appeared how a dragon would see it; everything was unusually crisp and clear, the colours bright and saturated. Little details jumped out at Eiryenne, like the texture of every blade of grass, the whiskers on the unicorn's muzzle, every nook and crevice in the distant mountain. With one sweeping glace, the dragon took note of it all. He appeared to be able to focus on both the foreground and background at once; no object in the image was blurry.

The scene changed abruptly, and now Danzi was flying over a battlefield. His mouth was stretched open in a savage snarl as he bathed the people below him in fire. They screamed, begging for mercy, but he continued to attack.

Eiryenne turned away. She'd seen enough of his massacres.

The girl wondered whether she could really trust him. The seeds of doubt planted both by Tairung and some of the dragon's own actions were starting to flourish now that her mind was idle. She had no choice but to go along with him until the end, obviously. It was clear that he wouldn't stop until he'd destroyed the necklace. But though she doubted that Danzi was as evil as Tairung suggested, she couldn't help but worry about what he'd said about Danzi leaving her to her doom afterward. Much as she didn't like the idea, she had to agree it seemed like something he'd do. The dragon's actions were driven by necessity, not kindness. He helped her because he had to; the Emperor was his enemy, and he wasn't going to let Varcroft have Tairung's army. He protected Eiryenne because there was no other way to safely move the necklace.

What, then, would he do once she no longer had that excuse?

Chapter 15 ~ Icy Showdown

"This place is usually crawling with soldiers," muttered Danzi. "Looks like they've all been called off to war."

It was the day after they left the cave, and the two riders now stood on a small plateau near the end of the mountain chain. Danzi had gotten off his horse and climbed up a rocky escarpment to peer down at the valley.

"It's clear," he said, sliding back down. "Let's go."

As Danzi and Eiryenne had continued to ride north, they found that the cold weather of the mountains didn't stop even once they'd left the foothills. Old wooden barracks stood on the valley floor, their doors and walls frosted with ice; a thin dusting of snow covered the ground. A chilling winter gale tore through the air, and darkening clouds warned of an oncoming blizzard.

Tairung was known for offsetting the seasons, Danzi had said. His active presence had stretched out autumn in the region, but after being cut off from the world in Danzi's crystal cave, the dark unicorn's aura ceased to influence the weather, and it went back to its regular, chilly January state. The dragon and the girl had emerged from their refuge to find themselves caught in the grip of winter.

Despite the warming amulet that Eiryenne now wore around her right wrist, she was cold. She shoved her freezing hands into her pockets, guiding Neil with her legs. If only there had been gloves or cloaks in Danzi's cave of treasures…

"If no one spots us by the time we round that tree," Danzi said, pointing to a big, gnarled oak ahead of them. "We'll try to fly the rest of the way. It's not far, and if this place is truly abandoned, we'll save some time."

They were halfway to the oak when a group of soldiers emerged from the trees downwind of them. A group of ogres and elves closed in on Danzi, while four men formed a wedge between him and Eiryenne.

She automatically reached for her sword, priming the blade with her magic until it glowed with purple and blue. Dodging the first man's swing, Eiryenne parried the next warrior's blow. Then she countered by turning and sliding her blade down his, moving his arm slightly to the side and then giving a slash to the exposed corner of his chest. It was a move drilled firmly into her muscle memory by Danzi's endless sparring sessions. Her blade bit deep, and he fell to his knees with a groan.

But her triumph was brief. In focusing her attention on one attacker, she'd gotten tunnel vision and blocked out the others. Someone's club grazed her back. She'd only avoided getting her spine crushed because Neil had seen the motion and spooked. Reeling, she struggled to stay in the saddle as the other two soldiers attacked her, one with a sword, the other with a long spear tipped with a curved blade—a glaive. Behind them, the third was readying his club for another swing.

Eiryenne jabbed Neil in the ribs, making him sidestep the glaive. Then there was a searing pain in her sword arm. The other soldier had attacked on her blind side, and his blade ripped her forearm open. She cried out and dropped her weapon. The man with the club smacked Neil on the flank with it. He gave a buck and bolted. Eiryenne was thrown from the saddle, her landing only slightly softened by the snow.

She was dimly aware of shouts and flashes of magic in the background as Danzi fought, but the other soldiers and mages were keeping him busy. He couldn't reach her. Eiryenne groped for her sword, realizing that her life was now in her own hands.

She saw the hilt and reached for it, but a large, black leather boot had come down over the handle, and she looked up into the sneering, scarred face of the Imperial swordsman that had wounded her. Blood ran down his blade almost as quickly as it spurted from her arm.

Eiryenne tried to make herself move, but her muscles had locked; she crouched there, frozen, in the bloodied snow.

The stones of her necklace had slipped out from under her jacket. They hung in front of her now, shimmering. Eiryenne couldn't help but think of how beautiful they seemed against the stark backdrop of winter.

She sensed rather than saw the other two soldiers approaching her from behind. Though she took note that none of her opponents were mages—they were saving all of them for the dragon—it was little consolation.

It was the sound of a blade whistling through the air that made her react. Without thinking, she put up the densest, most solid barrier she could manage, filling it with the essence of the colossal defences around Danzi's crystal cave.

She looked up to see the sword hovering in the air a few inches above her head, stopped by a shell of glimmering blue and purple light. The man wielding it paused, looking surprised. He hadn't expected her to be a hard kill.

Eiryenne grabbed the dagger from her belt. Instead of trying to launch her offensive spells, she coated the blade with them. In her mind she saw a broadsword brimming with flames and tried to capture even a tiny bit of its destructive power. Bright blue and purple lights began to dance along her blade.

Then the glaive hit her barrier. The spell shattered, broken pieces of glass-like light stinging the men's skin where it hit them. The swordsman dropped his blade as shards of magic as sharp as crystal struck his fingers.

The glaive wielder grimaced but kept his grip, his greater distance ensuring that he received less of the fallout. He recovered quickly, springing at Eiryenne with a mighty swing.

All her instincts screamed at her to jump away. But she knew that if she did that, he'd only have a greater advantage. The glaive had a reach of over seven feet; she'd never get far enough. The key to overcoming a weapon with such a great strike radius, Danzi had always told her, was to close the gap.

So, her heart in her mouth, she forced her legs to move toward the soldier even as he brought his weapon about. She dove into a roll beneath his strike, the wicked blade shearing through her hair, barely an inch away from her scalp.

Everything seemed to happen both too quickly and too slowly at the same time. Eiryenne almost felt numb. Her head was filled with a strange buzzing, the adrenalin making her incapable of coherent thought. Her body seemed to move independently, muscles automatically falling back on Danzi's emergency drills. She launched herself from the ground, winding up her arm, and plunged her glowing dagger into her opponent's gut. The big man's momentum worked against him; he literally ran into the blade, and it sank into his black tunic up to the hilt.

The man stumbled. He knocked her in the head with the shaft of his weapon. She wrenched her blade out and stabbed him again, blood splattering her arms and face.

He caught her gaze, and she watched his eyes lose focus and roll back in his head.

Then he fell.

Before she'd even realized what she'd done, the soldier who'd dropped his sword grabbed her in a headlock. The one with the club brought his arm up to swing.

Think, she told herself, though the crushing pressure at her windpipe was fogging her brain. *Think. What did Danzi say about headlocks?*

She jabbed the man in the side with her elbow, but he only tightened his grip as she came into contact with his armour. She tried again, putting magic into her elbow and trying to will it to be as hard and sharp as the crystals she'd almost fallen against in the cave. This time the man's armour shattered, and he loosened his grip just enough for her to slip down a few inches. Instead of crushing her skull, the club the other soldier swung rammed into her assailant's chest.

She twisted out of his grip as he collapsed, stumbling across the snow. The necklace had slid out from beneath her shirt during all the commotion; the stones now bounced lightly against the front of her jacket. The man with the club turned on her with an angry grunt, his first blow almost shattering her leg. She reached for her magic but found she had run dry.

Eiryenne rolled out of the way of the next blow then scrambled to her feet and took off. Her desperation mounted as the soldier drew closer, and her sword was still nowhere to be found. He'd overtake her in seconds. Realizing she was out of options, she dove over a snowbank, the club whistling through the air behind her and landing with a soft thump in the snow.

She tumbled down the bank's other side. As she came to a stop, her fingers closed on something hard: the bow that had slipped off Neil's saddle when he bolted.

Danzi trotted up just in time to see a lone soldier toppling off the crest of a tall snowbank with an arrow lodged in his chest.

Eiryenne appeared soon after, peering cautiously over the top and already starting to draw another arrow. Then, seeing that she, Danzi, and Chief were the only living beings in that clearing, she relaxed. Her bloody shoulders slumped in relief. She limped down the bank, clutching her wounded arm. Danzi waited patiently while she retrieved her sword and dagger, also bumping into her pack along the way.

Her hands shook, and she could not steady her breathing. Adrenaline was still pumping through her body. She couldn't believe what she'd just done. With trembling fingers, Eiryenne opened her pack and retrieved some herb leaves, taking a deep breath of their calming fragrance.

"More are on the way," Danzi said. He offered her a bloodied hand. "Neil ran off toward the hills. Get on."

Eiryenne took his hand and was pulled up onto the horse behind him. Without another word, Danzi kicked the gelding into a gallop.

"Can't we fly now?" she asked, lightly holding on to Danzi's waist to keep her balance. Even through his cloak, she could feel the heat of the fire magic that flowed through his veins.

"No. There's another group up there behind those rocks," he replied. "They'll be expecting me to make a mad dash for the cavern. They've positioned themselves to see any direct approach we try."

"What are we going to do?" she said, confused by their abrupt change of course. Instead of continuing down the path, Danzi had turned Chief in almost the opposite direction, choosing a route that skirted the trees at the base of the foothill and gradually began to climb it. "How do we get to the cavern without being ambushed?"

"They're not going to ambush us. *I'm* going to ambush *them*."

***

Danzi left the girl and the horse in the shadow of a rocky ridge, out of view of the squad of soldiers that they had snuck up on. He stayed in human shape as he began to run, shoulders ducked low as he sprinted from boulder to boulder. Some of the soldiers were beginning to turn, sensing Tairung, but not enough of them would realize the danger before it was too late.

His cloak rippled behind him as he ran, his legs pumping far faster than a human's, his strides taking him much farther. Danzi tried to size up his opponents as he approached. Those other soldiers had been sent to slow him down; these ones were dressed for the kill. There were griffins, demons, winged smilodons, Dyre wolves, elves, and ogres. Varcroft's usual mix for a hit squad. But what was unusual were the mages that he sensed. Danzi recognized elven and griffin magic, as well as that of the demons, but there were several stranger energies here as well. Something may have been familiar about one of them, yet he was positive he had not encountered this mage before. He was also surprised at the degree of power he sensed there, but if Varcroft was serious about taking him out, one or two of the Empire's top mages might be here.

The fire mage landed on a boulder, still out of sight, and gathered up his magic. The element of surprise would be his advantage, but briefly, and he intended to make as much of it as he could. A crippling first strike was crucial.

Danzi leaped onto a stack of fallen trees and unleashed his magic. A wave of fire rolled over the surprised soldiers, quickly devouring the first few rows.

Then he transformed.

The dragon leaped forward, fire rolling off his crimson scales like a molten waterfall, burning and ravaging all in his path. He grabbed a griffin around the neck and bit through its spine before slicing a demon's head right off with a single slash of his claws. But his few seconds of surprise were over; the soldiers were starting to fight back. The griffins who'd escaped his initial attack were taking flight; unlike the dragon, they preferred fighting from the air. Bursts of their wind magic shot toward Danzi, exploding when they met the fire that surrounded him.

He was halfway through a group of ogres when he noticed that most of the other beasts were edging back, clearing the space around him. An icy blast hit him from the side, almost quenching his fiery aura. Danzi whipped around in time to see an enormous, castle-sized boulder that crashed into him, knocking him flat. He rolled out of its way before it could completely crush him.

Scrambling to his feet, Danzi saw two new creatures enter the fray. The first was a stocky beast covered in white fur and tinted blue spines. Its hind legs were longer than its front, roughly arm-shaped limbs. It had a thick, short snout and a stubby tail ending in a silver bulb. Long silver claws hung over its giant paws, and fangs resembling icicles curled down from its top jaw. Its muzzle looked squashed in, disfigured, a mix of human and animal characteristics combined to give the creature a demonic appearance. Behind its fur were thick plates of icy blue armour.

It was an igarevin, a creature from the far north; way beyond the farthest reaches of the Empire. How Varcroft had gotten his hands on one was beyond him.

The boulder that had almost squashed Danzi broke and collapsed inward. Four pillars broke away from it, stretched to the ground and then grew, raising the rest of the rock above the snow. A single boulder moved up from the mass and split almost in half to form a head and jaws. Two white, crystalline starburst eyes unearthed themselves in the upheaval, along with jagged stone teeth, while more rocks formed sharply angled plates on its back and extended into a club-like tail. The rock creature towered above Danzi, dwarfing even his dragon form.

Hrmm. An igarevin and an oberon. Varcroft outdid himself this time, Danzi thought. He had to shift into human shape to avoid the oberon's hurtling tail. It smashed into the space where his dragon shoulders had been a second before.

The igarevin stepped forward and shifted also, becoming a pale-skinned man dressed in glittering white furs. "Give up, Daggoras. You stand no chance. Surrender yourself and the necklace, and we shall kill you quickly."

Danzi smirked. "Just who do you think I am?" He opened his hand, and small plumes of flame encircled it, dancing around his palm, hurtling faster and faster. Within a split second he'd built up the power he needed and hurled the ring of fire toward the silver-haired man.

An ice wall rose up in front of the igarevin man to absorb the blow.

"I *told* you that you shouldn't have bothered, Kutal," rumbled the oberon in a voice so deep and loud, it made the earth shake.

"Our custom dictates that even the damned should have a chance to surrender to their fate," the igarevin replied, casually rubbing his smooth chin. He spoke calmly, even as he made spears of ice jump out of the ground all around the dragon mage.

Danzi surrounded himself in a cocoon of fire, melting the ice on contact. The last spear almost made it through, disintegrating only when it was a few inches from his face. *Now* he realized where he'd sensed this magic before.

"The manacles," he growled. "That was *you*."

"That's right," said Kutal with a smirk. "Fine piece of work, wasn't it? I was surprised when I heard you'd managed to break free. No fire mage should have been able to break those bonds."

The oberon lumbered over to the trail that led down toward the cavern and sat there, blocking it, continuing to hurl rocks at Danzi. Boulders rose up from the earth as the ground gave way beneath Danzi's feet. He leaped high, narrowly avoiding another icy blast.

From the air, Danzi shot enough dragon fire at the ice mage to melt several icebergs. But pale blue light rose from Kutal's hands to quench the fire magic before it could reach him. His narrow, austere face betrayed no hint of concern. If anything, he looked very slightly amused, like a huntsman surveying the struggles of the great buck in his sights.

Danzi gritted his teeth. Brute strength would not be enough here.

Dragon Mage

The dragon mage landed on a group of downed trees. Focusing intently, he silently extended his energy, putting invisible fire in the trees and all the dried vegetation beneath the snow. Every blade of grass, every twig was soon inwardly smouldering. It took all his concentration to keep them all from igniting; his fire wanted to burn, but with great effort, he kept it in check. The amount of attention he gave the spell came at a price; two spades of ice nailed him to the tilted trunk at his back.

Thinking he had him, Kutal began to approach. He stepped over a bush. That was when it and everything else around him erupted. The monsters ran yowling as the fire blazed at their ankles and paws and leaped at their hides and fur. The oberon lifted a foot but appeared unharmed. Kutal jumped back, his pelts ablaze and his legs scorched. But then a heavy blue mist rose up around his body, extending to blanket the clearing and making the fires disappear as quickly as they'd arrived.

The wind had picked up; ice pellets, sharpened by Kutal's magic, rained down on their heads and bounced off the oberon. He didn't seem to care that they struck his own soldiers as well as the dragon mage.

With a wrench, Danzi broke free of the icy spears pinning him to the tree. Sharp pieces of ice flew as he shattered them. But since the spears had pierced his body all the way through, some jagged chunks of ice broke off inside him and continuing to chafe at his flesh. Ignoring the pain, Danzi stepped forward, fresh fire burning around his hands as he formed a new spell.

Now the ground between them turned into a sheet of ice, freezing the melted water around Danzi's boots and binding the leather to the ground. All the blue mist in the clearing seemed to condense and hover over his head while he tried to free himself. Then it turned into water and cascaded down onto him, quenching his fire and freezing solid once it had covered him completely. The oberon hoisted up a large boulder and threw it.

Danzi struggled to break free as sharp shards formed in the ice to pierce his cloak. Before they could reach his flesh, he dissolved into a burst of yellow fire, holding the shapeless form for a second or two longer than normal. The ice holding him started to melt as the dragon took on his true shape. He broke free of the ice and hurled himself into the air, the oberon's rock clipping his belly. Kutal, too, shifted. The igarevin lunged at Danzi, an icy halo forming around his front paws.

A tornado of flames formed around the red dragon. The vortex spun around him faster and faster, absorbing all Kutal's blows before sinking into the ground at a downward flick of his wings. Then Danzi growled a word in Draconic. A fiery symbol appeared on the earth next the ice mage.

There was a rumble. The earth began to shake; an indentation appeared in the snow, deepening before it quickly widened into a crack. Within seconds the crack grew and deepened down through the snow and to the dark earth. Even that gave way, opening a crevice down through all the layers of the earth and to a pool of bubbling, flaring magma. Spinning streamers of fire detached from it, swirling up toward the surface and releasing sparks and flashes of heat and light.

It all happened in barely a second; Kutal had no chance to react before the earth split open under him, dropping the ice mage into the inferno below.

Danzi smirked. He liked fighting in places with where dormant volcanoes and lines of earth magic were close to the surface. In most areas they were miles below and of little use to him.

Danzi now turned on the oberon, who lurched toward the hole and shoved its giant paws in there before the crack could close. With a grunt, it opened the ground again just as Danzi landed on its shoulder and blew fire into the creature's eyes. The beast roared and shook its charred head but didn't let go of the ground. More flames appeared on its back, forcing the creature to its knees. Danzi grabbed the back of its neck in his jaws and bit down with all his strength. Rocks broke on his teeth. The oberon continued to rumble with increasing distress as Danzi bit deeper into its neck, even stone yielding to his fangs.

He hoped these things had a spine.

Now a handful of griffins mobbed Danzi, forcing him away from the rocky creature. As he fought them off, he could see the other soldiers scouring the rocks, searching for Eiryenne.

The oberon, giving off a pained lowing, thrust its rocky paw down into the magma and scooped up Kutal, lifting him out of the blaze and dumping him onto the ground; the igarevin had frozen himself solid in an effort to escape the heat. The oberon lumbered back to block the trail, limping heavily. Its rocky skin was blackened and scorched, and its neck was deeply cracked where Danzi had mauled it.

Quickly thawing himself out, Kutal got up with a groan. His muzzle was dark with soot, and there were ferocious burns on his sides; his right hind leg had been burned off to the knee. Still, he managed to muster up enough energy to freeze the air around the fighting dragon's wings. Danzi fell to the ground with a thud. He scrambled to his feet immediately, fire glowing on the tip of his wide, forked tongue. He was getting tired, but so was the igarevin. He knew he still had a chance.

There were shouts from the side. The dragon turned as two ogres chased Eiryenne out from her hiding place. She rode hard, but Chief was having trouble with the icy ground.

Still, something seemed off. The dragon swept his gaze around his surroundings while Kutal prepared some kind of spell. It was only then that Danzi really noticed what the other mages were doing. Concealed behind an incoherent blur of magic that appeared to be a strangely constructed barrier if not examined too closely, they had drawn a two-lined circle covered with symbols around the place where Danzi and the ice mage fought.

Kutal cried out a word, and the space between the lines filled with icy magic that hardened until it was rock solid. The other mages then began to chant.

Danzi, realizing what was happening, started to run. It was only a few strides to get beyond the circle, but the ice beneath him grabbed at his claws with every step.

A shower of rocks came from the oberon, forcing Danzi to slow. He shifted back into human form to squeeze through the last gap.

Just then, every mage in the clearing cried out in unison. The circle surrounding Danzi began to glow with all the colours of their combined magic. Then, one by one, the mages fell to ground, dead. The spell they'd just done had cost them their lives.

The fire around Danzi's hands faded. Ice stopped melting around his feet. Water froze on the bottom of his boots and made him slip, falling to one knee.

"I haven't worked with the Emperor for that long," said Kutal. "But if there's one thing I like, it's the kind of loyalty he can *inspire* from his people." He chuckled, looking around at all the dead mages. Then he turned back to Danzi. "Binding a dragon's fire from him is no easy feat. But now there is nothing between you and my ice." He pinned Danzi to the ground with three long, icy spears. "Take a dragon's magic away, and he is defenceless."

"Not this dragon." Danzi scowled at him, drawing his sword with cold hands that were already starting to go numb and hacking at the ice with wide, intent swings. He had not survived this long by depending on any one asset. A very specialized warrior, no matter how strong, would eventually meet his downfall in the wrong conditions. Generalization of skills was crucial in this world. If he didn't have his fire, he still had his sword, his hands, his wit. If Plan A failed, there was always Plan B, Plan C, and so on. And at the end of the list there was Plan X.

His left hand went to the medallion that hung around his neck, hidden beneath his jacket. Danzi wished he could call on its power by choice. So far, it had only activated twice in his life, to save him from an unbreakable bondage. But try as he might, he could not get its white fire to appear again.

Trapped in human form without his magic and facing the most powerful ice mage he'd ever met, Danzi knew he had little choice but to go with Plan X. He didn't like what he was about to do, but the direness of the battle always dictated the desperation of the action.

Eiryenne drew level with him, still chased by the ogres. She hadn't avoided a fight; one of the ogres had two arrows in its rear, while the other had had a bow broken over its head. The wooden pieces were still there, tangled in its coarse hair.

Kutal looked at the oberon. "Do you still want to kill him, or shall I?"

Danzi bounded toward the girl, vaulting onto the horse's back behind her. He reached around her and grabbed the stones that hung from her neck. Chief reared as a pale green light bubbled around Danzi's fingers then travelled up his arm and shot out of his sword. Time seemed to stand still as it lit up everything in the clearing, from the oberon to the ice mage, the circle on the ground and the rest of the soldiers. For a split second they were bathed in a ghostly light that seemed to shine right through their skin and illuminate their skeletons.

Then they all exploded.

Chapter 16 ~ The Cavern

When the dust cleared, there was nothing left there to show that anyone else had ever stood on that mountainside. No ash, no bones, nothing.

Eiryenne stared at the scene with wide eyes. This, then, was the destructive power of Tairung.

Danzi tore his fingers away from the stones and sat back, panting. When the dragon mage had first leaped onto Chief behind her, he had been cold as ice. Now that the circle had been wiped out, Eiryenne could feel Danzi's regular warmth returning.

They looked up at the sky at the same time. Distant shapes were appearing among the clouds. Unfamiliar cries reached Eiryenne's ears. She shuddered as she realized that in those couple of seconds that Danzi had held the stones, Tairung had been able to send out a call that was heard across the entire Empire.

Behind her, Danzi began to shift. The fire gripped her as well, lifting her from Chief's saddle. Next thing she knew, she was in the dragon's claws, soaring upward. Danzi pumped his wings, trying to ride the turbulent currents of air. The storm had begun in earnest now, and it showered them with a mixture of icy rain and snow. Eiryenne was rocked up and down in his grip with each beat of his wings, and sometimes between, as the gale mounted.

Ghostly grey demons began to float out of the bloom, unbothered by the wind. Larger shadows followed them: griffins, winged tigers, and other even more terrifying beasts. She realized that the griffins were controlling the air around them with their wind magic, creating smooth areas for themselves and their companions to glide through.

Danzi angled his wings and slipped behind a bank of clouds. He tightened his grip on the girl and began a series of wild evasive manoeuvres, making sharp turns and gut-wrenching dives to avoid the jets of magic from his pursuers. At one point he flew in a tight loop upside-down, coming up behind a demon to spray flames at its underside. Then he righted himself and took off again, flying as fast as he could.

To call the flight bumpy would have been an understatement: painful bruises formed on Eiryenne's head as it slammed against the dragon's scales. Her fingers were raw from being clenched against his forelimb, and her neck felt like it would snap from being jostled to and fro so roughly.

Then Danzi tucked his wings against his sides and dove straight down. As he dropped out of the clouds, Eiryenne could see a wide, gaping hole in the earth that sped toward them. In a few seconds he was through. It was deep, but the sides were narrow.

As the ground came into view, the tunnel widened into a cavern, and Danzi opened his wings. Eiryenne closed her eyes as they came to a bone-jarring stop just a few feet off the ground. He dropped her onto the floor and landed heavily.

"Welcome to Boyevin Cavern," he said, looking around. "Stay there, I'm going to goad the Firedrake. When I give you the signal, pass me the necklace."

With those words he turned to walk across the cavern until his silhouette melted into the shadows. Eiryenne could hear his claws loudly scraping the rock as he walked. She realized he was doing it on purpose.

She took off the necklace and then held the stones up at eye level, wanting to take one last look at them before they were gone. As she traced the dark blue swirls, she sighed. Such a pity that something so beautiful had to be disposed of.

Then she blinked. At the centre of the largest gem she could see a small chip of black—a fragment of Tairung's horn. It was embedded so deep inside the rock that she hadn't seen it before. Now it stood out, glowing green.

Green, with a hint of orange.

Then a blackness began to surround the piece of horn; it spread until it trickled to the edges of the stone.

In her mind's eye she saw the mad unicorn standing in front of her. He looked triumphant; at the end of his broken horn he held a spark of Danzi's dragon fire, evidently snagged during their brief exchange. The grey markings on his fur swirled with a renewed excitement, and the demonic shadows surrounding him morphed into one another so quickly that it was impossible to make out a single shape.

"This should be enough," he chuckled. "The dragon had a tight focus; I'll give you that. But a split second, that split-second right after the blast, he let his guard down. And as his magic came back, I grabbed this." The fire on his horn began to crackle and spark.

In the stone in her hand, Eiryenne saw the blackness, flowing like ink from the horn chip, start to condense into a line. A crack appeared on the surface of the rock.

"You might destroy my army's souls," Tairung said, nodding to the smaller, adjacent stones. "But you won't be destroying *me* today."

Eiryenne opened her mouth to call for Danzi, but the chain jumped out of her hands and twisted around her throat so tightly that she couldn't breathe. Her surroundings began to fade. They got blurrier as the beast in front of her got more solid.

The girl looked up at the black unicorn. She was too tired to be afraid. She'd used up all her strength, both emotional and magical. But after all she'd done, Tairung was still going to escape at the last second.

All her efforts were in vain. Her parents had died for nothing.

A new emotion formed in the turmoil of her thoughts: anger. And something else. A growing speck of cold, hard hatred. She latched onto it like a solid point in a sea of chaos.

"*No,*" she said, not even knowing where the determination in her voice came from. "You're going to die today, Tairung. I'll see to that."

She forced her shaking muscles to move. Reaching up, she seized the accursed beast around the muzzle. Tairung paused and looked down at her. There was amusement in his mad eyes.

"Do you honestly think that you, a trainee mage who hasn't even seen two decades, have a chance against the Shadow Unicorn?" he said with a deep chuckle.

Eiryenne strained until her consciousness found the familiar spark of fire atop Tairung's horn. She grabbed it. "Me? Of course not."

The crack in the rock stopped growing. Instead, the blackness began to flow into the girl's hands.

"But I know someone who can." She was dimly aware of thundering footfalls coming from the other side of the cavern. Eiryenne knew that she couldn't stop Tairung; she just had to stall him for long enough.

With one toss of his head, the unicorn shook her off, and the fire on his horn blazed black. "Oh, really? And what can he do?"

The black fire on his horn threatened to fill her vision. One of the demonic shadows that swirled about him broke off to sink into her skin instead. In her hands, the blackness trickled from the stones to blacken her fingers. But then she sensed familiar warmth on her right, a figure blazing with orange and red fire that had touched her shoulder. Gritting her teeth, Eiryenne tipped the stones into Danzi's waiting hands.

In a flash of dragon fire, Tairung faded from her sight. The chain unwound itself from her neck, and she fell to her knees, breathing hard. The blackness that had entered her skin from the stones didn't disappear. It continued to spread, hungrily blanketing every inch of her body.

There was a deafening rumble that made the earth shake. What she thought was the wall of the cavern began to move. When she looked more closely, she realized that the black, sharp pieces of rock were claws, and more rock continued up to form the body of a gigantic, six-footed monster. There was magma glowing beneath its rocky hide, but the magma was ash grey. Danzi shifted and spat a bolt of fire at its side. As soon as it hit, his magic greyed and disappeared, absorbed by the colourless, smokeless lava.

The Firedrake's size dwarfed the oberon they'd faced. Even in his true form, Danzi looked tiny next to it. His transformation seemed to stir up more activity from the monster; it reared a head as large as a mountaintop, with a cavernous, gaping maw that seemed to suck the life out of the very air. Several rows of giant, boulder-like teeth gnashed together with a thud that shook Eiryenne's bones.

To her horror, the dragon was flying right into the Firedrake's mouth. But as Danzi landed on its jaw, he shape-shifted just before the jaws smashed together. The Firedrake's teeth were obviously not meant for gulping down anything much smaller than a dragon, because they were so huge and widely spaced that there was more than enough room for Danzi to move through as a man. Despite the fifty-foot teeth thudding shut on either side of him, the dragon mage did not appear to be worried.

The Firedrake opened its jaws, and Danzi moved deeper into its mouth, timing his steps so that he could cross over each row of teeth while its jaws were still open and have an empty space to stand or walk in when they snapped shut. As he went farther, the rows of teeth became smaller, forcing him to shorten his strides, until he was almost out of sight, down on one knee in a narrow gap near the back of its throat.

Eiryenne saw him raise the necklace, which he'd been carrying by the chain, and touch its stones. Green light briefly flowed around his fingers. Then he raised his hand and sent a blast of Tairung's magic directly down the Firedrake's throat. Its chewing motion stopped, and it pitched forward, giving a deep, guttural screeching, like plates of rock rubbing together. Then Danzi tossed the necklace down its throat. The Firedrake swallowed and belched green fumes. The fire mage began to retrace his steps, having to hurry because the monster was gnashing its teeth with renewed speed and vigour.

When he was at the edge of its mouth, Danzi drew his sword. The blade flickered combination of green and orange. Then he jumped out and in midair, sent a tsunami of pale green light blasting over the Firedrake. It roared and began to melt, quickly dissolving into the ground. As with the soldiers, there was no debris to indicate that it had ever been there.

Danzi flipped over in the air to avoid a falling boulder, one of several that the creature's thunderous cry had dislodged. Then he shifted into his true shape and glided to the ground.

Eiryenne heaved a sigh of relief. It was over. They'd done it.

Only now did she really become aware of the paralyzing darkness that had taken over her body. Her skin had darkened until it was blackish grey; her hands had gone completely black, and her insides felt like they were being mashed together. Her breathing was getting shallower and shallower as a phantom hand squeezed her chest. Tairung was going to have the last laugh after all.

Danzi moved closer until he was standing over her. The girl could see a reflection of herself in his amber eyes.

She thought that the prospect of death would scare her, but she felt no fear as her vision began to fade. Even if this was the end, Eiryenne decided she had no regrets. She'd seen and done things that most ordinary people could only dream of. She'd done her part to help stop a great evil force from rising. By helping to destroy Tairung, she'd saved countless lives.

So she looked up at the magnificent red dragon, savage but beautiful, his brilliant scales a dark gold-touched crimson in the gloom, his fierce amber eyes drawing in her gaze as they blazed brighter than the light at the end of the tunnel above them. As far as last sights went, she decided she could do far worse.

"Give it up, Tairung," he whispered. "You're through."

Tairung, or rather one of his shadowy demons, laughed maniacally inside Eiryenne's head. *Not quite, Danzellius,* he sneered. *This one will come with us to the grave. We'll eat up her soul nice and slowly.*

Danzi shifted back into his human shape. *No,* he said. *This one comes with me. I've decided that I'm keeping her.* His lips didn't move, but his voice echoed clearly in Eiryenne's head that the demon heard him, and so did she. Danzi knelt beside her and seemed to hesitate for a second. Then he reached into his tattered jacket, and from his inner pockets he pulled out a dazzling, narrow strip of something white.

Eiryenne's vision began to clear as she focused her gaze on the object in Danzi's hand. It looked like a piece of bone, with smooth ripples travelling up its length in a tight spiral. It gleamed with a silvery white halo, driving back the shadows at the edge of her vision.

With a jolt, Eiryenne realized what it must be. It was almost the same as it had looked in the storybook and the exact same as it had been in Danzi's dream.

A unicorn horn.

Danzi reached out and put the end to her temple. A silvery blue aura extended from it as an unfamiliar but not at all unpleasant magic streamed from the point of contact, feeling all at once like both the freshest of spring air and the purest of mountain streams. It began clearing away the shadows that swirled around the girl's body. Colour came back into her skin and the paralysis left her muscles as the demon that tried to possess her shrieked and fled, dissipating into a puff of smoke when the horn's essence reached it.

"Mention that to anyone and I will kill you," Danzi said when he was done, tucking the horn back into his jacket again. He slipped it back inside his jacket to a pocket inside his vest.

Eiryenne's lips felt like she hadn't used them for ages. "U-understood," she mumbled with a weak smile.

Danzi transformed and grabbed her in his left front paw. He jumped into the air from a standing start on his other three legs and began the sloping vertical descent back to the outside world. The walls of the tunnel seemed wider now; he could spread his wings almost fully.

"Now what?" Eiryenne said slowly. Surely, he hadn't saved her soul from Tairung's demons just to leave her to the nearest soldiers.

"Now we fly across half the Empire with almost all of Varcroft's soldiers after us," the dragon replied. Then he smirked. "All in a day's work."

She sensed him start to gather his strength; molten sparks jumped over the dragon's hide. He was surrounded by a faint red aura; his scales practically hummed with power.

Eiryenne tried to settle herself more comfortably in his grip as the dragon rose out of the cavern. As expected, the skies were crowded. Demons of all kinds, flying tigers, griffins, and even some winged horses all stood at the ready, waiting for their targets to emerge. Dyre wolves, ogres, elves, and centaurs stood at the cavern's rim. Every soldier who wasn't in either of the wars had to be here. But no one, it seemed, had dared to venture into the Firedrake's lair.

A thin web of fire surrounded Eiryenne. She soon saw why.

"Let the fun begin," he muttered. Then he tossed his head and roared. A wall of fire rolled off his wings and paws to scorch enemies on either side at the same time as a blast of it exited his jaws. It passed harmlessly over the barrier he'd put on Eiryenne but stopped the soldiers' spells in their tracks and sent burning bodies tumbling into the cavern.

Several fiery explosions later, Danzi had broken a hole through the angry mass in the sky. Surrounding himself with a large barrier of yellow and crimson flames, he charged through and finally broke free of the throng.

Eiryenne got glimpses of multicoloured flashes of light as the soldiers attacked, but only a few of their spells made it through to Danzi. These beasts and people had not come here prepared to kill a dragon; they'd rushed over chasing Tairung's call. It was likely the force left to defend and patrol Varcroft's home turf would not be the most powerful when the Emperor was stretched out between two wars; that would explain the great variety of opponents that met them outside the cavern.

Eiryenne found herself feeling very thankful that the Emperor had other battles to contend with. Otherwise, they'd have been greeted by his entire army, and even Danzi would be hard pressed to escape then.

Tumultuous winds made for another bone-jarring flight, especially as Danzi barrel-rolled around griffins and dove or banked sharply to dodge demon spells. At one-point Eiryenne tucked her face into her jacket and closed her eyes, tired of the merciless, icy wind that whipped her cheeks.

The unmistakable feeling of free-fall made her look up. Danzi was diving down into a network of canyons and trenches, hoping to slow some of his pursuers. The wind was weaker here in the shelter of the canyon and raging turbulence at its tops stopped the winged beasts from flying there. Danzi followed the passage, flying close to the ground, twisting and turning along with the canyon. Some of the demons who followed were not so agile; on more than one occasion Eiryenne heard them smash into the wall at a particularly sharp turn. The walls were getting so narrow that Danzi had to fly at an angle just to maintain enough room to keep his wings spread.

Then, sensing a change in the air currents, Danzi rose sharply and caught an updraft. The wind was strong, almost knocking the dragon against the rocks as it hurled him out of the canyon. He began losing his grip on Eiryenne, as if the howling gusts sought to rip her from his claws. She slid through the dragon's paw until he had her only by her feet, and the force of a wrenching turn made her head smash into his shoulder, hard. The girl lost consciousness within seconds.

***

She woke to a blur of orange lights and the wind in her ears. Her head pounded, and it took her a second to realize that she was looking at a sunrise. The outer rim of the sun had just started to crest the tops of the hills, sending rays of yellow light streaming down through the morning mist and colouring the clouds orange and pink.

The storm had passed, but it was still windy. Eiryenne looked around. Danzi's claws were around her waist again, though he had her in his right paw now rather than his left. There were still one or two demons flying after them in the distance, but it was a significantly smaller amount than she remembered. The rest must have been taken out by storm or dragon fire.

"Where are we going?" she asked, still gazing at the horizon.

"The Resistance camp. They should find some use for you there."

"What made you change your mind?" Eiryenne said before she could stop herself. She looked up at the dragon. The morning sunlight made his scales appear gilded. The ridges over his eyes that resembled eyebrows were rimmed with gold. He raised one of these now as he glanced at her.

"I trained you," he said with a shrug. "And I don't like to see my efforts go to waste."

Eiryenne glanced over her shoulder again; the demons started to fade into the distance. At first, she wondered why new beasts weren't flocking to join their fellows. Then her hand went to her neck, and she realized there was nothing there. The days of being a magnet for danger were over. No one would come after her anymore. Her heart soared as she realized she was free.

About the Author

The author, Arisha Grabtchak, graduated from Dalhousie University with B.Sc. with a double major in Biology and Creative Writing and Honors in Biology in 2015. She self published her first book, Doom of the Teachers when she was 17 in 2011 and distributed it mainly to friends. Writing was her passion. Arisha completed three novels that are parts of the series Red Dragon Chronicles. The novel Dragon Mage is the first one from the series. Arisha also made a few digital drawings related to the story. She was a gifted and multitalented artist creating realistic digital paintings that received high scores from her peers. She was an accomplished scuba diver and a horseback rider. Ocean and horses were her two favorite hobbies. Her plans were very big and ambitious. She shot three short movies in which she acted as a director, an actor and a cameraperson. She dreamed about all her novels to be published and seeing movies based on them. Arisha passed away in 2016 at the age of 23. Her legacy lives in her books that have been published with the support of her family.

ALL THINGS THAT MATTER PRESS

FOR MORE INFORMATION ON TITLES AVAILABLE FROM
ALL THINGS THAT MATTER PRESS, GO TO
http://allthingsthatmatterpress.com
or contact us at
allthingsthatmatterpress@gmail.com

If you enjoyed this book, please post a review on Amazon.com and
your favorite social media sites.
Thank you!

www.ingramcontent.com/pod-product-compliance
Lightning Source LLC
Chambersburg PA
CBHW021219260626
47172CB00002B/514